HER FROZEN PROMISES

A ROCKY POINT WEDDING BOOK FOUR

VANIA RHEAULT

❀ Created with Vellum

ABOUT THE BOOK

Autumn still loves Cole . . . despite the fact he made a terrible mistake.

He gave her sister a baby, and she can never forgive him, even though he still loves her, too.

All Cole ever wanted was Autumn, but his weren't the only mistakes that kept them apart.

Now they're both in Rocky Point free to be together, but is there too much bad history standing in their way?

Resentment and regret are only the start.

A killer on the loose may be their end.

CHAPTER ONE

Sitting behind his desk, Cole McClure leaned back in his webbed office chair and watched Autumn across the bullpen.

She'd begun logging off, her routine the same to end the day. Shut down her computer, take one last look in her inbox positioned on the corner of her desk, put finished projects in her outbox, shove anything she'd work on at home into a file, and pick up her purse and jacket.

He knew her every movement, could picture her doing those things even when he turned away to answer a colleague's question or answer his phone.

It hurt to look at her. He'd have thought that with so many years that had gone by his feelings for her would have faded, but it seemed every time he looked at her the throbbing in his chest intensified.

He wanted to march over to her desk, yank her into his arms, and kiss her senseless.

But he wouldn't.

Couldn't.

He stood, his chair squeaking in relief as it gave up his weight, and put his jacket on.

He'd walk her to her car, even if she gave him shit for it. That asshole was still hanging around, and it gave him a sick feeling in his gut.

The cops said the guy wasn't breaking the law, standing in the cold, harassing Autumn, and it pissed him off they wouldn't stop the fucking jerk.

It still razzed him she'd been engaged to the prick, though, he conceded as he weaved around desks to reach Autumn's, his choices hadn't been much better.

Some would even say they'd been worse. Much worse.

"Ready to go?" he asked as she slid her arms through the sleeves of her jacket.

"Not that it should matter to you, but yes, I am."

He bit back a retort. He wasn't the only one who fucked up.

"It matters to me because you do," he said patiently, slinging the strap of her laptop bag over his shoulder. He was already carrying his messenger bag and camera case. "You look nice. Going somewhere later?"

Jealousy burned, but if she wanted to date, he couldn't stop her. She hadn't seemed interested in anyone since moving back to Rocky Point, but people could be alone for only so long. She'd already proven she wanted to be a part of a couple.

She focused her large blue eyes onto him and tugged mittens onto her hands. "Marnie's having us meet to make the flower centerpieces that will go on the reception tables. I'm behind on the blog. Will you be around to take pictures?"

"Not tonight. I have Ty."

"Right."

Bringing up Ty was always a risky endeavor. Autumn loved her nephew, but the little boy represented his biggest mistake.

He scanned the old department store's parking lot. Several years ago the newspaper purchased the building and gutted it, turning the huge open space into new offices. Snowflakes fell lazily from the sky, and they glittered on the ground in a thick blanket.

A bulb in one of the light poles had either been shot out or simply burnt out, and he didn't like the dark corner and what could hide in the shadows. Huge piles of snow leftover from the latest blizzard made good hiding places.

"I'll take a few with my phone, then," she said, walking with him to her car.

He didn't give a shit about their little party or who would take pictures. "Fine."

She slanted him a glance, her springy curls poking out of the hood she pulled over her head.

He wanted to kiss her, tell her to forget about everything. Tell her that they were the ones who should be getting married on Saturday.

All he did was open her car door and shove her bag in the backseat.

He held up his hand as she drove away, but she didn't return the gesture.

She turned a corner and her car disappeared.

He looked away and met Buck Drayton's eyes. The slime was leaning against the burnt-out light pole, his steely eyes fixed on him.

The cops said not to engage. Ignore him and hope he grew bored enough to move on.

People who lashed out were the ones who paid.

He didn't have time to sit in a jail cell because he

bashed the guy's nose in, no matter how satisfying that would be.

He worked for a newspaper, for Christ's sake.

The pen was mightier than the sword.

He said the one thing he knew would agitate Buck to hell and back.

"She's mine."

Adrenaline pumping through his veins, he drove to Ty's mother's house. She didn't own the house, she was housesitting for her parents while they were on an extended European vacation. His ex-father-in-law had bought stock at the right time, dumped it at an even better time, and Summer's mom and dad became the only members of Rocky Point's millionaire's club.

If his bank account had all the money the Bennett's did, he wouldn't live here, either.

He parked in the wide driveway. The blue flicker of the TV glowed through the huge picture window in the living room.

Leaving the vehicle running to keep the insides warm for Ty, he trotted inside. After a day of watching him, Summer gave him up in the evenings without trouble, and his packed diaper bag already sat next to the door.

"Daddy!" Ty's chubby legs carried him across the carpeted floor and he launched himself into his arms.

His son's sticky kiss swept away Autumn's coolness. He couldn't resent Ty for being born.

When Autumn looked at Ty, she saw the family he could have, *should* have, given her. Short of finding a time machine or rubbing a magic lamp and asking the genie to grant him a do-over, there wasn't anything he could do about it, and when Ty started babbling about *Paw Patrol*, he knew he wouldn't anyway.

Not even if it meant he could have Autumn.

"Did you see my sister today?" his ex-wife asked.

Only eighteen months separated Summer from Autumn, and believing that Summer's nearly identical features made them similar on the inside as well could be added to his long list of poor choices.

"We work in the same building, Summer. Of course I did."

"Did you talk to her?"

He didn't want to get into it. Over and over again. Cole boosted Ty on his arm and said, "No."

Summer nodded in satisfaction, and determination glinted in her eyes.

"I'll feed Ty dinner and be back in time to tuck him in."

"Whatever."

He liked to think her dismissive attitude came from her trust in his ability to take care of their son, but the truth was, she liked being home alone and didn't care when he took Ty.

He bundled the little boy in his winter jacket and the *Paw Patrol* boots he'd ordered online.

Summer didn't say goodbye . . . to either of them.

Buckling Ty into the car seat he always kept in his backseat, he kissed his little boy on the top of his head.

"We're going to see Auntie," he said, watching Ty's reaction in the rearview mirror.

"Auntie A!" Ty shouted, pumping a fist.

Ty spent a lot of time with Autumn, almost as much as he spent with him, but Leah was staying in Autumn's spare room and busy doing wedding activities, she hadn't been babysitting Ty as often as she usually did. Ty missed her.

"I know how you feel, buddy, but we're going to Auntie Beth's. She's making your favorite."

"Skettie."

"You got it."

His little sister lived in the nicer residential section of town and he drove in that direction, his headlights cutting through the dark.

Rocky Point was divided into the have and have-nots, though that line blurred when the paper mill closed and the town's economy tanked.

Beth, her husband Russ, and their two daughters lived on a well-kept street in a middle-class neighborhood where fortunate two-income families could afford to live.

Autumn had bought a house in the poorer part of town. Her parents offered to help her when she moved back to Rocky Point, but she'd declined, determined to make it on her own.

It was just another thing he loved about her, and he was never happier than when he brought Ty to her house to visit.

With her puttering in the kitchen and he and Ty playing in the living room, it was as close to domestic bliss as he'd ever gotten. It always ended when he had to bring Ty back to Summer and Autumn turned off her porch light as he backed out of her driveway, leaving her yard and his heart in complete darkness.

He parked in front of their garage and killed the engine.

He enjoyed spending time with his sister and her family, and one Sunday every month their parents joined them too. While he was married, Summer used to go, but her prickly attitude created a tense atmosphere and no one complained when she stopped.

"Come on, buddy," he said, unbuckling his son's straps. "I'm starving."

He knocked on the door and Beth let him in, a dishtowel laying over her shoulder.

"Hey, kiddo," she said, holding out her hands. Ty eagerly fell into her arms. "How was your day, dear?" she teased, setting Ty on the floor and unzipping his jacket.

His sister liked joking, always trying to draw a smile out of her somber brother, but this particular joke got old the first time she said it. The woman he loved waiting for him to come home, dinner on the stove. Not that he thought that's where a woman belonged, but the picture, the feeling, the *family*, he would never have.

"Oh, same old, same old." He hung his jacket next to Ty's and shoved the diaper bag near his dress shoes.

Beth eyed the bag as Ty ran into the living room to hunt down his cousins. "Still not potty trained?"

"He's only three and some change, let him be."

"Summer won't do it," Beth accurately guessed.

He followed her into the kitchen and she pulled a bottle of beer out of the fridge and set it on the table.

Gratefully, he pried the cap off and took a long drink. He'd had a hell of a day. He came up for air and said, "She's too busy making sure I'm staying away from Autumn."

Beth added pasta to a huge pot of boiling water. "I still don't understand what you were thinking."

"You and me both."

She gave the noodles a brisk stir and sank into a seat next to him at the table. "No, really. What were you thinking?"

"Autumn had gotten engaged," he said uneasily.

"So it was payback."

"That's not—" He clamped his mouth shut.

"Ah-huh," Beth said. "You wanted to hurt her, and you did. Whenever I run into her I can see it on her face. But she wasn't the only one you hurt."

He leaned back in his seat, took another swig of his beer, and tried to relax as Ty's happy shrieks pierced the air.

He hurt, too.

He'd have to fix it, that's all. Never mind he'd been trying for years.

Blocking out his sister's insistence Ty needed to be rid of his diapers, he pretended he was with Autumn. That she was running her fingers through his hair and telling him she loved him.

That everything was as it should be.

Autumn pushed out of her car and tentatively scanned the resort's parking lot. She'd seen Buck at the newspaper office and fear dried her mouth. He could have followed her here, but only the low hum of a snowmobile carrying across the lake greeted her.

Christmas lights decorated a couple of the evergreens near the front entrance, and she appreciated the peaceful atmosphere, taking a moment to breathe in the cold air before being surrounded by the girls.

Odd one out now, but she couldn't be jealous or angry. She already loved Leah like a sister and it made her happy she'd decided to stay in Rocky Point. She and Jared were such a good match. The man sparkled whenever she saw him.

She grabbed the bag that had her iPad in it out of the backseat. She hoped her blog posts weren't wearing on her friends' nerves. If she told herself the truth, she was getting tired of writing about wedding stuff, though the online editor was pleased with the consistent content and the pictures were bringing in a record number of hits as the wedding series went on.

"Where's Marnie putting centerpieces together?" Autumn asked Sophia, the slim front desk agent.

"The Poplar Meeting Room has been blocked off," she said, tapping at her keyboard. "Appetizer trays are scheduled to be served in about forty-five minutes."

"Thanks."

She didn't need the signs to find the small meeting room Marnie reserved. The doors were closed, and pushing one open, she peered into the room.

Leah, Gail, Marnie, James's mother, Linda, and Callie sat at a large circular table, a huge mound of flowers in the center of it.

"Come in," Gail said, waving a long-stemmed wineglass that was filled to the brim with a deep, dark red. "We have forty centerpieces to put together and we've only just started."

She forced a smile, hoping she didn't look tortured by the thought, and sank into a seat next to Marnie. "How are you?"

Tears filled Marnie's eyes. "Hey."

Unwinding her scarf from around her neck, she asked, "What's wrong?"

"I got my period today," Marnie whispered, poking at a flower.

Her subdued behavior took Autumn off-guard. She couldn't remember seeing Marnie without her usual happy glow. She rubbed her friend's back in sympathy and said, "I'm sorry, sweetie. You have plenty of time to get pregnant. That's what the honeymoon's for, right?"

"I guess so," she muttered.

Gail poured more wine into a half-empty glass sitting in front of her daughter. "Autumn's right. There's plenty of time. You're not even officially trying yet. You can't start stressing out now or you won't have any fun." She wiggled her eyebrows and Marnie laughed.

"Mom!"

"What? You think I don't know how it works? I had you, didn't I?"

She poured wine into a glass and tried not to let the baby talk hurt her. It was difficult to think about children when the man she'd chosen to be their father hadn't chosen her.

The mood lightened, and Gail read a list off her phone. "We need centerpieces for the wedding party table, guest tables, and smaller bouquets for the high-tops that are being used as conversation stops, the cake table, the guest book table, and the gift table."

Everyone groaned, and Callie said, "We need more wine."

"Truer words have never been spoken," Linda said, nodding at Callie.

Leah scooted into a seat next to her. "You look tired."

"Long day at work."

"What about that guy bothering you? Have you seen him lately?"

She slid a squat black vase toward herself and plopped the ball of Styrofoam that would keep the flowers in place into it. "I haven't seen him today," she lied.

"Good."

Buck Drayton was another thing she was tired of thinking about.

"Did you guys hear Logan and Ivy got married last night?" Marnie asked.

She snapped her head up.

"No!" Callie gasped. "Really? God, that's so romantic."

"Yeah, in her mom's hospital room. The guys are partying at the Viking tonight to celebrate."

"What's Ivy doing?" Leah asked.

Marnie shrugged.

"We should do something for her. Throw her a small party or something," she said, lifting a wineglass full of rosé to her mouth.

"We don't have time," Marnie said, stabbing a flower into a foam ball.

"Don't turn Bridezilla now," Gail said, frowning, and Marnie blushed. "Ivy's had a hard time and she doesn't have many friends. Logan's mother's in town, and I'm sure she'd love to help put something together for her new daughter-in-law. Take some credit if it will make you feel better. If Logan hadn't told James he'd be a groomsman, they may never have reconciled. Logan is James's best friend. Be happy for them, honey."

Marnie blew out a sigh. "You're right, I know you are. Blame PMS or something."

"That's my girl. You're not pregnant, drink some wine. You're going through withdrawal." Gail pushed the full glass into Marnie's hand, the liquid sloshing precariously close to the rim. "They're going to be dealing with her mother's accident along with everything else. Rosie's going to be in hot water once she's released from the hospital."

Autumn listened to the conversation but didn't join in.

She spoke in a soft whisper to Leah instead. "How did you get to the resort?"

Leah finished a centerpiece, tying a red bow around the squat vase, and placed it on a table behind them. "Briar drove me over. I spent most of the day at the store."

"How's that going?"

"Good. Helen's teaching me a lot, but the books are horrible. She's been doing them herself. The first thing I did when Briar picked me up was look online for an accountant. God. I don't need the IRS on my butt. I don't want to think about what he's going to find." Leah shuddered.

She laughed. "I hope you don't think you bit off more than you can chew."

"No, I love it, I really do. And for once in my life, I know that if I need anything, I have help, and all I have to do is ask."

She clinked her glass against Leah's. "Definitely." She loved Leah's shine. She looked a million times happier than when she met her a week ago.

She wished she could find that kind of happiness.

Cole wanted to patch things up between them, but whenever he tried, she shut him down. How could he think they had a future? The past was too messy and their mistakes weren't content to stay there.

Gossip floated around her, and she itched to take notes to post on the blog. She didn't want to miss anything but she was here as Marnie's friend, not as a reporter, and she tamped back the urge to scribble.

An hour into their evening, she stood and asked Marnie's permission to take pictures of the centerpieces.

Marnie rolled eyes. "Yeah, sure, but I don't know who's going to be interested in that."

"The answer would surprise you," she said wryly.

Walking around the table, she took a few pictures of the girls making the centerpieces and a couple photos of the finished product.

Putting her phone back into her bag, she wrote a mental note to interview Ivy and Logan about their surprise wedding. The news had come out of left field, when in the past, she would have been the first to know. She was losing her edge.

She'd always had that drive to ferret out news, but lately she struggled to find the point in it all. Blogging about centerpieces and the kind of dress Marnie would wear when she walked down the aisle. Who cared? Maybe people living here, but in Decatur, she could have been reporting on real issues. News that mattered.

Lifestyles would always be a popular part of the paper, but there wasn't anything like having a byline above the fold.

Like the article she wrote about Mitch and his place, or lack thereof, in the community. Articles like those were the kinds of pieces she wanted to write. News that made a difference.

She blogged about important issues, too, but she wouldn't be winning a Pulitzer anytime soon.

If she wasn't going to have a personal life, she could at least have a satisfying professional one.

She just didn't know how without leaving Rocky Point, and the thought of moving away from Cole and Ty hurt her heart. She loved both of them, so much. They were her family.

Her sister was another matter.

One she could do without.

It neared midnight by the time they finished the red and green centerpieces, and Gail and Linda packed them into boxes, saying the resort would store them until the reception. Marnie waved goodnight, still a little melancholy, and Callie bounced down the hallway toward Mitch's room, eager to see him.

She brought Leah back to her house and they talked about the wedding while she drove the empty roads. It was nice having a roommate. Leah felt bad about taking up her spare bedroom, but Autumn told her she could stay as long as she liked. Months, if that's how long it took her and Jared to figure out their living situation. She slept better knowing she wasn't alone.

She parked in her small garage and turned her car off.

"I hope you don't have to go in early," Leah said, unbuckling her seatbelt.

"You should talk. You'll get six hours and rush to the store before I can make coffee."

"It's Christmas. We're going through stock like crazy," Leah said, following her into the house, "and I want people to know it's in good hands."

"Everyone knows that already. You've done an amazing job and Helen looks like a different person. You've changed a lot of lives since coming to Rocky Point, Leah."

Inside the tiny foyer, Leah blushed and took her jacket off. "Thanks. This town has changed my life, too. When I accepted Marnie's invitation, I had no idea my whole world would be turned around and upside down."

"It suits you." She hung her coat in the small closet near the door. "I need to congratulate Ivy. I honestly had no idea she and Logan got married last night. Absolutely none. What do you think we should do for her? Gail wasn't kidding when she said Ivy had it rough, and because of the trouble her mother's in, it won't get better anytime soon. At least Logan will be around to help her. That's a lot more than she had before."

"I talked to Ivy a little bit, and my life wasn't the only one that changed because of Marnie's wedding. Marnie's an angel to all of us." Leah covered her mouth with her hand. "I'm sorry, Autumn."

"There's nothing to be sorry for. I'm happy for you and Jared, and I've always liked Logan. He had a hard childhood and Ivy softened a lot of those blows. Figuratively speaking. They belong together."

"But you and Cole . . ."

"There's a lot of crap keeping us apart, and it will take more than a few conversations and 'I'm sorrys' to get past it. If he would have told me before he . . ." She rubbed her eyes, suddenly exhausted. If he would have just said something, she could have warned him what kind of person Summer was. Not that he would have believed her. Like Laurie marrying Amy instead of Jo in *Little Women*, Cole had *wanted*, and he'd done whatever he could to get it.

She sank onto the couch and brushed her hand over her cats' soft fur. They didn't acknowledge her, the snooty little things.

"There's nothing that can't be fixed," Leah said, leaning against the archway that connected the kitchen to the living room. "Soon we'll be dress shopping for you, too. Something's bound to change."

"I don't see how. We can't move forward. Thinking about it is like going around in circles. I end up where I start."

"I thought that, too, when it seemed like Jared and I weren't going to make it, but Cole loves you. I can see it when he looks at you. That can't be for nothing." She yawned. "I need to get some sleep. Jared's going to pick me up in the morning and drive me to the store. Goodnight, sweetie."

"Goodnight."

She sat alone in the living room and stared at the Christmas tree sitting in the corner. A few of Ty's presents were already piled beneath it wrapped in *Thomas the Tank Engine* wrapping paper.

No, there didn't seem to be any solution to her dilemma.

She turned out the lights and movement outside caught her eye.

Buck leaned against a beat-up truck parked in her driveway.

Dread rolled around her stomach and she yanked the curtains closed to block him out.

Huddled in bed, she wished Cole would come spend the night with her.

The sad part was, he would if she asked.

But she couldn't.

Cole parked in the Viking's lot needing a tall, cold beer to drink away his sister's words and Summer's warning when he'd dropped Ty off.

Summer bringing up Autumn every five minutes only made him think of her more. No, that wasn't true. He didn't need any help thinking about her pale skin and bright blue eyes. Soft lips. Cupping her breasts in his hands.

They'd made love only once, long before she'd gotten engaged, before he'd moved back to Rocky Point.

He'd always loved her.

It was Autumn who'd been all about her career.

He'd wanted a home. A wife and kids.

She'd wanted a byline.

They didn't have either.

A cheer greeted him as he stepped inside the dark bar, a party taking him by surprise. He'd been expecting a quiet evening, a corner to lick his wounds.

Not tonight.

James and Logan held court in the center of the room and it brought him back to high school where James Fox, king of Rocky Point High, would lord over the cafeteria with his friends by his side.

He hadn't been a loyal subject or friend of James's, and the "Cole!" hollered across the bar almost knocked him off his feet.

He wanted to tell James to fuck off and maybe ten years ago he would have, but tonight it didn't matter and he dropped into the chair James kicked out for him.

"What's going on?" he asked, taking his jacket off.

"Logan and Ivy got hitched last night. We're celebrating."

Logan grinned and held up his left hand.

"Congratulations," he shouted over Toby Keith and about ten other people surrounding their table. He recognized James's father, Marnie's, a handful of other wedding guests, and Mitch Sinclair.

"Thanks," Logan shouted in return.

"He's drunk," he said, "and happier than hell by the looks of it. You're not mad he stole your thunder?"

James poured him a glass of beer from one of the pitchers in the center of the table. "Nah, that's a chick thing. Logan deserved this."

"Can I take some pics?" he asked, reaching for the camera that went with him everywhere.

"Yeah, sure. That'd be great."

He took a few snaps, Logan shitfaced, but yeah, happier than hell.

He had nothing bad to say about Logan, and he raised his glass in a toast. Ivy was a nice woman, though he didn't know her well. She worked all the time and he rarely saw her around town.

Autumn would go nuts when she discovered she'd been scooped. Nothing usually got by her, and hearing second-hand Ivy and Logan got married would tick her off. No doubt that's what they'd be gossiping about tonight while they put centerpieces together.

Toby finished wailing and no one fed the machine more quarters. Thank God. There was only so much country he could stand.

"How's it going?" James asked.

"Fine. Why?" he asked, guarded.

"No reason. Can't a guy make conversation?"

"Yeah. Sure." He sipped his beer. "Wedding stuff going good?"

"Yeah, I guess so. That's more for the ladies, right? I just show up?"

His cocked his head. "In theory, but you gotta put a little more heart into it, bro."

"He's got heart," Jared said, inserting himself into the conversation and slapping James's back, "but he's starting to get cold feet."

"It's not like you didn't," James said good-naturedly.

"I didn't, but I should have. Should have called the whole thing off. My stupid little head was too much in love."

"Wrong head?" he asked, his lips twitching.

Jared barked out a laugh. "Probably. Can't regret it though, right?"

He knew what Jared meant. Without their marriages, mistakes or not, Briar and Ty wouldn't be here. He shrugged.

"What'd you marry Summer for? Didn't last five years," Jared said, moving to a chair closer to him and James.

He decided on honesty. "I wanted Autumn. Couldn't have her so I took the next best thing. That's what I thought, anyway."

"No?" Logan asked, butting into the conversation.

"The only thing the same about them are their noses." And he realized it much too late.

"Don't beat yourself up. Nobody stays married forever anymore. You take what you can get and when the relationship goes south, you do your best to move on," Jared said, pouring more beer into his glass.

"Shut up," James growled. "Leah hears you say that, and it'll break her heart. That's the cynical Rita-busted-my-balls guy talking. You don't put a ring on it without believing you're going to do your absolute damnedest to be the best husband you can be."

That sounded more like James. The booze was making everyone melancholy, and he glowered. He was the only one at the table who deserved to feel that way.

"Yeah, well, sometimes the person you marry won't let you do that." Beer curdled in his stomach. "I didn't marry Summer thinking I'd divorce her. It wasn't my fault she made our marriage so miserable I had to get out no matter what."

Jared nodded. "Agreed. I tried my best and it wasn't good enough."

"Because Rita's a bitch," Logan said. "She hated it here

and always wanted more than what she had. She should have told you that before you got married."

Jared glared. "She's not a bitch . . . wanting something more doesn't make her a bitch. We should have been more honest with each other, that's all. But it's a moot point now, isn't it?"

"Not when she's still under your roof." Logan smirked. "I bet that's comfortable for everyone."

Strike melancholy. Try hostile. He winced.

"What's going on? This doesn't sound like either of you. Jared, I've seen the way you look at Leah, and James? What the hell, man. Marnie's gold."

"Divorce sucks," Jared said, "and I don't want to go through it again."

"I don't want to go through it, period."

"Aren't you in marriage counseling or some fuck with your pastor?" he asked.

James grimaced. "Yeah, but we only agreed to get a discount on our marriage license."

"But no red flags are popping up, are they? You're actually using the sessions to talk things out?"

"They've been going great," James mumbled.

"Then I don't get it."

"She was right under my nose the whole time. Why didn't I tell her sooner?"

"Did you know sooner?"

"No."

"Then what were you going to do? It's different if you loved her but were too big of a coward to say anything."

"Like you and Autumn?" Logan asked.

"Hey." He straightened. They could be dicks to each other but he wasn't participating.

"What? It's true, isn't it? Everyone knows you're in love

with her. Why didn't you say anything? We all make mistakes. Say you're sorry and move on."

"Yeah, I'm sure was easy for you, hotshot," he snapped. Logan had fucking nerve. "Telling Ivy to fuck off for eighteen years and then think she's going to forgive you with a pathetic 'I'm sorry.' I hope she made you work for it, you asshole." He turned on Jared. "And you. Talk to your parents. They've been going strong for forty years. Take a lesson." Angrily, he pushed away from the table. They didn't know how good they had it. "Stop looking for trouble where there is none. You all have women who love the fuck out of you. Jesus Christ." He jerked on his jacket and yanked his camera case off the floor. He wasn't going to listen to any more shit. He could drink at home.

A silence had fallen over the bar and he slammed out the door, the *bang* echoing across the quiet parking lot.

He rammed his key into the ignition, his breath coming out in angry puffs.

James and his cold feet.

Jared already taking Leah for granted.

Logan, a smug prick who had a ring on his finger.

Only Mitch had stayed silent, watchful. A guy like him and a hot chick like Callie. He was a nice guy, but eerie as fuck.

Mitch had more brains in his head than all the others at the table combined. He knew he was lucky God dropped Callie in his lap. Wouldn't take her for granted for a single second.

James and Jared and their privilege. Rita dumping her family to chase the blaze of city lights. Wanting it all and throwing it away in the process. Logan leaving a woman who'd given him everything. He was lucky Ivy waited around.

God, people were so fucking stupid.

He drove to Autumn's house, dark except for colored lights shining behind the blinds. The Christmas tree she and Ty decorated a couple of weeks ago.

If he hadn't married Summer, he never would have had Ty. He loved him, and that was the end of the conversation as far as he was concerned. Even if it shackled him to her for the rest of his godforsaken life.

He parked and shut his lights off.

He wondered what Autumn would do if he knocked on her door. Invited himself in. Covered her mouth with his, insisted on it because she would fight him. Spit at him like one of her cats, and the thought of a rough tumble made him hard.

His fingers twisted in her hair, their teeth gnashing together. Forcing her to tell him she loved him.

It was the truth.

Maybe Logan had a point after all.

They'd been dancing around each other for years. Summer and Ty made it necessary.

If they could admit they still had feelings for each other . . . that would be a start, wouldn't it?

A start of what, he didn't know, but a start moving in the right direction.

Better than standing still.

In a pile of his own shit.

A light flickered on, and Autumn moved the curtains aside.

Looking to see if Buck was watching her.

"Fuck."

He was no better than that shithead, stalking her, waiting for her to take one misstep.

He pushed out of the car, stood and stared at the window, meeting Autumn's eyes through the frozen night.

He held up a gloved hand.

It took her a moment. A calculated moment.

She placed her hand on the glass.

He nodded.

The curtain fell back into place.

The light went dark.

He drove home.

CHAPTER TWO

Autumn scooped up her hair, turned to the side to see how it would look pinned into an updo, then let it fall and settle, framing her face. Too much work.

Her footfalls echoed through her empty house. Leah had left a while ago to put out more freight, and Autumn took her time going to the office. She didn't want to see him.

Something had compelled her to check her driveway one more time, expecting to see Buck, but Cole had sat and watched her house instead.

Like her thoughts had summoned him while she was trying to fall asleep.

Now she'd have to face him at the paper and she had no idea what to say.

What does a woman say to the man she loved but still betrayed?

What does a woman say when she looks into his eyes and sees nothing but what their future could have been if she hadn't been so stupid?

She forced herself to smile.

Their predicament wasn't as serious as that. Nothing life-threatening.

Only wasted time.

As she made a mental list of the calls she would have to make that day, the blog posts she would have to write, the articles she would have to outline, she grabbed her bags, shut and locked the door, crossed her snowy walkway, and stepped into the dark garage.

Ivy's party headed the list.

Something tonight, if she could manage it.

Marnie's bachelorette party was scheduled for the day after next, the rehearsal dinner Friday night, and then the wedding Saturday, early afternoon. It would be a busy week.

Unfortunately, as good as everyone's intentions were, if she couldn't find an available space tonight, they may not be able to have anything for Ivy at all.

She climbed into her car and opened her garage door. Thank God her driveway was empty this morning, besides the tracks Buck's truck dredged into the snow. He was tres-passing on her property and she should take pictures, but she thought of it too late and her car wheels ran over them. If she wanted him to stop, she needed to be smarter. She sighed. At least the drive to the newspaper offices was uneventful.

Cole caught her eye the moment she stepped into the bullpen.

He looked like shit. Tired, worried. He straightened, already wanting to talk.

She couldn't. Not yet.

In the breakroom, she poured a cup of coffee and snagged a cranberry scone, and then settled at her desk, the hum of voices and keyboards clicking washing over her in a familiar wave.

She belonged here.

At least she knew of one place she did.

She knew of other places too, but she had yet to secure a position there.

In Cole's life. In his arms. In his bed.

Across the room, he spoke on the phone, an old landline that had a receiver and rotary dial. He'd bought the ugly thing off eBay saying he liked the satisfaction of slamming the receiver down after an aggravating conversation.

She told him he'd have to do more than report sports then, as hanging up on an uncooperative source was a more satisfying scenario than getting angry over another Vikings loss. He'd scowled, and for a second it had been just the two of them, their love of news, their distant love for each other, and nothing else.

Nibbling on her scone, she began making calls to find a venue for Ivy's party. Evergreen Hill, the Rocky Point Bar and Grill. The Pointe Supper Club. She called Desiree at the resort to no avail. No one had availability.

She called The North Star as a last hope, a small but elegant restaurant built on an island attached to the edge of Rocky Point by a narrow bridge. A popular place that offered gorgeous evening dining al fresco in the summer, they were full all year round.

"Actually, we had a cancellation tonight," the hostess said. "We have a small meeting room that can seat fifteen. Limited menu, but a full bar is available. Would that suit?"

"Thank God, yes," she breathed. She tried to race through who would attend Ivy's party, hoping fifteen would be enough.

"It's reserved until seven-thirty. Please allow the

busboys time to refresh the room. We can book you from eight to midnight?"

"Yes, that's perfect. Thank you. Here's my credit card to hold the space. I appreciate it very much."

She hung up and texted Leah the good news.

I'll let everyone know. Leah replied. *I have more time than you.*

She doubted that since Christmas was less than two weeks away, but she did the hard part and she'd let Leah do the rest since she offered.

Make sure they know it's women only. The men had their fun last night.

Leah sent her a thumbs up.

Sighing in relief, she checked that task off the list and worked on a couple of blog posts, including the boring centerpiece writeup. She'd wait to write about Ivy and Logan. She wanted to interview them together.

She managed to avoid Cole until lunch. He stood near her desk, his hands shoved deep into his pockets, a frown on his face.

"What?" she asked curtly.

"I want to talk to you."

"There's nothing to talk about."

"Yes, there is."

"No, there's not."

"Yes, there is."

"No, there's not."

He gripped her upper arm. "Yes. There is."

He yanked her out of her seat and she squealed in protest. An older woman sitting at her desk near her who edited recipes for the Lifestyles section raised her eyebrows. "Play nice, kids."

Usually Cole, self-contained and calm, never let his temper show, but he was shaking as he dragged her down the hallway and into a storage closet full of office supplies.

He shut the door behind them and she leaned against the wall, crossing her arms over her breasts.

"What are we doing in here?"

"We need to talk," he said, glaring.

She lifted her chin. "There's nothing hashing out the past will change."

"You're wrong."

He drew her to him, a hand at her lower back, and she let him. Their bodies pressed together, his chest warm and strong, his arms a safety net.

A soft moan escaped her and she burrowed into him. It'd been too long since someone had touched her. Too long since she'd been kissed.

He traced his finger along the bow of her upper lip and heat flooded her panties.

"Something has to break," he whispered.

That snapped her out of her daze. "You mean besides my heart?"

"Besides ours." He brushed his lips over hers and she whimpered. She'd never forget how it felt when he kissed her. Like the lake, deep and dark. Forking his fingers through her curls, he mumbled against her lips, "Come home with me."

"When?" she asked, tempted.

"Tonight."

She pushed him away. "I can't. We're throwing a party for Ivy at The North Star. I set it up this morning."

He blew out a frustrated sigh. "Right now, then."

"No. I have work to do."

"I don't care." He leaned into her and whispered in her ear. "I want to fuck you, Autumn. Hard and fast, and I want to feel you come on my cock while you cry my name."

Jerking out of his arms, she said, "Crass. And I'm not interested. Go fuck Summer. You're good at that."

He grabbed her hand and yanked her out of the storage room and into the hall.

The receptionist who was coming out of the women's restroom frowned at them, puzzled. "Were you looking for more pens?"

"Mind your own business," he snapped.

She sucked in a breath, surprised he would speak to her like that, and hurried to her desk.

"That was rude," she said, trying to free her hand. She didn't like this Cole, but his anger made her heart race. Finally, he was showing something. A spark. An emotion that wasn't manufactured happiness.

"Get your stuff," he ordered, nudging her toward her desk. "We're leaving."

Pausing by her chair, she considered going with him. They wouldn't have sex, but they could talk. He was right about that. Something had to change. The stress of being around him, the emotions that flooded her every time she met his eyes. That had to change.

"Fine, but I'm not sleeping with you." She logged off her computer and slipped on her jacket.

"Whatever you say," he said, reaching to pick up her bag and purse.

They'd danced around each other for years. Being

together was nothing new but the rage radiating from him was, and a friend hurried across the room. "Are you okay?"

"Yeah. Don't worry about it. He's having a bad day. We're going to get a bite to eat. I'll see you later."

He turned around, halfway across the bullpen. "Autumn."

"Coming." She blushed.

Her friend laughed, shooing her away. "I get it now. Finally."

"That was embarrassing," she complained, following him to his car.

She sank into the passenger seat, Ty's car seat deepening the hole in her heart.

Shivering, she latched her seatbelt. She shouldn't have worn a skirt, and her feet were frozen, snow wetting her tights.

He didn't say anything as he started the car and cranked the heater.

She shut it off. "Are you trying to freeze me to death?"

He scowled all the way across town.

It'd been months since she stepped into his little house, and the scent of old pizza permeated the air. Her stomach rumbled.

"Are you going to feed me, at least, since you dragged me here?"

"Shut up."

Her eyes widened, but he approached her and she held her ground. She didn't flinch when he skimmed a finger along her jaw.

It hurt to look at her.

His heart thumped, vibrating pain throughout his body.

"I love you, Autumn." The words came from the depths of his soul, and he held out his vulnerability like a fragile flower, begging her to take it, to keep it safe.

"Fuck you," she said, raising a hand.

He caught her wrist, stopping the fury in her arm before her palm could connect with his cheek. "Not so different from your sister after all."

He crushed her to him, hoping for a struggle, hoping for a fight, and she didn't disappoint, furiously turning her head to the side, preventing him from kissing her.

Tearing at her jacket, a puffy thing that had a fake fur trim along the hood, he swept the material away and cupped her breast through her thin blouse. "I need to touch you," he said, trapping her in place, his leg between hers, pinning her to the wall.

"What about what I need?" she asked through gritted teeth.

"Here." He shoved her hand to his aching cock. "I need to be inside you. Now."

She hesitated only a moment and then flew at him, her lips colliding with his, her hands grappling with his belt buckle.

She kicked off her shoes as she scrabbled to undo the button of his slacks, and he broke away to tug the tights off her legs. He threw aside her panties, too, a white scrap of lace that didn't cover anything, and wadded her voluminous skirt at her waist.

His mouth covered her, his teeth scraping over her clit, and she cried out. Spurred on by the sound, he rammed two fingers inside her. She came, her hands clutching his hair, urging him closer.

He drew out her orgasm, his tongue playing with her clit, and her legs trembled.

When she stopped shivering, he lifted his head from between her thighs and wiped his mouth with the back of his hand, her cum dripping down his chin.

That's what he wanted, that's what he needed. Evidence she still cared. That under the nonchalance and silent stares, under the smoke, embers still burned.

"My turn," he said, pushing his pants down his ass, his cock springing free of his briefs.

Autumn.

Nothing else existed in his mind.

Lifting her against the wall, in one smooth stroke, he impaled her, her core so wet he nearly lost his mind.

He plunged into her, hard and fast, the way he imagined it. Her arms wrapped around his neck, a sob on her lips with every deep thrust.

This was what he fantasized about. Against this very wall. Bending her over the kitchen table, the armrest of the couch. Against the headboard of his bed. He'd taken her everywhere, and his dreams weren't enough.

They couldn't compete with the real thing.

Biting the sensitive skin of her neck, he came, pumping into her, knowledge hazy in the back of his mind he hadn't asked her if this was okay, hadn't asked if she was on the Pill, hadn't used a condom, and frankly, not caring because feeling Autumn bare, nothing between them, was worth every consequence.

He'd learned a long time ago nothing he did came without.

"I'm not apologizing," he said, his tremors subsiding.

She hugged him, her legs tight around his hips. "I don't want you to."

"Good."

He kicked off his pants and briefs and carried her to his bedroom, stepping over dirty clothes and Ty's toys.

Spur of the moment or he would have cleaned.

He couldn't let Autumn see Ty's cars or the mood would be gone, her anger would come back, and she'd try to walk home in her silly shoes and skirt.

Still connected, he laid her on the messy comforter and rested his body on top of hers.

Nuzzled her mouth with his.

He'd made so many mistakes. The first was leaving her behind in Decatur. He should have said something sooner. He'd known he loved her but he'd been too big of a stupid fool and hadn't admitted it to himself.

Until it was too late.

He lapped at her, licking her mouth, moving his lips to her jaw and down her neck.

His cock stirred and began to stiffen.

He'd never have enough of her, and gently, back and forth, in and out, he rocked, the orgasm building steadily in his gut.

She whimpered and closed her eyes.

"Tell me you love me," he rasped.

Her eyes fluttered open, denial and pain burning hot.

"No." He thrust and the tip of his cock hit her center. "Tell me the truth."

Autumn held his head between her hands, tears dripping down her temples. "I love you."

"Sweetheart."

He pulled out and undressed her, unbuttoning her blouse, floating kisses over her collarbone, to her breasts and stomach, and slid the skirt off her legs. She laid splayed across his bed, pink and glistening, her heart in her eyes.

While she watched, he finished undressing and laid beside her.

She hugged him, a leg over his hip, the tip of his cock searching for its target.

He let her roll him onto his back, straddle him, and fill herself.

She tipped her head back as she rode, undulating her hips, his cock buried deep inside her softness.

Uninhibited, she took from him.

He wanted her to take, as much as she wanted, as much as he could give, because then maybe she'd realize she couldn't live without him.

He needed her, and he had to make her see it.

As she rocked, he found her clit and helped her come. She quaked, tears trickling down her cheeks.

Gripping her hips, he followed.

He covered her with a sheet and she met his eyes.

He braced to hear words spoken in anger, or worse, defeat, but all she said was, "This is nice," and he relaxed beside her, resting his hand on her belly.

"We didn't use anything. Are you on the Pill?"

She placed her hand on top of his. "No."

"Okay." There wasn't anything more he could say. They both knew how sex worked, and even if she wanted to keep a pregnancy a secret, she'd never be able to. He saw her every day. He wouldn't press the issue, no matter the promises and reassurances he desperately wanted her to whisper in his ear, and instead, he cuddled into her side. "Thank you."

"Yeah."

He got it. Regret wouldn't come right now while they were naked, his cum drying on the insides of her thighs, her breasts tender after his man-handling. No, the guilt, the shame she'd slept with her sister's ex-husband, would come later. Deep in the night. Maybe when she'd wake and go into the living room to look for Buck. It would come, slow but sharp. She'd feel helpless and alone, and he wouldn't be able to stop it because he would be the cause.

He twisted his fingers in her silky hair and fluttered kisses over her cheeks. "I stopped at the Viking last night. The guys were there partying." It hadn't occurred to him to feel slighted because he hadn't been invited. He may not have shown up anyway.

"Logan and Ivy got married," Autumn said, smoothing his fingers over his stubble.

"Yeah. He's a lucky son of a bitch."

A smile played with her mouth. "Why do you say that?"

"It was so easy for him. Say a few, 'I'm sorrys' and she opens her arms and that's it. A ring on her finger and a signed marriage certificate in little over a week. Like he hadn't done anything."

She wiggled deeper under the comforter. "Do you think she's wrong?"

"I think eighteen years of nothing deserves more."

"They have a lot of history."

"And that should be enough to save them?"

"Ivy thought so."

He skimmed his fingers up her thigh and over her pelvic bone. Stopped at her belly button. "What do you think? What would it take to save us?"

"Summer won't allow it."

"What if Summer were out of the equation?" He

circled one of her nipples with the pad of his thumb. It pebbled under his touch and his stomach tightened.

She arched her back. "What do you plan on doing? Killing her and throwing her body into the lake? She's unhappy, and her misery loves company. I could have told you that, if you would have asked."

"I hated you for getting engaged. I didn't want to talk to you."

He lowered his head, his lips barely touching hers, his breath wafting over her skin.

She swallowed. "You were gone, Cole."

"Decatur's only three hours away. You couldn't have invited me to the city for a coffee, asked me to meet in Marengo to have dinner, or drove to see me and asked to go for a walk? Tell me in person that another man asked you to share your life with him and you said yes? I didn't warrant that amount of courtesy."

"I didn't know."

He blew out a sigh. "That was my mistake. For not telling you, for not saying it out loud, anyway, for depending on some kind of unspoken agreement and for not breaking the silence afterward. You weren't the only one who had a broken heart back then."

She kissed him, guiding his hand between her legs and widening her thighs, inviting him in. He slid two fingers inside her. Wet. His and hers. "Even with Summer gone, if it was just the two of us . . . but we have to think about Ty. Anything we do will hurt him. Summer will make sure of it. Leave it alone and love me, one last time."

"I don't have any condoms."

She met his eyes, her blue irises so full of things he didn't want to name. "Does that matter now?"

"Yes, to me it does."

"I'll handle it."

He grabbed her chin, his fingers sticky, and forced her to look at him. "I love you, Autumn. If we made a baby this afternoon, I want it. Don't you dare."

Her pupils dilated, out of focus, fuzzy. Something flickered across her face. Something he couldn't identify, and it scared the hell out of him.

"Okay."

He let her nudge his body on top of hers, let her slip him inside her, let her give him the afternoon as if it would be their last. But it wouldn't be.

Not by a long shot.

Autumn stood in the shower, as hot as she could stand it and scrubbed her skin until it bled.

Washed away Cole's touch, washed away his words, washed away his love.

Water blinded her, or was that her tears?

It didn't matter.

She'd let him love her, sweetly, slowly, and somber, he'd taken her back to her car in the newspaper's parking lot.

He'd pressed a kiss to her hand and let her step out of the car without saying anything.

Her tights had felt funny, her skirt and blouse wrinkled.

Buck had been in the parking lot, peering at her from around the corner of the building, He'd noticed her flushed cheeks and wet eyes, had narrowed his, his hands clenched at his sides as if he'd known what she'd spent the last few hours doing.

As if he could smell Cole's cum as it trickled out of her and seeped into her panties.

She stood under the hot spray, rinsed Cole's cologne and kisses down the drain.

She'd let him believe that if Ty hadn't been born, there was a chance they could have fixed things. She'd let him think it because part of it was true. Children shouldn't pay for adults' mistakes. Ty was already growing up in a broken family.

Because of Cole. Because of her.

But there was more to it, and it harbored black in her heart.

Summer had Cole first.

It was something she would never be able to forgive him for, and no amount of apology would change her mind.

Out of anyone in Rocky Point he could have slept with and given a child, he'd chosen the one person who hated her.

He could cry, he could say he loved her, he could make his stupid promises, but she would never be able to forgive him for giving her sister everything she ever wanted.

"Ivy's excited," Leah said, standing next to her in the small bathroom. "I don't know if it's for the party or if it's because she doesn't have to work."

Laughing, she scrunched her curls using texturizing product. "Probably both. This might be the only reception she'll have, unless they marry in a church later on. Even then, though, she's been so isolated, she'd probably feel like she didn't have anyone to invite."

Outside, a horn honked, and Leah started. "Oh, I forgot

to tell you that Marnie's giving me a ride. I hope that's okay. I don't want you to feel like I need you to drive me everywhere, and she has the cake, so I said I'd help."

"The cake?" She hadn't thought to order a cake.

"She picked up a sheet cake from the grocery store. I hope you don't mind?" Leah asked, frowning faintly.

"No, not at all. I'm just surprised."

"She said she felt bad for the way she acted last night. She was disappointed her period came, that's all."

"It's probably better this way. Now she can celebrate at her reception." She smoothed her dress down her belly.

After she came home, she'd looked at her work planner and tried to remember when she last had her period. She'd hoped glancing through her activities last month would jog her memory, but it hadn't. She couldn't remember because she wasn't sexually active and normally didn't give her time of the month a second thought. In the end, she guessed this was as good as time as any to get pregnant and all she could do was hope for the best.

She didn't know what that was.

Another honk.

"You're not mad?"

"Of course not. I like having you here but don't feel like we have to be joined at the hip."

"Okay. I . . . haven't had friends. I don't know how to act."

She squeezed Leah's arm. "You're doing just fine. Marnie needs help, so don't worry about it. But you better get out there or you'll find out firsthand that she isn't the most patient of the human species."

Leah laughed. "I already know that. I'll see you soon!"

The door shut, and she was left alone in the silence.

She followed fifteen minutes later, tucking her heels

into her bag and wearing boots in the snow. Buck wasn't lurking around, at least, not that she could see, and she let out a relieved sigh.

It had been a long time since she'd been to The North Star. She didn't date and the newspaper was too cheap to host events at the elegant restaurant. The icy roads were unfamiliar in the dark, and at one point, she turned a curve too fast. Her car's back tires skidded onto the shoulder of the road, and a startled gasp lodged in her throat. She didn't relax her grip on the steering wheel until she parked in the restaurant's parking lot.

Marnie and Leah were already there, the chocolate cake sitting on a side table in the corner of the room. Elora, Logan's mother, sat next to Gail, and Callie laughed at something Linda said. Leah hadn't forgotten anyone. Even Ruby Sinclair sat near Callie, which made sense since Ivy and Mitch had been friends for years.

She hung up her jacket, kicked off her snow boots, and put on the heels that matched her black lace dress. She sat at the table and said to Ivy, "I'm sorry your mother couldn't be here."

Ivy squeezed her hand. "Thank you for doing this. I didn't expect it. I can help pay . . ."

"No, don't be silly. You're our friend and we wanted to do something for you. Besides, we can't let the boys have all the fun."

Blushing, Ivy said, "Okay. I'm sorry. Thank you."

"How's your mom doing?" She smiled her thanks at Leah who poured her a glass of wine.

"She's doing better, but I don't know what's going to happen once she's released. She didn't hurt anyone but she was driving with an expired license and her blood alcohol level was through the roof. The crash didn't damage the building, thank God, but my car's totaled. I'm so grateful I didn't tell her Logan bought me a new one. She thought all we had was the old Camry. Things could have been a lot more expensive for me, I mean, for us. Logan insists that we're in this together. It's nice not to be alone."

"No, you're definitely not alone, and if I can help with anything, let me know. And of course, I want to interview you and Logan for the blog. Everyone's going to want to hear about your secret wedding," she teased, and Ivy giggled, glowing.

She sipped her wine and almost choked on it when Ruby touched her shoulder. She didn't have any contact with Mitch's mother, and it surprised her.

"I want to thank you for that piece you did on Mitch. People have started treating him a lot better and I don't care if it's guilt or God's grace, but it's made a difference. Too little too late, since we're moving, but you defended him. I have to admit, I didn't like you and your blog, but we appreciate you doing that. Chip and I both do," Ruby said, referring to Mitch's dad.

She was used to the negative way some people thought of reporters and didn't take Ruby's comment personally. "It was no trouble, Mrs. Sinclair. I was happy I had the opportunity to make a difference in someone's life. How are you and Mr. Sinclair doing? Are you looking at houses in Decatur?"

"Here," Leah said, whispering in her ear. "The waitress dropped off the menus."

"Thanks." Autumn set the menu aside as Ruby answered her question.

"We are. And we're able to look at something a little out of our price range thanks to the online donation campaign Callie's father set up for us. People donated the full amount and then some." Tears filled Ruby's eyes. "That Ed Dunlop, he's going to serve some time, no doubt about that."

God. She'd missed so much in the past few days.

"That's wonderful, and I'm happy for you. Marnie's wedding has changed a lot of lives."

Marnie heard her name across the small room and grinned. She looked happier than she had last night.

She tipped her wineglass in Marnie's direction.

"It sure has. I can't tell you how proud I am of Callie. She's the love of Mitch's life."

"And he's mine," Callie said, leaning into the conversation.

Her life hadn't changed, she thought, tapping a list of people into her phone she needed to interview. She could run some ideas by her editor and she could possibly do a piece on Ruby and Chip's house hunting, or at the very least, write a short article on the generosity of others and note that the donation campaign would help them start their lives over in a city a little more forgiving.

No, her life would stay the same. Babysitting Ty when her sister grew tired of watching him, dancing around Cole and the relationship they couldn't have, working a meaningless job.

Nothing mind-blowing like finding a partner, her one true love as Ruby put it, because Marnie had wanted to marry in her hometown.

She caught up with gossip, listening to Ruby talk about going through what was left of their house for items to salvage, and with misty eyes, Callie updated everyone about her brother. He'd checked himself out of rehab and was dating a nurse he met at the facility. He applied at a telephone company repairing the lines, something outdoors where he could breathe and not feel closed-in.

Marnie reminded them about their dress fittings, and Elora drew Linda and Gail into a conversation about how town had changed over the years.

Leah explained how she was changing up the Supply Company, but Ivy kept to herself, taking it all in.

"It's a bit to get used to," she commiserated over a piece of cake and a cup of coffee.

"They've all been so great."

"Overwhelming, but great."

"I just feel . . ." Ivy played with her fork.

She tilted her head. "What?"

Ivy lowered her voice. As the guest of honor, she sat at the head of the table, Autumn to her left. Elora sat at her right, but she was speaking to Gail and not listening to them.

"I feel like this is because of Logan. No one looked at me before he came to town. I had Mitch. That's it."

Heat stained her cheeks. "You're saying this feels fake."

"Yeah." Ivy shrugged and looked down at her empty cake plate.

"I'm not going to try to justify our behavior. I'm sure Mitch feels the same way. He and Callie are in a relationship now, and all of a sudden he's being included in things he wouldn't have been otherwise."

"Yeah, he's said that."

"But Marnie's been gone since high school and Callie's lived in Decatur all her life. Leah's new here, too. If there's anyone at the table you should blame, it's me. I never took the time to get to know you and I'm sorry about that. People have a way of coming into our lives when we least expect it or when we happen to need them. You'll be living in Decatur with Logan, and I'm sure you'll do a lot with

Marnie and James. Callie and Mitch too, once they get settled."

"Yeah."

"Don't write off friendships because you question their motives."

"I've been alone for a long time. Some of that was by choice, I know that, but it's hard to ask for help. It's difficult to admit you can't do everything on your own."

She covered Ivy's hand with hers. "You don't have to try anymore, and maybe that doesn't feel like it means anything right now, but one day it will."

"Thanks."

"You're welcome."

After every last crumb of cake had been devoured and every last drop of coffee had been consumed, she stayed behind to settle the bill. When Ivy wasn't around, the girls would split the check, and to distract her, they hurried her out of the restaurant in a cloud of cheerful goodbyes. She signed the credit card slip and stood uncertainly in the lobby near a brilliant Christmas tree.

She should go home, but she didn't feel like it. Instead, she sat at a high-top in the bar, ordered a low ball of whiskey, and slid her iPad out of her bag. She'd write up the blog post about Ivy's dinner, add the pictures she took, and schedule it for tomorrow.

Ivy poked her head into the bar just as she was about to open the newspaper's blogsite. She shuffled over, a concerned frown on her face. "You didn't come outside."

"No. Leah said Jared was going to pick her up and that I didn't need to give her a ride back to my house. They don't get to see each other much and I didn't feel like going home quite yet. Do you want to stay and have a drink?"

"Sure, if you don't mind."

She gestured to the seat across from hers at the small table.

"I'll have a spiked hot chocolate," Ivy told the waitress as she wiggled awkwardly onto the tall stool. She hung her jacket off the back of the chair.

"You didn't want to go home, either?" she asked.

"Elora's staying at the cabin until after Marnie's wedding and Logan moved into my apartment. I texted him, but he's sleeping."

"You fell into being half of a couple pretty quickly."

Ivy shrugged. "It's easy to do when you love someone."

She thought back to her and Cole's conversation, pushed aside the feeling of the hard wall against her back, his fingers digging into her hips, his lips on hers.

The words on his breath. *I love you, Autumn.*

The waitress set a large mug in front of Ivy towering with whipped cream and sprinkles.

"Very adult," she teased.

"I haven't had much fun in the past few years. I might as well."

"I'm sorry."

"It's okay. Part of that was my fault. I should have gotten my mom help a long time ago. I shouldered it because I felt like I deserved it. I was paying for something that wasn't mine to pay for, and Logan helped me realize that."

She closed her iPad and pushed it aside. "Can I ask you something?"

"Sure."

Running her fingertip over the rim of her glass, she asked, "Why did you forgive him so quickly? How? He left you and for eighteen years you didn't hear a word from him, but he came back to Rocky Point and all it took was a few days, a few kisses, and you were married. How did you let go of your pride? How did you forgive?"

Ivy tipped her head back and took a deep breath.

She was trying not to cry and Autumn gave her time to tamp down her tears.

"Logan went through a lot as a kid. I grew up with him while he grew up with *that*. The day he left is a day I'll never forget for as long as I live. The push of leaving to get out of town, the pull of staying to be with me. In the end, getting away from Gunner won and I'll never blame him for that. How can I resent him for all that he's accomplished? Maybe if he'd turned into an addict or followed in Gunner's footsteps, married and beat his wife every day, then came back looking for forgiveness? No, I wouldn't forgive. All that time wasted when he could have stayed here with me. But he turned his life around. He made that time away from me worth it."

"But what if . . . what if he'd married. Had a baby with her, but realized he'd made a mistake? Then what? He chose another woman over you. He gave her a baby, then what would you do?"

"This is about Cole. He married your sister, right? A few years ago?"

"Yeah." She sipped her drink.

"Weren't you engaged? Isn't that what the gossip says? Is that true, too?"

"It's true, but I couldn't go through with it. It isn't . . . proper to think about another man while your fiancé's fucking you."

She liked to say it like that. It took the emotion out of the intimacy.

"You blame him for getting married when you were engaged. I don't understand."

Ivy made her feel like a fool and a hypocrite. "Maybe it's not the marrying part. Maybe it's because he married Summer."

"He wanted you and he settled for the next best thing. You're not flattered?"

She scoffed. "No."

"How do you think *she* feels? She knows he married her thinking he was getting second best. Did she love him that much she looked past it?"

"She married him to get back at me. We've never gotten along and if Cole would have told me instead of keeping it a secret, I could've warned him. Not that he would have believed me, he would have accused me of sour grapes, but at least I could have tried."

Ivy sipped her hot chocolate. "Maybe there was more to it than that. Logan was running away, and because I know what he was running from, I don't blame him. Was Cole running away? Hiding from your engagement? Or . . . *to* something? He was lonely and thought he'd lost you to another man. Maybe he thought Summer would give him what he wanted with you. Have you talked to him about it?"

"I don't want to hear what he has to say."

"Then maybe you should. Ask him what he was feeling, what happened. His answer might surprise you. If you listen."

"He'll give me excuses."

"If he loves you, that's not what they'd be." She pushed her empty mug away. "I hope you don't get cold at night."

She shook her head. "I don't understand what you mean."

"You can keep your self-respect and your dignity if they're that important to you, but they won't keep you warm when you're lying in bed, alone. I'm going home to my husband. The man I chose to forgive. None of us are perfect, and if you hold Cole to perfection, he'll always fail. Guilt makes us do stupid things. Be careful."

"I don't feel guilty."

"Yes, you do, because you don't want to admit you're wrong." She paused. "Drive home safely, and Thank you for the party."

Ivy weaved her way around the empty tables and stepped into the lobby.

Maybe Ivy had a point. Maybe she *was* expecting too much from Cole, she'd certainly made her own mistakes, but it didn't change the fact that as Ty's mother, Summer would always be in the picture. The idea of her and Cole having kids . . . their baby would be Ty's brother and cousin. It put a bad taste in her mouth.

She packed her bag and bundled into her jacket, scarf, and mittens, and changed out of her pumps and into her boots. Only a handful of cars remained in the restaurant's parking lot, and she stood in the snow alone. She listened for a sign that Buck was waiting, lurking behind a tree, but nothing made a sound besides the echoing of a lone vehicle on the highway.

She let her car warm up for five minutes and then drove out of the parking lot, shivering. She didn't want to wait any longer, even if her car protested and she was frozen to the bone.

Headlights immediately came up behind her, blinding her.

"Too bad," she murmured. She wasn't going to speed on these icy roads in the dark. He'd have to be patient until he could lose her closer to town.

She drove a steady thirty miles per hour, five miles under the speed limit. The road curved, and she didn't want to take the turns too fast like she did on the way there. The frozen lake stretched on both sides of her covered in snow.

The driver was relentless, butting up so close behind her she wondered if he wanted to run her off the road.

Her gaze flew to the rearview mirror. If Buck was driving, that could very well be his intention.

Cautiously, she pressed on the gas pedal a little harder, increasing her speed by a few miles an hour. It didn't help.

The truck only increased its speed, too.

Shit.

The truck's bumper nudged her, and her car jerked forward.

Her heart started pounding. "What the hell?"

She stomped on the gas and shot forward, the tires finding purchase on a patch of snow. Her hands trembled as she gripped the steering wheel.

The truck kept pace and hit her again, but this time her car slid on a section of ice.

She began to fishtail in the middle of the empty road and she did what every person on the face of this earth says not to do. She slammed on the brakes and grappled with the wheel praying to God she could keep her car on the road.

It didn't work and she spun in a circle, the trees and the stars whipping around in a frightening streak. Her car skidded off the shoulder of the road and dredged into the snowdrifts that hugged the shore.

The engine sputtered and died.

The truck's driver stopped in the middle of the highway.

Trapped, he could do whatever he wanted to her.

Gunning the engine, he drove on, and tears of relief dripped down her face.

She reached behind her, and her hands shaking, she

grabbed her purse. She needed to call for help. Her car was stuck, and even if it wasn't, she was too skittish to drive anymore tonight.

She could call Leah, but Leah would still be with Jared. She should call the cops and report the accident, but she only wanted Cole, and pressing his number in her Recents, hoped he didn't have Ty overnight.

CHAPTER THREE

Bad news came in the middle of the night. Working for the paper and being a jack-of-all-trades at the television station taught him that, but being a father had brought that lesson home in spades. There was nothing more terrifying than when Summer would call him crying, asking him to go to the ER with her because Ty's temperature was out of control and he wouldn't stop crying.

Nothing mattered in those minutes driving to the hospital, nothing mattered more than holding his son while the doctor brought Ty's fever down, while the pain in his ears subsided.

When his phone buzzed under his pillow waking him at almost two o'clock in the morning, thoughts of Ty were quick to surface and he was already reaching for a shirt before he answered.

Autumn's number glowed in his dark bedroom, and his heart sank lower yet.

This wasn't a booty call.

"Autumn."

"Cole," she whimpered, and his heart cracked.

"What is it, baby? Tell me what you need."

"I'm in the ditch. Buck . . . I think—"

"Are you hurt?"

One-handed, he pulled on jeans and a sweatshirt and quickly looked on the floor for his socks.

"No. I don't think . . . he drove away. I'm so cold."

"I'm calling the cops, but I'll patch them in. Don't hang up. Stay on the line with me, sweetheart. Stay on the phone with me until I get there."

He enabled three-way calling and dialed nine-one-one. He searched for his earbuds and connected them to his phone while the dispatch asked the nature of his emergency. "I'm on the phone with . . ." Who was Autumn to him? A friend? A girlfriend? A lover? If he had his way, she'd be his wife, but she wasn't. "I'm on the phone with Autumn Bennett, a reporter for the *Journal*. She's been in an accident on Highway 51. I'm calling on her behalf. She called me first."

"Is she on the line with us, sir? Can she tell us where she's at? Is she hurt?"

"Autumn, honey, can you tell dispatch where you are?"

He needed to know too because she sure as hell wasn't going to go through this alone.

"I don't know . . . bridge . . ."

"Okay, sweetheart, that's good enough. She's near the bridge on Highway 51. She was driving home from The North Star."

"I ascertained that, sir," the dispatch said dryly. "Ma'am, are you hurt?"

Waiting for her to answer, he gritted his teeth. He put on his jacket, boots, hat, and mittens. Looked for his keys that should have been on the counter but were in the pocket of his coat. He bit back an oath.

"Shaken up."

"Stay on the line, we have emergency services en route."

He didn't say anything while dispatch gathered more information. Nothing about how much he loved her, nothing about how if something happened to her, his whole life would implode. He made do listening to Autumn's shallow breathing and answered the dispatch's questions the best he could about the make and model of her car, her description, and if she had any health concerns.

It bothered him he knew more about her sister than he knew about her, and he promised himself that would change.

The roads were empty at that time of night, the town's lights a weak glow in the sky.

Riding the edge of impatience and caution, he broke the speed limit but he still didn't outrun the cops who were already at the scene of Autumn's accident.

He parked behind a cruiser, the blue and red lights flashing, casting an eerie glow over the snow and the trees that bordered the highway.

He sagged against his car at the sight.

Had it been any other season, Autumn's vehicle would have been submerged in the water. She must have been going pretty damned fast trying to outrun that asshole.

Fury rose in his chest, but he swallowed it back. Autumn was more important now, and no one had helped her get out of the car.

He followed two uniforms wading through the snow.

An officer who was standing on the shoulder of the road shouted at him. "Hey! This could be a crime scene. Get the hell out of there."

"She's my girlfriend," he yelled in reply, as if that made a difference. Besides, this wasn't a crime scene. The instigator of this accident was long gone, and he was willing to bet Autumn wouldn't be able to describe the truck, much less know a plate number. No, all this looked like was a woman going too fast on slippery roads and lost control of her car.

She'd probably been drinking at dinner, too, and he hoped they didn't give her a breathalyzer test. She'd pass, she wouldn't drink heavily and drive, but any alcohol in her system wouldn't work in her favor.

It took both cops to open her door, one kicking snow away while the other yanked.

Autumn released her seatbelt and scrambled out of the car, her eyes locking on his, and she stumbled through the snow and flung herself into his arms.

He caught her, standing in knee-deep drifts, and he held her, pressing his lips to her hair. A dozen horrible scenarios skipped through his head, and he hugged her tighter than he ever had before, tighter than she'd ever let him, while he pushed back the burn behind his eyelids.

An officer wrote notes and declared it a one-vehicle accident, just like Cole knew he would, and sent them on their way. "I'll arrange a tow," he said, shrugging, his gaze scanning Autumn's car. "It'll take some work to pull it out of there. Halfway to Canada, looks like." He scoffed. "Lucky it wasn't summer."

Autumn shivered in his arms, and he bit back a fountain of swearwords he wanted to unleash on the cop. He looked like he didn't give a damn about anything but going back to the station and having a cup of coffee.

"Get in the car," he told Autumn. "I left it running."

"My bags . . ."

"I'll get them, sweetheart."

On shaky legs she trudged to his car, and she huddled in the passenger's seat, her eyes closed.

"She called me and said someone was on her tail," he said, unwilling to let it go.

"There aren't any street cameras around here," the cop said, his breath coming out of his mouth in a white puff. "Can't do much without a witness or a plate."

He knew this. "I want it documented. She's being stalked by an ex, and she's reported it several times. He did this, and I want it documented."

"We can note your concerns." The cop zeroed in on his face. "You're McClure. You take pictures for the paper."

"Yeah, and Autumn's a reporter. She wouldn't make this up."

The cop nodded. "Okay, but there's still not a lot we can do. Has she filed a restraining order?"

"I don't know."

"She should do that, and keep a journal, list the times he harasses her. The more physical evidence she can gather, the better."

"Okay, thanks." It was the best he was going to get.

He waded through the snow and grabbed her work bag and purse out of the backseat. The cops drove away, and since they didn't bother, he took pictures of Autumn's car stuck in the snow. She had to have been going sixty if not more to have skidded so far off the road, and fear roiled greasily in his gut.

Her car could have flipped over, and who knew how long she would have been alone, hanging upside down, unable to reach her phone.

Reining in his anger, he threw her bags into the backseat next to his camera case and slammed into the car. None of this was her fault and chewing her out wouldn't help.

He drove her to his house. Leah would take care of her, if he asked, but he wanted to keep an eye on her himself.

Without a complaint she followed him inside, and he knew she was in shock.

Had it been only this afternoon he'd made love to her against the wall in the kitchen?

He helped her take off her jacket, kneeled at her feet and pulled off her boots.

He adjusted the thermostat and led her to his bedroom where he undressed her, unzipping her cocktail dress and tugging the pantyhose down her thighs.

Nothing sexual about this, not tonight.

He left her bra and panties on and slipped a pair of sweatpants over her trembling legs and a sweatshirt over her head.

With a gentle nudge to her shoulder, she crawled into bed, and he climbed in after her, cuddling her to him, pressing his lips to her temple.

"You can't do that to me," he whispered. She shook in his arms. "I need you."

She lifted her head. "I'm sorry."

"Don't be. It's not your fault and we're going to make damn sure the cops know that. This is bullshit. You could have gotten hurt tonight, seriously hurt."

"He was on my bumper, he even hit me. If you check, maybe there's something . . ."

"I will. Autumn, you're not going anywhere alone, not anymore. It's too dangerous."

She snuggled into him, and he curled his body around her. "Cole, will you make love to me?"

He eased his hand under his Vikings sweatshirt and felt her shiver beneath his palm. "No. There's no way I'm taking from you tonight. You already think I'm an asshole. No reason to give you more proof."

Her light laugh floated through the darkness. "I don't think you're an asshole."

"Yes, you do. Now go to sleep. Tell me if you hurt. I have some muscle relaxers leftover from when I sprained my back last fall."

"Thanks."

He kissed her cheek.

She drifted off, but he laid awake until the sun came up, imaging her trapped in her car, no way to call for help, and even though she was next to him, safe, he couldn't get the vision out of his head, no matter how hard he tried.

The next morning Cole dropped her off on the way to the paper. They'd sat in her driveway, silent. She didn't know what to say, and neither had he, only mumbling a "Be careful and call if you need anything." He'd kissed her hard, crushing his mouth to hers, a hand to the back of her head. Finally, he released her, her lips stinging, and he watched her unlock the door and go into her house. Only then did he drive away. She hadn't had time to think about what Ivy told her, but her warning sparked in the shadows of her heart. No, her pride and dignity didn't keep her warm at night, but she still wasn't sure if that was Cole's place, no matter how willing she was to forgive.

She wasn't sore enough to need medication, but a hot shower went a long way toward loosening up her back and neck. Dressed in yoga pants and a tank top she threw on off her bedroom floor, she called the paper and requested to work from home.

Leah hustled into the kitchen looking crisp in a pair of black dress pants and a blue button-down shirt, her hair pinned into a twist.

"What happened to you last night? You didn't come home. Spend the night with Cole?" she asked, her eyebrows raised, a steaming mug of coffee paused at her lips.

"Yeah, but not for a romp, as your saucy grin suggests. Someone ran me off the road last night. He picked me up and brought me back to his house. I was in a bit of a shock, and he wanted to make sure I was okay."

Coffee sloshed over the rim of Leah's mug. "Good Lord, are you all right? What happened?"

"I think it was Buck, but I don't have any evidence. The driver had his brights on and I couldn't see who it was. Bashed into me and made me skid off the road. I was lucky."

"Yeah, you were. Sliding on the ice like that is scarier than hell. When I did it driving from Marengo, my heart felt like it was going to stop. Thank God Cole heard his phone when you called. After Jared dropped me off, I fell into bed and didn't hear anything until you took a shower."

She smiled faintly. "He's always been good in an emergency."

"What are you going to do? Do you need a ride to the paper? Jared's picking me up in a few minutes and wouldn't mind."

"No, but thanks. I'm going to work from home and wait for the shop to call about my car. They had to pull it out of the ditch and they're going to look to see if anything underneath was damaged."

"Let me know, will you? And if it was Buck, we need to talk about this. You can't be going anywhere alone."

"That's what Cole said last night."

"He's right. Oh, there's Jared. Let's do something tonight. Just the two of us. Stream a movie and make some popcorn. Crawl into our pajamas and watch a chick flick."

"That sounds amazing, but we can't. No more free evenings for a while, Miss Bridesmaid. We have dress fittings when you're done with work. Remember?"

"After, then. How long can it take?"

"This is Marnie we're talking about. It will take all night. But, on the bright side, we might go to the Viking afterward. You haven't been there yet, have you?"

Leah shook her head. "Not yet. I better get going. I'll text Marnie about the time. Maybe Jared or Briar can drop me off at the boutique and I won't have to bother anybody to give me a ride. Text me about your car."

"I will. Have a good day."

"You too. Be careful." Leah hugged her. "You're my best friend. Stay in one piece."

"I plan to," she promised, but with Buck literally on her tail, doing so would be a lot easier said than done.

Cole couldn't concentrate. No one needed him to take pictures, and by noon he'd finished his short sports pieces. The senior curling club was having some exciting times this winter. He loved this town, but God, sometimes it was such a drag. Every once in a while he wondered how much longer Autumn would put up with the slow-paced life.

He never should have left her.

Needing a distraction, he poked his head into the WDAZ offices, but they sent him on his way.

That left him with the afternoon free. Normally he'd spend time with Ty, and around the holidays that meant looking at lights, watching Christmas cartoons, and hanging out at Beth's. Reading a book while his son napped on his chest.

But he couldn't force himself to drive to Summer's and look at a face that so spookily resembled Autumn's he'd start crying.

He'd buried it under anger, but her car accident scared the shit out of him. Knowing to keep it to himself, he hadn't told her how grateful he was she'd spent the night. That she'd woken up in his bed, that she allowed him to cuddle her a little, sprinkle kisses all over her face in relief.

Parked in her driveway, he'd watched her go inside and lock the door behind her. Without her car, she'd call in and write her blog posts at home.

She'd never agree to stay with someone at all times. That wasn't like her, though the run-in with Buck would make her more aware, more careful. He'd make sure she filed a restraining order and started keeping track of when that bastard showed up around town, but she wouldn't give up her independence.

He wrote a mental note to ask her how much of this she'd told her contact in the police department. They were friends, she and Layla, and maybe Layla had her back.

At home, his bed still messy and Autumn's dress and pantyhose still laying on his floor, he put on his outdoor gear and grabbed his camera equipment.

Mitch said he'd put a salt lick behind the resort and if he wanted to photograph deer, that would be the place.

One day he wanted to publish a coffee table book of Minnesota wildlife. The project gave him an excuse to be outside alone and sort through his thoughts, and he hadn't needed it more than he did today.

He should have known better than to chose a high-traffic trail, and sitting on a fallen long, Mitch waved at him as he shuffled over the snow. Sighing impatiently, he hauled his bag's strap up his shoulder, squinted into the sun, and lifted his hand in return.

Mitch was okay. Picked up a cute little thing because of Marnie's wedding. She filled out a dress pretty good, and if she could see Mitch as a person after the accident, she had a heart of gold under the rack.

"Hey," Mitch said. "Looking for deer?"

"Not with you yelling, I'm not."

"Eh. I've been sitting here for a bit. They aren't around. Head past the cabins, you might find some."

"Thanks."

Mitch had given him a natural out, but he sat on the log and eyed a red squirrel running up a tree. Squirrels wouldn't sell books. Anyone could look outside and see one. He left his camera in his bag.

"Taking a break?" he asked. Might as well make conversation.

"Yeah. All anyone wants to do is talk. The wedding, Mom and Dad's house. What we're going to do in Decatur, when Callie and I are getting married, how many kids we're gonna have. All I want to do is unclog a drain in peace, but repairs at the resort are surprisingly slow. Desiree's having a panic attack. She can't find anyone to replace me."

"Things are changing for you here. You don't have to leave."

Mitch kicked at the snow. "Callie's family lives in Decatur. Mom and Dad are excited about the move, and thanks to that donation campaign Callie's dad set up, they're looking at some decent houses. They deserve it. Things are okay, but I think old feelings would come back and maybe in a year I'd want to move after all. I might as well go now."

"Probably right."

"You gave the guys an earful the other night," Mitch said, staring past the trees to the lake beyond. "I like what you had to say. Those guys, they take a good life for granted. I probably did too, before the accident. Logan surprised me."

Cole shrugged and wryly lifted a corner of his mouth. "I took things for granted, too. I thought Autumn would be around forever without having to tell her I was in love with her. Turned out she couldn't read my mind any more than I could read hers. From what I've seen, James and Marnie are okay. Jared's still shaken up by his divorce, but Leah will smooth him out. I know Logan the least of all of them. In high school, he kept to himself when he wasn't with Ivy. But look," he said, pulling his camera out of its case, "you can tell a lot by how people act around each other when they don't know they're being watched."

He showed Mitch a few pictures off his digital camera roll.

James and Marnie stealing kisses.

Jared, his hand frozen near Leah's face, pushing back a piece of her hair, how tender the moment was, the look in both their eyes. That was at Marnie's meet and greet. It had started even back then.

"Do you have any of Callie and me?" Mitch asked.

"Ah, yeah, let me keep going. Here's a picture of Logan and Ivy." Ivy leaned over the bar wearing her work uniform while Logan cradled her face in his hands, placing a delicate kiss on her mouth. "You can't make up feeling like that."

He scrolled through a few more pictures. Autumn looking regal but tired, Ty giggling. Crap, he needed to back these up. "Here's one of you and Callie."

Mitch sat near the fireplace in the lounge, his toolbox on the floor, a coffee mug on the table next to his chair. Callie sat on his lap and she was whispering something in his ear, making him smile.

"See how your hand is on her leg, possessive, but not too hard. You want to keep her there, but you won't force her to stay. She has her arms around your neck, and she's leaning in, telling you a secret. You weren't looking at the camera, so I can't see it in your eyes, but that's sweet body language right there. You two love each other. A stranger looking at this picture would know it in a heartbeat."

Mitch cleared his throat. "You know a lot about that."

"I took a few Psychology and Sociology classes. The way people interact with each other has always intrigued me. I got annoyed at the Viking because those guys were listening to doubt, not their hearts." He clicked past a few more photos of Autumn. He took more pictures of her than he should. "See Jared's parents? I took this the morning he came back after his plane crash. We were at the resort eating breakfast."

He tilted the camera, clearing the glare off the screen.

Jared's parents huddled together, his dad's arm wrapped around his mother's shoulders, and he was pressing a kiss to her cheek. Their eyes were closed, and Jared's mother's hand clutched at her husband's shirt. He wished he could remember their names.

"They didn't worry apart. When Jared was missing, they worried together. I could have taken pictures of them then, too, because I was at Jared's house waiting with everyone else, but their grief was too personal. This is personal, too, but it's a celebration about Jared being alive, that he was okay. They celebrated their son's safe return together."

"You're good at that. What are you going to do with them?"

"Print them out. Maybe Autumn can make photo books after the wedding as gifts. I'm not the wedding's photographer, but I enjoy taking them anyway."

"Do you have pictures of my parents?"

"No. Sorry. We haven't been to the same events, but I have pictures of your house, after the fire, I mean, if you want them."

"I would, thanks. You're not in any."

He laughed. "The curse of the one always being behind the camera." He ran through a few more until he came to the end, Autumn's car slanted sideways in the deep snow.

"What's that?" Mitch asked.

"Oh, Autumn was in an accident last night." The photo dried his throat.

"Is she okay?"

"Yeah. Slid off the road. Some jackass wasn't giving her space on the highway and she panicked."

"You care about her. I don't need a camera to see that."

"I made some mistakes. We both did. Now we're paying. It is what it is."

Mitch nodded. "Some things you can't fix. I can't bring those girls back. My parents can't get those years back people in town stole harassing them because I'm their son. We made a mistake staying here and we can't get that time back. If you made a mistake and you know you can't fix it, there's no point in trying. Learn from it and move on. That's what I'm doing. It's all anyone can do. How would you move on?"

He cut Mitch a sharp glance. "You're asking me to think about a life without Autumn in it."

"She's not, is she?"

"Not in the way I want her to be."

"And you just said she can't be. So why not cut her loose?"

He paused. Up until that point, it wasn't something he'd considered doing, but maybe, even though he was madly in love with her, he should have. Summer would always be in his life, as Ty's mother, as his ex-wife. For another fifteen years she'd be entitled to a portion of his paycheck.

He was asking too much of Autumn to accept that.

Rubbing it in her face every day that he'd chosen her sister instead of simply opening his mouth and telling her that when she accepted Buck's proposal she'd broken his heart.

Maybe it was time to admit their mistakes were too big to fix.

"I'll think about it. Some stuff has to get resolved before I let her be."

"Then figure out what you want and what it takes to get it."

If he stayed on the path he was on now, what he wanted would require a miracle and he didn't see that happening.

"Yeah. I'll catch you later."

"Go look for those deer."

He set out toward the wooded area behind the cabins.

He settled in a pile of snow near a log that would support his camera. He'd sit for a while, watch and wait. See what would greet him in the silence of the sunny afternoon.

Watch and wait.

Cut the ties, cut her loose.

Hope that Ty would be enough to keep him anchored to the ground when he let Autumn float away.

After Leah bounced out of the house, and there was no other way to describe it, Autumn opened the newspaper's blogsite.

Her talk with Ivy had taken a good two hours' worth of work from her, and she'd have to recoup those hours this morning.

Ivy didn't tell her what she didn't already know. Forgive and forget or shrivel up into an old, bitter prune.

There was no doubt Cole loved her. The question was how long he'd let her push him away before he gave up.

Sipping coffee, she typed out her blog posts and added the pictures.

Cole didn't call to check on her, and she was both annoyed and relieved. She wanted him to care, but she wanted to deal with this herself. It was her mess, her ex-fiancé. She'd figure it out.

Or die trying.

Her fingers stilled on the keyboard.

Buck wasn't that dangerous.

He used to love her once.

A little after noon, one of the dealership's mechanics called. Her car's undercarriage hadn't sustained any damage and she could pick it up at her convenience.

Like Leah, she didn't want to bother anyone, and she asked if someone at the dealership could pick her up. Cole was working and Marnie was too busy doing wedding things to run her around town. Callie might be helping

Marnie, and Summer never did anything for anyone if she didn't benefit from it.

The mechanic said he'd send the courtesy car in fifteen minutes.

She quickly changed out of her wrinkled yoga pants and was waiting on the sidewalk when a white car that had the dealership's logo on the passenger door coasted to a stop in front of her house. They made idle chitchat, the kid saying he was taking classes at the community college and that his mom liked her blog posts.

Smiling weakly, she thanked him and wished she enjoyed writing them as much as people seemed to like reading them.

The charge came to fifty dollars and they refilled her fluids and washed it, too. She found her car in the lot and crouched to inspect her rear bumper. It looked fine. No dent, not even a small scratch.

She sucked in the cold air and rested her forehead against the trunk.

No evidence. No witnesses.

It was like it didn't happen.

Except that she'd called Cole, and he'd come for her. Brought her home and spooned her all night.

She hadn't imagined that.

Hadn't imagined his arms around her, kissing her good morning. Hadn't imagined him giving her a cup of coffee exactly the way she liked it.

Hadn't imagined his worried frown when he dropped her off at her house. Hadn't imagined his kiss.

Her phone rang, jerking her back to the dealership's cold parking lot, and she pulled it out of her purse.

Summer.

She wanted something. Even if she would've heard about her accident, she wouldn't be asking if she was okay.

"Hello?" She sighed as she unlocked her door and slid behind the wheel, relieved to have her car back. Being stranded meant feeling helpless.

"Cole isn't answering his phone."

She shivered in her seat. The engine turned over without a problem and hummed. The vents blew out cold air, the radio was turned on low, playing a Christmas carol. Everything was normal except the unease she felt. She'd need a few days to shake off Buck chasing her.

"Autumn?" Summer asked sharply.

"He's probably at work. You keep threatening us, making sure we don't see each other, so why do you think I know where he is?" *Or that I would tell you?*

"Can you come get Ty? You haven't seen him since that skinny woman moved in with you."

"I have things to do." She hated saying no. No doubt Ty was bored watching TV. He wasn't potty trained and a preschool wouldn't take him until he was.

She'd called around asking because he was at an age where he could use some friends that weren't on the other side of a TV screen. She'd do it, but Summer limited time with Ty like a starving man rationed his meager supplies.

It hurt more than she'd admit.

"Bring him with you."

Marnie and the others wouldn't mind if she brought Ty to the dress fitting later. Maybe she could get a hold of Cole before then.

No. She wouldn't dump her nephew. Not when she hadn't seen him in a few days. She missed the little guy.

"And can you keep him overnight? I have a date tonight."

She stifled a scoff. It all made sense now.

"I'll pack him up," her sister continued, oblivious to her lack of agreement.

The line disconnected.

"You're welcome," she muttered.

Reluctantly, heat finally blew out of the vents. She tossed her phone onto the seat and scanned the parking lot.

She didn't see Buck. No trace of him this morning. Maybe he thought he'd gone too far last night and decided to leave her alone.

She drove through town to the richie-rich section of Rocky Point. Cole called it that, though it wasn't so rich anymore. Not since the paper mill closed.

The SUV their parents bought Summer for her birthday was parked in the first stall of the garage. She rarely went anywhere unless she decided to go to the Viking to play pool or the VFW for Bingo, and that was only when the need to party outweighed her want to punish Cole by keeping Ty away from him.

Without knocking, she let herself inside.

Ty ran across the living room.

"Hey, buddy," she said, kneeling, his sticky hands tangling in her hair as she hugged him.

It hurt to remember that anything she did to Summer affected Ty, too. Poor little boy caught in the middle of three adults who couldn't get along.

She buried her face in his sweet, soft neck. "I missed you."

"Auntie A," he said, sighing.

"You wanna go get some food?" she asked, the tangy yet sugary scent of canned pasta lingering on his shirt.

She could do better.

"French fries!"

"Sure." And a vegetable.

"Hello to you, too," Summer said bitterly, watching the exchange, her arms crossed over her breasts.

"Hey, Summer." She forced the words out. "Hot date, you said?"

"Yeah. Might be a late morning, if you know what I mean."

Frowning, she said, "I'll see what I can do. Some of us have jobs."

"Cut the crap. You work from home. Your job is just an excuse not to help me with Ty."

She put Ty's jacket on, wiggling his arms through the sleeves, and shoved his *Paw Patrol* boots onto his feet. One of his socks had a hole in the toe.

"Whatever you want to think. I'm not arguing with you in front of him. I'll bring him home tomorrow." Or maybe not at all.

She hefted the diaper bag onto her shoulder and picked Ty up, securing him on her hip. His body molded to hers, and he wrapped his arms around her neck.

Not even a bye or a kiss for Mommy, she thought, not that Summer gave Ty time to do so. The minute she stepped onto the porch, Summer slammed and locked the door, the deadbolt sliding into place.

"Wow."

Ty kicked at the snow while she struggled to strap in the car seat she kept in the trunk. The fresh air would do him good, and his little cheeks were rosy when she buckled him in.

She texted Leah and asked if she could take a break and eat a quick lunch at the diner with them.

Leah agreed and said she could be there in ten minutes.

"I couldn't pass up the chance to see this cutie," Leah

said, jiggling a Supply Company bag, the plastic crinkling. "We got some of the cutest sweaters in, and more stuffed animals. If it doesn't fit, let me know and I'll exchange it. I had to guess, and I'm not very good at that." Leah blushed and took off her jacket. She helped Ty with his and tugged his t-shirt over his protruding toddler belly, tickling him in the process. He laughed.

Summer hadn't taken the time to shop for him in a while, and his shirt barely fit. She bit back a naughty word and hung her jacket on the back of her chair.

"How much do I owe you?" she asked as Leah lifted Ty into a booster seat.

"Nothing, don't be silly. I hope he likes the dog. I kept one, too."

Ty played with the Alaskan husky wearing a Santa hat while Autumn texted Cole. *I have Ty. I'm keeping him overnight,* she typed, *unless you want him. Summer has a hot date.* She ended the text with a vomiting emoji.

Thank you, was all he texted in return. Huh. He must be at work and busy, or crabby she had Ty.

She shrugged it off. She spent all the time she could with Ty and wouldn't feel bad about it. She loved her nephew, and Cole knew she did.

She wished things had turned out differently, that's all.

"How are you feeling?" Leah asked, picking up her mug. "Is your car okay?"

"Yeah. No lasting damage to me, or the car. No evidence, either, that someone bashed into me."

"The police can't do anything."

It wasn't a question.

"Nope. I filed a restraining order but I haven't been keeping track of when Buck's been watching me. If I can't provide a little evidence, then the judge might not grant it.

Cole has maybe spotted him, and Callie's seen him standing outside the newspaper offices, so that will help, but I need to do better and make note of it myself. What do you want to eat, Ty?" she asked, skimming the menu. "Chicken strips?"

"Yeah!"

"Okay. I know, fries, too, but you have to have something good for you. Like some broccoli, or peas. Can't live on SpaghettiOs, even though Mama tries."

Leah wrinkled her nose. "Gross."

"You're telling me." Autumn chose chicken strips too, in case Ty wanted more off her plate.

He usually did.

"Well, thank God nothing else happened," Leah said. "Max likes picking on me. I know it's not the same, but it's stressful when people won't leave you alone. Do you think he still loves you and that's why he keeps showing up?"

"I have no idea. When I broke off our engagement, he took it hard and begged me to stay. He became violent when he realized I wouldn't change my mind. I moved here thinking I was starting a new life with Cole." She lowered her voice, but Ty was blowing bubbles in his chocolate milk and wasn't listening. "I think the first time I saw him was about a year ago, longer, maybe. Cole and I were fighting, and he kissed me in the newspaper's parking lot. Rough, you know? Hot. I pulled away to catch my breath, and Buck was standing there, staring, hate in his eyes. I think he wanted a second chance, though by then a couple years had passed."

"You left him and he hasn't forgiven you."

"I guess not. I don't like being unforgettable . . . not like that. I wish he'd go back to Decatur."

"Have you seen him today?"

"No. It's like he knows exactly how far he can go without making me freak out."

"Or he knows exactly how far to take you before you freak out because he'd rather have you on the brink than actually breaking down. I've been there. The expectation, the foreboding, the dread, it's worse than the actual doing."

"Yeah."

Leah brushed her hand through Ty's blond curls.

He was one hundred percent Summer. Cole was nowhere to be found in his sweet little face.

"Is Ty safe with you? After the accident?"

She stiffened. "I haven't seen Buck today," she repeated. "I don't think he'd do anything to me if he saw Ty. We talked about having kids, and he looked forward to it."

Leah leaned away to give the waitress space as she set their plates in front of them and said, "I wish I had a car. You shouldn't be alone."

"I'll be okay. Everyone's busy, and I don't expect people to take time out of their day to babysit me. I texted Cole that I'm keeping Ty until tomorrow and he'll show up when he's free. I have to bring Ty to the dress fitting later, but I don't think Marnie will mind."

Leah tapped Ty on the nose, and he grinned, his mouth full of fries. "He won't be any trouble."

"I don't think so, either."

They finished their lunch gossiping about Marnie, the wedding, rehashing Ivy's dinner, and Leah asked her how the blog was coming along.

Having Ty would set her back, and she needed to get going on the interviews she hadn't been able to do this morning without her car.

They finished lunch on a high note, Leah scrambling out of her chair when she realized forty-five minutes had passed. "Helen's going to kill me. I told her I wouldn't be long. We've been crazy busy since the second we opened."

"I'll see you tonight? About five?"

"Yep, I'll be there. Helen said she'd close the store tonight. She's going to help me while I move, and I couldn't be more grateful."

"You're doing a great job. I'll see you later."

"You bet. Bye, Ty," she sang, and he giggled. She gave him a smacking kiss on the cheek and rushed out of the diner.

It was amazing what falling in love and moving to a new place could do for a person, she marveled. God, she wanted to find her happy place, too.

She and Ty finished their lunch, his eyelids drooping more and more after every bite.

"I guess that's a no to dessert," she said, flagging down the waitress to pay the check. "Let's go home and we'll both take a nap."

Holding Ty in her arms, she cautiously stepped out of the diner and onto the empty sidewalk. She didn't see Buck.

Her heart calmed to a normal rhythm, and with Ty sleeping in his car seat, she drove home.

Cole packed up his camera as the sun began to sink into the horizon.

Stiff and frozen to the bone, he welcomed the numbness.

It all seemed so . . . not pointless, but . . . futile. Nothing would change. Summer would always threaten him and use

Ty as a bargaining chip to get her way. Summer and Autumn would always be sisters.

Unless the situation escalated and the cops could finally do something about him, Buck would always be around, just out of reach, avoiding the arrest he deserved.

At least Ty was in good hands this afternoon.

Autumn loved Ty, and it brought him to his knees in gratitude.

And made him love her more.

Letting his car warm up, he checked his phone. A text from Autumn told him they were at EvaMay's Boutique downtown.

He brought his camera inside. He cared about bridesmaid dresses as much as he cared about reception centerpieces, but Autumn would want some pictures to post on the blog, even if she had to use them after the wedding because Marnie didn't want the dresses revealed before the ceremony.

The scent of roses hit him when he stepped into the boutique and orchestrated Christmas music tinkled throughout the store.

Ty ran around in a little tux, and he blinked in surprise then laughed. "What's this?" he asked.

Autumn blushed. "Marnie asked if Ty could be their ring bearer. I said she'd need to ask you, but she insisted that he at least try one on since he was already here. I think he likes it."

"Indeed."

Ty ran around the boutique, stopping to swing his hips in front of a three-paneled mirror and then taking off again. EvaMay ran after him, and he squealed.

"Or the attention," Autumn added, laughing. "I'll talk to Summer, if you don't mind."

"I don't care, but good luck convincing her to let him do anything *you* want him to do."

"I know, but she's like any selfish person. I'll just twist it so she'll believe it was her idea, and she'll get another night free on top of it."

He didn't want to talk about Summer anymore. She already occupied more of his life than he wanted her to. "You look nice in that color."

"Candy Apple Red," Marnie said, stepping out of a fitting room completely decked out as a Bride with a capital B. She looked ready to pose in a magazine spread. "I wanted something festive, and the color suits all the girls."

"You look great, Marnie," he said, his throat dry. This was how couples should marry. A huge fanfare.

It's how he'd marry Autumn, if he ever got the chance, but that chance seemed farther away with every day that passed. She'd wear a poufy dress, he'd wear a grown-up version of the tux his son wore, and they'd seal the deal in front of their family and friends. He'd say, "Look at this woman who could forgive anything to share her life with a guy who doesn't deserve her but will spend the rest of his life trying to do right by her and his son."

Ty wrapped his arms around his leg and pressed a hard kiss to his thigh. Before he could say anything, Ty bolted off and hid in the middle of a rounder full dresses. Leah played peekaboo wearing her red dress, her hair pinned into a twist.

Jared would have her pregnant before too long. She looked too happy playing with Ty not to want one of her own. He'd heard the stories of how she'd grown up, but every second she spent in Rocky Point seemed to make that disappear.

He took a few snaps of her and Ty playing, and then

focused his lens on Autumn who leaned against the counter speaking to EvaMay.

She looked beautiful in red. Her blonde curls were tucked into a twist similar to Leah's, a sprig of poinsettia fastened in her hair, a ruby bracelet glittered on her wrist, and the tips of her gold shoes peeked from under the dress's hem.

Marnie deemed the dresses a perfect fit, and amidst many giggles, he grabbed Ty around his waist and helped Autumn change him into elastic-waist jeans and a *Paw Patrol* shirt. "New clothes?"

He couldn't imagine Summer buying their son anything, and he was proven right when she said, "I bought them a few days ago. A store in Marengo had a holiday sale online and they came today. What he was dressed in when I picked him up . . . God."

He swallowed past the burn. Definitely more than what he deserved. "Thank you."

She gave Ty a graham cracker, and munching, he stomped off. She held his hand. "You don't have to thank me for loving him."

"Yes, I do. You could easily . . ." He had to stop.

"He needs more than Summer. Her heart isn't in it. And you need the help. Even if I felt that way . . . he's my nephew. I like to think I'd be adult about it."

"Leah's grandmother was adult about it," he said, rubbing his thumb over her knuckles. "Duty doesn't replace love."

"I guess not."

"Come home with me tonight. You and Ty. Please? I need the time with you."

Refusal shined in her eyes and she parted her lips, but he placed a finger over them to stop it. "Please."

She paused, then nodded. "Let me change."

He sat with Ty in his lap and read a *Paw Patrol* book, also new, he found in Ty's diaper bag, while Autumn dressed.

Impatiently, he waited through the plans and the good-byes, and Autumn gave Leah the keys to her car. Locking the door behind them, EvaMay waved, and Ty waved back. Cole lifted a hand and she walked away, turning off the boutique's lights.

"He might be hungry," Autumn said as they walked across the small parking lot to his car. "We had lunch at the diner with Leah, but that was a while ago."

"I have hamburger in the fridge to make meatloaf, and potatoes for mashed, if that's okay?"

"Yeah. That sounds fine."

Cole scanned the street, always on the lookout for Buck, but he didn't see anyone except someone letting their dog pee against a streetlight.

Ty babbled in the backseat about Leah, Autumn, and Auntie B thrown in for good measure.

Nothing about Mommy. He should have felt terrible, that he'd made such a poor choice, but all it did was make him sad Ty had such a weak relationship with the woman who'd given birth to him that she didn't rate a mention when he talked about women in his life he loved.

Autumn told him about her day, and he blocked out the thought that this was the way it should have been all along. Autumn by his side, their child in the backseat, driving home after an evening out as a family.

He blocked them out, pushed them back, and wanted to damn Autumn all to hell when she held his hand.

He squeezed.

They cooked dinner while Ty sat at the table and

colored, and after they ate, she gave the little boy a bath. He cleaned the kitchen, Ty's happy squeals echoing through his house.

So natural.

Need gripped him by the throat and wouldn't let go.

They piled into his bed to read books, and Ty drifted off smelling of baby shampoo and diaper rash cream.

"I am so sorry," he whispered.

She cupped his cheek and smoothed her thumb over his lips. "Put Ty in his crib."

He settled his son into his crib with the new dog Leah gave him, turned off the light, and slipped between the warm sheets. Autumn's naked body curled around him.

He made love to her that night, and while Ty slept in the bedroom down the hall, he pretended.

Pretended Autumn was his wife, that she'd give him another baby, a little girl this time, and tears filled his eyes because he knew that was all it was.

A game of make-believe.

CHAPTER FOUR

Autumn's cell phone chimed and she stifled a groan. Last night she'd set her alarm for seven, and she shut it off before it woke Cole.

He'd fallen right to sleep after they made love, but she laid awake past midnight, trying to think of a way out of their mess.

Summer, obviously, was the key player.

In his desperate attempt to distance himself from Summer as quickly as he could, when they divorced, Cole had given her full physical custody of the baby not yet born.

Likely, he never thought she'd turn into such a poor excuse of a mother and regretted it.

She'd talk to him about suing Summer for shared custody, at the very least. They were giving her power when she shouldn't have it.

It wasn't up to Summer if she and Cole saw each other, but if he did take that step, she had to be prepared to take it with him. If they married, she'd be Ty's stepmom. Did she want that responsibility? She loved Ty, but he wasn't hers.

And what was last night? Christ. Was she trying to get pregnant? Another round of lovemaking without protection. He never asked and she hadn't thought about it until it was too late, and by too late she meant he was moaning her name while he came, hot and fast.

Just like that, while he was still inside her, a vision of babies plopped into her head. Not sugarplums. Those would have been a little more realistic what with all the Christmas music playing around town.

It wasn't like she was letting her biological clock have its way, like Marnie trying to get pregnant as soon as she could. She didn't hear the ticking. Taking care of Ty muffled the sound.

She was asking for trouble.

Not one time in the history of anything did a baby make a situation better.

She had to work, support herself. Cole already gave up part of his pay to support a child.

She shifted, and the insides of her thighs were sticky.

Grow up, Autumn.

Cole nuzzled her cheek and sprinkled kisses over her jaw. "Good morning."

She tamped down her annoyance.

It took two, and last night she'd been a willing participant.

She turned her head and their lips met. "Good morning. Do you have to go in?"

"Yeah. You?" He palmed her breast and she leaned into his touch.

"I 'worked from home' the last two days. I need to go in."

"I'll ask Beth to watch Ty. I'm going to assume Summer will be MIA most of the day."

"You know her better than I do." She couldn't keep the hurt out of her voice, even when his thumb skimmed her nipple and it hardened in arousal.

"She's always going to be a wedge between us, isn't she?" he asked, his hand sliding down her ribcage.

"I don't see how she can't be. She's my sister, and you screwed her. Gave her something—"

"That you didn't want from me," he said, jerking away.

"You didn't tell me."

"I know, and I'll regret it for the rest of my life, but the fact is, you knew. You knew and still said yes to that fucking creep who won't leave you alone. I'm not the only one to blame here." He sat on the edge of the bed and raked his fingers through his hair.

"He's not in your life, Cole. He's in mine."

He scoffed. "What a stupid thing to say. Whatever affects you affects me because I love you."

She wrapped her arms around him. "That's sweet."

"It's not sweet. It's pathetic and true."

She nibbled his neck and gripped his erection. He moaned deep in his throat, under her lips. "Make love to me, before Ty wakes up."

It was only after when she was beneath him, while he twitched inside her, that she said, "We haven't been using anything."

"Good," he growled.

All day that one word did a happy dance around her stupid, foolish heart.

Grow the fuck up, Autumn.

Beth opened the door in bare feet, yoga pants, an old sweatshirt that fell down one shoulder, and a secret in her eyes.

Cole's nieces were at school, only a week and a half until Christmas break.

"Hi, sweetheart," Beth said to Ty who rewarded her with a grin full of baby teeth.

"Hi, Auntie B."

"The TV's on, kiddo."

He took the jacket and boots off his squirming little boy who was impatient to watch his favorite show. "Thanks for babysitting Ty today. Sorry I'm later than I said I'd be. I had to drop Autumn off at home."

"Oh?" she asked, her head tilted in speculation.

"Summer dumped Ty on her yesterday and she ended up spending the night."

"Playing house?"

"Kind of."

"The blush on your cheeks says yes," she said, padding into the kitchen.

"Maybe a little," he admitted, but he'd never tell her how good it had felt.

She poured a cup of coffee, set it in front of him, plated a cinnamon roll, and heated it in the microwave.

His mouth watered. No one baked as well as Beth, except their mother.

"Better be careful," she said. "One Bennett sister already messed you up."

"Autumn isn't like Summer."

She sat crisscross on the chair near him. "I know. She can hurt you worse. Listen, I have something to talk to you about, and you might get mad at first but promise to listen to all of it before you explode, okay?"

He sipped his coffee and tried not to panic. He didn't need any more complications. Dealing with Summer, trying to be a good dad, and controlling his obsession with Autumn so it stayed at a manageable degree used up all his emotional energy. "I can't make any promises."

Beth hopped off her chair and paced the warm, cozy kitchen. "Russ was offered a teaching job in Denver. Tenth grade history. Better pay, a shorter summer, but more days off during the school year. They had a football coaching position open up the day they called, and they threw that in there, too."

His heart slammed in his chest. "You're moving."

"He'd be stupid not to take it, so yeah. He said yes. There're better job opportunities for me and I won't have to transcribe anymore. I was getting tired of it anyway."

"When are you going?"

"After school lets out. We'll have all summer to settle in. We already called a realtor and asked about putting the house up for sale. We figured it would take that long to get even a couple nibbles. The housing market here sucks."

"What if it sells right away?" He forced himself to think. What would he do without his sister around? Ty would miss her like crazy.

"Mom and Dad said it'd be okay if we squatted in their basement. It'd be a crush, but I'd gladly deal if our house sold that fast."

"You've thought a lot about it."

"Yeah, we have, but . . . this is the part you have to listen to. Don't get upset."

He tightened his hand on his coffee mug.

"We want to take Ty with us."

He reared back, sweat covering every inch of his skin. "What? Why?"

She stood in front of him, her hands on her hips. "Because we think he needs consistency. Being bounced around among you, Summer, me, and Autumn, that's not a life for a kid. He'd have his own room. The girls would be his siblings. We'd find him a great preschool. He'd have a mom and dad."

"Fuck you. He has a mom and dad."

She scowled. "Really? You're going to sit there and tell me Summer acts like a mom? You're going to lie and tell me she loves him? I know you do your best, but how much time do you give him between taking pictures for the paper and doing odd jobs at the station? You're always hustling because you have no choice."

There wasn't anything she said that wasn't true, and that made him all the more ashamed.

In a quieter voice, she said, "Let us take him."

He shook his head. "I can't. Ty's mine. Summer may not love him, but I do. I'd miss him too much."

She blew out a sigh. "Then come with us. You have a great CV. You'd be able to find something in no time. *Ty needs stability.* He needs a schedule, kids to play with, maybe you could get him a dog. When was the last time he played outside? Went for a walk and picked up sticks? He needs more, Cole."

He looked out the kitchen's picture window to his sister's backyard. His nieces had a huge swing set to play on and a family of snowmen stood guard.

When did Ty play outside? When he had time, which, as his sister pointed out, wasn't often, or when Autumn squared off against her sister and brought him to the playground or the beach.

"There's too much snow to pick up sticks."

"You know what I mean. You're deflecting."

He knew he was. "Summer would never go for it."

Flinging her arms out, Beth said, "She doesn't care! Buy her off. Tell her you'll still give her money every month. Payment to take care of Ty when she doesn't have to take care of him? She'd be stupid to say no. And trust me, she's mean, lazy, and vindictive, but she's not stupid."

"Autumn—" he started, grasping at straws.

"Come on, big brother. If you two were going to make it, don't you think you would've gotten your shit together by now?"

"You don't know anything about it."

"I know you've been dancing around each other since she came back. I know Summer would go ballistic if you two tried to have a relationship. I know that no matter how much you say you love her, she'll always be the one who accepted another man's proposal and to spite her, you married her sister and gave her the baby that should have been hers."

The *Paw Patrol* theme song drifted to them and Ty's "Ruff! Ruff!" made him smile.

Beth was right, in so many ways, and all of a sudden, Autumn's letting him make love to her didn't change much.

Summer would always be in their way.

A rotten apple spoiling the barrel that represented their lives.

Wasn't Ty's wellbeing more important than his relationship, or lack thereof, with Autumn?

Of course it was.

That's what happened when people brought children into the world. Their needs came first.

"I'd like to have you with us. You and Ty are my family, and I'll miss you. But Russ and the girls are my family too, and we need this."

"I don't know if Summer would go for it."

"Stop saying that. You know she doesn't care. She'll be glad she doesn't have Ty dragging her down. All she wants to do is party."

"Okay," he said, straightening, and for the first time in years, the spark of possibility fired in his soul. "I'll force Summer to agree, and we'll go."

She squealed. "Really? I'm so happy! You have no idea how relieved I am."

He'd tell Autumn today. That way she could plan to spend as much time with Ty as she wanted before they left Rocky Point.

"What kind of jobs are out that way?" he asked. "How's the housing market? You'll have better luck dumping yours than I will. Who's your realtor?"

She tugged on his arm. "Russ and I have been researching a little already. Let's go look at what we found."

This was the right choice, he told himself, following her into her home office. This was the right choice for him and Ty.

He could buy Summer off and she could do whatever the hell she wanted. Autumn could move back to Decatur and write the kinds of articles she wanted to write.

This move would be best for everyone.

It was a win-win situation.

Cole stepped into the newspaper's offices looking forward to the future, and he hadn't had a reason to do that in a long time. He'd been stuck in a rut of appeasing Summer, groveling at Autumn's feet, and trying to eke out a living in Rocky Point, only to give Summer half of it so she could go home with whatever guy she met at the bar that night.

It wasn't a way to live and he could finally change it.

Autumn sat at her desk, typing on her desktop, earbuds in her ears.

This move would be good for her, too. She felt tied to Rocky Point because of Ty. He liked to think she stayed to be with him, too, but he didn't know how true that was. Now she could make her own plans, put time and energy into a career she could be proud of.

He'd miss her, though. Her blonde curls, her elegant figure. Her smarts and sense of humor. Eventually he'd find a woman without so much baggage and they could build a future without the past showing its ugly head at every turn.

"Hey, I need to talk to you a second."

She ignored him, typing.

"Hey." He touched her shoulder.

She jerked in surprise and yanked out her earbuds. "Sorry. I'm transcribing an interview. What did you say?"

"I need to talk to you."

She rose halfway out of her seat. "Was Beth not able to watch Ty? Is he in the car?"

"No. I just came from there, actually. He's fine, but she told me some news and I want to pass it along. Do you have a minute?"

"Yeah. Sure."

She knew something was wrong, and it sent slithers of apprehension down his spine. This talk wouldn't go well, but then again, he shouldn't have expected it to. He had to do what was best for Ty, and this move *was* for the best. The quick perusal of jobs Denver offered told him that in about ten seconds. Not only was the pay better, but there was also more opportunity. Autumn wasn't the only one spinning her wheels in this crappy little town.

He led her to an empty conference room and shut the door, keeping the shades drawn over the windows. He didn't want anyone gawking at them.

"What's going on?"

"You should sit down."

She narrowed her eyes. "No, I think I'll stand."

"Okay. Whatever. I talked to Beth this morning and she said a high school in Denver offered Russ a teaching and coaching position starting the next school year. He took it, Autumn. They're moving over the summer."

A smile trembled on her lips. "That's great, but Ty will miss them. He loved playing with the girls."

He shook his head. "He's not going to miss them. Beth asked me to look at jobs, and we're moving too. I won't have to piecemeal projects around the station and the paper to earn scraps. I already applied for a cameraman job at one of the TV stations. The opportunities are there. In fact, I can move ahead of Beth and Russ and that will give her and the girls a place to stay if their house sells faster than they think. Russ needs to finish out the school year, but he already put in his notice."

Her throat worked, her lips parting like a fish. "But, Summer—"

"Do you really think Summer's going to care? She uses Ty as a weapon to make me do what she wants. She'll never let us have a relationship and I'm giving up. I'll still pay her alimony, I'll still pay her child support. She won't turn down money for a kid she doesn't have to take care of anymore. You know as well as I do she'll agree before the words are even out of my mouth. She's a greedy, selfish bitch, and the last thing she wants to be is Ty's mom."

"But this morning you said . . ."

"I said what?" He needed the anger to keep from breaking down and changing his mind. His life without Autumn . . . no one said doing what was best would be easy.

"You said you loved me," she finished on a whisper, the words almost too low to hear across the conference room.

He had to keep distance between them or he'd crush her to him and take it all back.

"I do, but that doesn't change facts, does it? My love hasn't done a damned thing. You still resent I married Summer, and that we had a child together. Ty will always come between us. You'll always see the baby we didn't have, and no matter how sorry I am, I'll never be able to make it up to you. Ty will always remind you of my crappy choices. I don't need that for him, either."

Her eyes sparked. "I would never—"

"You would never take it out on him and I appreciate that more than I can say, but this is between you and me. We have no future, and we've known that for a long time. The move will do you good, too. You won't have to stay here. Move back to Decatur, or to an even a bigger city. New York. Los Angeles. London. You're too smart to write about bridesmaid dresses. Chase that Pulitzer, Autumn. You deserve it. That piece you did on Mitch was amazing. That's what you should be writing. Don't let us hold you back."

She said nothing, but tears filled her eyes.

"I need to tell Summer. If she gives me a hard time, I'll take her to court. I'm tired of being her puppet. You'll be character witness, won't you? If it comes to that."

She barely nodded her head.

"Thank you. You know this is the right thing to do. Summer was never his mother."

And neither were you.

The horrible words weren't spoken by either of them, but they hung in the air and his stomach churned.

"What about . . ." Her hand dropped to her belly.

She wouldn't want his baby, not now. It'd only be a consolation prize.

He gritted his teeth.

Gripping the doorknob, he said, "You said you'd handle it."

He turned his back on her and let himself out of the room.

Not one sound followed him.

Autumn walked back to her desk in a daze. The words hadn't hit her yet. Cole moving away, taking Ty. It wasn't so odd. People moved all the time, accepting better jobs, wanting better weather. It shouldn't have been a surprise to her, really.

Get away from Summer.

Get away from her.

Ty would thrive without Summer treating him like an inconvenience. She acted like the little boy was a burden and had since she'd given birth. Eventually, he'd come to realize that and it would hurt him. No, there wouldn't be any love lost between Summer and her son.

And honestly, she hadn't done her best by him, either, mostly because she didn't want to deal with her sister. What kind of person did that make her?

Cole had every right to start a new life in Denver, and with Beth and Russ there, Ty would have the consistency and stability he lacked being shuffled around to whoever could watch him when Summer didn't want to.

She didn't blame him for taking a golden opportunity, not when it dangled so sparkly in front of him, but he'd lied. He didn't love her. If he had, he could have at least let her down more gently.

Instead of telling her to get an abortion if she ended up pregnant.

She sank into her chair and woke up her computer. What had she been writing about? Ivy and Logan's interview.

"Chase that Pulitzer, Autumn."

Hadn't she thought it? Dreamed about it. Cole and Ty leaving was a gift. She could turn her own career around. Put her heart into her work because Ty would be safe and wouldn't need her anymore. Cole never had, and accepting Buck's proposal, she'd told him she didn't need him either. Maybe it was time to listen.

She could date, marry someone who would travel the world with her, reporting on scandals and war. Instead of interviewing other people, they would want to interview her, ask about her glamorous international lifestyle, and at sixty, seventy, someone would write her biography, praise her for giving up a family to uncover the truth. Then she'd retire, settle by the ocean, Greece, maybe, and she'd never think about this stupid little town and all the stupid people in it.

She was so much better than all of this.

But she didn't get up, she didn't turn her notice in to the editor.

Calmly, her hand steady, she turned the recording back on and started typing out her friends' interview, and as her heart cracked, little by little, she used Logan's and Ivy's happiness to block out the world.

She waited until she was alone in the office, the bullpen cleared out for the night.

That's when the tears came, and not knowing where else to go, she crawled under her desk. Her back pressed against the metal, she cried into her knees.

Hiding behind his computer monitor the entire day, Cole hadn't approached her, not to say he changed his mind, not to say that he was leaving but that she should keep Ty.

And not, she'd hoped in such a dark corner of her heart she hadn't admitted it to herself, not to ask her to go with them.

Things would be okay, she tried to tell herself. Cole was doing this for her, too. She couldn't be an international reporter living in Denver. She might as well stay here. That's why he didn't ask her to go. He wanted her to chase her dreams.

She used the hem of her blouse to dry her eyes. She had to pull herself together. Marnie's bachelorette party was tonight and she wanted to cross the border into Canada to mix it up.

Marnie had warned everyone months ago, and she renewed her passport specifically for the occasion. She didn't go anywhere else.

But she could now.

She crawled out from underneath her desk and the

janitor sweeping the floor dropped his broom in surprise. The wooden handle clattered onto the floor.

"Sorry," she muttered. "I dropped something."

He shook his head, resumed his sweeping, and didn't look at her again.

She packed her bag and shoved her arms through the sleeves of her jacket. Greece was sounding better and better.

Her car was the only vehicle in the parking lot, and it tilted at an odd angle. She trudged across the snow and groaned. One of her tires was flat.

Wait.

She dropped to her knees and covered her mouth, stifling a moan. Someone slashed her tire. A knife's silver handle glittered in the light floating across the lot.

It didn't take her much time to guess who'd done it. There wouldn't be prints on the knife, but there was only one person who had a vendetta against her.

She pulled her phone out of her purse. She'd call Cole and he'd—

No. She wouldn't call Cole. He'd done more than tell her he was leaving and taking Ty with him. He'd broken up with her, too. If things moved as quickly as it sounded like they would, he and Ty could be moving well before spring. His house would sell without any trouble. He'd done most of the remodeling himself and once they saw the inside, they'd fall in love in an instant. No, he didn't have to worry about selling his house or getting a job. She'd seen his résumé. He could ask Leah to help him, and she'd have him hired out in five minutes.

Tears pricked her eyes.

So easy for him to walk away.

There was no point in calling the police, they wouldn't

be able to do anything, and on her cell, she searched for the number to call a tow. The bored dispatch said it would be a while. Their only truck was pulling someone out of a ditch.

She didn't care she'd have to wait. The cold air would wake her up and hopefully shake her out of her shock. She needed something to knock some sense into her . . . she was stupid thinking she and Cole could have a relationship.

She wiggled the knife out of her tire and turned it over in her hands. A switchblade. It looked brand new.

Unfamiliar with knives, she didn't know how to shove the blade inside the handle. She wrestled with it, and the razor-sharp edge sliced a deep gash into her palm. Pain raced up her arm.

She whimpered and fresh tears wet her cheeks.

She wasn't macabre, but her and Cole's conversation put her in a bad place. When he moved, he'd be taking her heart. She'd need years to get over him, if she ever did. She could picture herself turning into a ghost. A tragic, heart-broken ghost, drifting from story to story, her own a mystery to those who cared to look.

Blood ran down her wrist and dripped into the snow. She couldn't stop staring at it.

A car backfired in the street and she jumped. She had to snap out of it.

She threw the knife in a snowbank. No one would see it, not for a while. Maybe not until spring. If it snowed again, the snowplow would bury it even more.

Using an antibacterial towelette she dug out of her purse, she wiped her palm and tried to stop the bleeding by wadding a ball of tissues in her fist. It hurt like a son of a bitch, but it was the best she could do. While she waited for the tow, she kicked snow over the blood.

The truck arrived, but instead of towing her car to the

shop, the driver changed her tire using the spare in the trunk. An hour and a half after finding the knife shoved into her tire, she was letting her car warm up, her flat on the way to the shop to be repaired.

Her hand ached, but she didn't think she needed stitches. The bleeding stopped, and examining the cut in the dome light, she decided a bandage would be good enough and it would heal on its own.

That suited her. She didn't need anyone lecturing her about her own stupidity, or the fact she'd covered up a crime.

Though Buck's actions hadn't interested the police so far, and she hadn't heard anything about the status of the restraining order, either.

For all intents and purposes, she was on her own.

That was okay because she'd be just fine.

She didn't hear from Cole, though she'd harbored a secret hope he'd call and tell her it had all been a big mistake, that he hadn't meant it, that he'd miss her too much if he left. But as she applied makeup in her little bathroom with Leah, pretending to be giddy and happy while they danced to Madonna, he was probably polishing his résumé or researching family law attorneys in Marengo or Decatur because he'd meant it when he said he wanted Ty away from Summer.

He didn't need an attorney to take him away from her.

Strapping him into his car seat and driving away would work just fine.

She sat on the edge of the tub and Leah stopped dancing. She couldn't pretend to be happy, but she couldn't let her personal problems interfere with Marnie's bachelorette party. She had to get through this weekend, this wedding, then she could make her own plans.

"Are you okay?" Leah asked, concerned.

"It's nothing. Sometimes I get tired, you know?"

Leah turned the music off. "I know. I also know that in those situations, you have to try to think of small things you can do to make it better. Tomorrow morning we'll sit down, you and me, and we'll talk it out. Cole, your sister, Buck. All of it. And if you have to take a break, my apartment in the city's available. Stay as long as you need to. See a show, do some sight-seeing. Whatever. Clear your head."

She hadn't expected Leah to understand so completely, so totally, to even offer a getaway, and she wiped her cheeks, her bandage scratching her skin. "Thank you."

"You've helped me so much since I came to Rocky Point and you've turned into my best friend. Whatever you need me to do, just ask."

"I will." She forced a laugh. She couldn't be a downer tonight. This was Marnie's time. "Come on, we better get moving so we're not late." She turned Madonna on again, the eighties music bouncing off the tiles.

She'd felt shiny and new in Cole's arms, just that morning.

It seemed so long ago now.

Autumn hadn't crossed the border in years. She had no reason to, and growing up in Rocky Point, she took it for granted Canada was so close. When she'd visit during college breaks, she and some of her friends would cross because the legal drinking age was lower than in Minnesota and they'd hit the town, but as an adult who didn't need accommodations to drink, crossing into Canada was the last thing on her mind.

The group caravanned through the border crossing, paying the toll and letting the patrols search their cars.

They were waved on without a problem, strict reminders that driving while intoxicated was against the law, but an old man who had an amused grin on his face said to, "Have a good time."

If this had been her party, she wouldn't have bothered with the inconvenience. Passports, tolls, driving in a city she wasn't familiar with, it all seemed too much for a bachelorette party, but a new nightclub had opened over the summer and Marnie wanted to give it a try. Unlike the men, she said, a pit that had greasy wings and an old pool table wasn't enough.

After playing tug of war with a pair of pantyhose, a slinky skirt, and a barely-there top, she thought jeans, a t-shirt, a pitcher of beer, and enough grease to raise her cholesterol by a few points sounded heavenly.

She was always on the lookout for things to blog about, though, and she'd find the manager and tell him or her she'd write a positive review in the *Journal*. Maybe they'd get a round of free drinks out of it.

Besides, Leah wiggled excitedly in her seat, and she shook her head, pleased her friend was having such a good time.

They parked in a full lot adjacent to the building, and she paid the cover charge to walk in the door. God. She'd be broke by the time this wedding was over. She loved Marnie, but she'd have to turn to some of her freelance gigs to make up the money she spent over these two weeks.

They checked their coats, another charge, and she stepped into the dark club, Leah by her side looking around and bobbing to the techno beat throbbing against the walls.

"This place looks great!" Leah yelled into her ear.

"You don't have clubs like this in New York?" she asked, her eyebrows raised in disbelief.

Leah shrugged. "Sure, but I never went. I never had the time or anyone to go with."

"I'm too old for this," Ivy said, flinching.

She agreed. "You and me both."

"I'm gonna go find me some beefcake," Gail declared, shooting off into the crowd, and Linda wasn't far behind.

"Oh, Mama," Marnie said, her eyes wide.

"Lord Jesus," she muttered.

"What? You don't want any beefcake?" Callie asked, nudging her shoulder.

"The only way I take my beef is in the form of a hamburger or a thick, juicy steak."

"How about a drink then?" Callie asked, laughing.

"Perfect."

Marnie led the way, confident wearing a skin-tight black dress and about a million necklaces hanging around her neck.

She didn't miss the appreciative glances Marnie's curves earned her, but Marnie didn't pay them any attention.

It wouldn't hurt to be on the lookout for a new guy. Someone to talk to over a drink. Someone to go to a movie with. She and Cole been dancing on and off for so long she'd forgotten there were other men out there. Available ones who hadn't fucked her sister, though that number in Rocky Point seemed to be dwindling.

Marnie was lucky and found an empty banquette in the back corner, and a waitress took their orders. To make it easy on her, Marnie ordered a couple pitchers of Cosmopolitans, and the waitress blew her a kiss.

That was a considerable amount of vodka, but she and Leah had taken her car and she didn't plan on drinking that much.

The waitress served them their drinks, though she was only able to take a couple sips before Callie pulled her onto the dance floor. "Come on! This is my favorite song!"

"It is?" she asked, her blood already humming. She couldn't recognize the main beat over the bass, but she, Leah, and Ivy followed Callie onto the crowded dance floor.

The voices of the patrons who hooted and hollered in time with the music or tried to hold conversations washed over her as she gyrated, her hands waving in the air.

Marnie joined them and shouted, "Keep an eye out for the moms, okay? They haven't been here before, either."

She nodded, but the nightclub seemed safe enough. Clean, the neon lights bright, the people on the dance floor looked like respectable citizens out on the town to have fun and nothing more.

When she'd lived in Decatur and did short news stories for the *Herald,* she'd visited some of the seedier dance clubs and stripper joints looking for a runaway teen. Filthy floors and waitresses who smoked crack and gave blowjobs on the side were common. Drug deals in the bathrooms. Dirty managers who skimmed from the registers. Overpriced, watered-down drinks.

The runaway had turned up a month later. She'd taken a Greyhound bus to Wisconsin.

She danced until it felt like her feet were going to fall off. She'd worn her highest heels, determined after Cole's news to enjoy herself.

She staggered back to the table and poured more of the martini into a glass. She wasn't sure if it was hers, but they were all friends, so it didn't matter. Parched, she downed the sweet liquid, and the vodka hit her like a one-two punch.

An Alexandra Stan song ripped through the club. This song she did know, and she joined her group and danced some more.

Marnie giggled when Gail and Linda found them in the middle of the dance floor, and the older ladies danced too, holding brightly colored drinks above their heads.

The song ended and she broke away to find the restrooms. They were clean and well lit, and several women stood in front the long mirrors reapplying their makeup.

She washed her hands, fluffed her hair, and freshened her lip gloss.

"Love that top, honey," a tall Black woman said, her own blouse sparkling under the fluorescent lights.

"Thanks. I bought it at Macy's. I like yours, too."

The woman grinned. "I bought mine at the same place. Have fun," she said, teetering on heels higher than hers out the door and into the hallway.

She turned back to the mirror.

She wasn't so bad. Maybe her curly hair looked dated, but short of growing it out, there wasn't much she could do with it. Color it? She'd always wanted to try being a redhead. Or pink streaks. Prove to everyone she hadn't lost her fun.

She'd held on to her figure, and she didn't spend time in the sun. Maybe a little bitterness had etched into her face, faint frown lines hugging her mouth. She shoved the corners of her lips into a smile.

Maybe she needed a vacation. She could visit her parents after the wedding. They'd be more than happy to buy her a plane ticket. She could write a couple of travel pieces and shop them around. What she needed to do was focus on what she wanted out of her career and go after it. Nothing was in her way now. Get paid to travel? There were worse things. Though getting her foot in the door at Condé Nast seemed about as possible as winning the lottery. Maybe she'd start her own travel blog. Apply for a couple of writing grants or finally accept the money her parents kept offering her. If it was good enough for Summer, it should be good enough for her, too.

A tipsy woman stumbled into her and she sighed. Not the best place for self-contemplation.

She went back to the table.

"Autumn, will you go to the bar and order more Cosmos?" Marnie asked. "Since you're already up?"

"Sure. No problem."

"Thanks."

She stood in the crowded line and waited her turn. The bartender was cute and she lifted onto her tiptoes and leaned over the bar. She ordered four more pitchers and asked if they could be put on the tab Marnie started. He nodded and grinned, and her job done, she twirled around and bashed into a man standing behind her.

"Whoa! Where are you going in such a hurry?" he asked, laughing and grabbing a hold of her elbow, his hand warm. Humor and a touch of concern twinkled in his eyes. "Are you okay?" He guided her to an empty space near the wall.

"Yes, I'm sorry."

"Don't be. I'm Phillip."

"Autumn," she said, holding out her hand.

He lightly squeezed. "Pretty."

No, you are, she thought. And he was. His blond hair was combed off his forehead, a sexy five o'clock shadow covered his jaw, and he wore a navy dress shirt and a navy and silver tie loose around his neck.

His accent sounded more American than Canadian, but she didn't know him and a man who looked this good wouldn't be left alone in a small town like Rocky Point. He belonged on this side of the border.

"Are you free?" he asked, speaking into her ear. His cologne hinted of sandalwood and she breathed in.

"I'm available, but never free," she said, but she wasn't kidding. She had a broken heart and that always came with a price.

"Ah, I like that," he said, chuckling. "Come, I'll buy you a drink."

"I'm with some friends. I was just ordering another round."

"I won't take up much of your time, I promise. Did you know there's a VIP lounge upstairs? Quieter."

She found nothing suspicious in his eyes, and when he tugged on her hand he hadn't let go of, she followed.

She and Phillip passed their table and she paused, Marnie telling an exaggerated story, her hands flying everywhere as she laughed.

"Tell them you're with me, if it will make you feel better," Phillip said, reading her hesitation.

"It would, thanks. I'll be right back."

She told Leah she'd met someone and was going to have

a drink. Leah leaned around her to see whom Autumn was talking about and said, "He looks nice. Sexy in a suit."

"Yeah, he is."

Marnie raised her glass and said, "Good luck."

She didn't think luck would be necessary to have a drink and a little conversation, but she replied, "Thanks."

Gail glared. "Be careful. You have half an hour, then we're checking on you," and she nodded, appreciating she had people who cared about her and wanted to keep her safe.

Cole's callous way of dumping her and saying he was taking Ty away had torn her down, but Phillip's blue eyes conveyed a warmth and comfort she wanted to wrap herself in.

They went up the stairs, his hand hovering over the small of her back.

A gentleman, too, she thought, and smiled her thanks when they reached the top.

"Those are some killer heels you're wearing," Phillip said, holding her hand.

She curled her fingers around his. "They're my fuck-me shoes."

"I'm sure they do the job quite nicely," he said as they walked across the black concrete floor.

Another bar was built into the long wall, but Phillip led her past it and the line of people waiting to order drinks.

He pushed an unmarked door open and allowed her to step into another part of the club, a lounge that had more banquettes, areas that were sectioned off by black silk curtains, and waitresses that didn't seem so busy. "This is Starburst's VIP lounge. What do you think?"

"The whole club's wonderful," she said truthfully. "Very trendy."

"We wanted a safe place where people could go and have fun. No drug deals in the bathrooms. We didn't want women scared that assholes were going to fuck with their drinks or rape them in the parking lot."

"We?" she asked, following him to a small, empty banquette tucked into a dark corner. He sat close to her and rested his arm along the back of the booth, his fingertips flitting over her bare shoulder.

"My brother and I own this club." A waitress approached them and he asked, "What would you like to drink?"

"We were drinking Cosmos downstairs." She liked the feel of his fingers as they played on her skin, and she melted into the bench, the booze relaxing her. Who cared if Cole dumped her? Who cared if she'd never see Ty again after they moved to Colorado? She was thirty-six years old and it was time to stop living for what could have been. That was done and there was nothing she could do about it.

"Would you like some champagne?"

"That sounds nice," she said and nearly choked when he told the waitress, "A bottle of Veuve Clicquot."

"Phillip—"

He chuckled. "Don't worry, it's not as expensive as it sounds. We don't carry the ultra-good stuff. We stock our clubs based on location and average median income. No one around here would order a fifteen-hundred dollar bottle of champagne. It would be a waste to offer it."

She sighed. "Thank God."

"Though, I think you're worth it," he murmured, leaning toward her.

"Are you trying to flatter me?"

"Yes. Am I doing a good job?"

"You are."

The waitress came back holding an ice bucket, the bottle of champagne, and two flutes. "I can pour, Jules. I'm sure you have other things to do."

"Yes, Mr. Hatton," she said, twirling on a heel.

"She's not a server," he said, pulling the bottle out of the ice. Someone had already uncorked it. "She's the manager. We're training her to take over when my brother and I leave to open another club."

"You don't live here?" she asked, disappointment and relief tangling inside her. She wasn't ready to date anyone, but it would've been nice to have someone nearby. Someone as affable as Phillip who wouldn't require so much work to be with.

"No. Well, we have been since we opened the club, but we're planning our next location. Our headquarters are in Vancouver, British Columbia."

"I wondered where you were from. You don't sound Canadian."

"My brother and I moved around a lot when we were children. A few years in boarding school in the UK, and we summered in Belize. Skiing in the Alps, that kind of thing."

"You come from money."

"A little."

He offered her a flute, and she wrapped her trembling hand around it.

"Do I make you nervous? I assure you, I won't hurt you."

"No, it isn't that. I'm not . . . I told you I'm available, and it's true, but it hasn't been that long since." Twelve hours.

"Ah. I knew there was someone lurking in the shadows of those sad eyes. He was a fool to let you get away."

"Men can be, can't they?"

"Yes. Perhaps you'll allow me to cleanse the palette, so to speak," he said, placing his flute on the table.

"What do you mean?"

"I'd like to kiss you, Autumn."

A kiss wouldn't hurt, not his, not tonight. "All right."

Phillip covered her mouth with his, gently, one hand resting on the back of her neck, the other caressing her cheek.

The kindness surprised her, and she leaned into him, craving attention that wasn't full of bitterness, anger, and regret.

He broke the kiss and brushed a curl away from her face. "Now tell me about the man who would give this up. Did he leave you for another woman?"

"No. He's moving to get away from my sister."

Phillip raised his eyebrows, and she smiled, rueful. She told him about their history, skimming over this morning when they'd made love and not four hours later him telling her he was moving and taking Ty.

"He doesn't love you enough to fight?" Phillip asked, his thumb smoothing over her bottom lip. "I would move heaven and earth to keep the woman I loved."

She lifted a shoulder. "He says he does, but we've been through this for many years and he's tired. So am I. My parents are on an extended holiday in Italy, and I'm thinking about joining them. I need time to myself."

"What do you do?"

"I'm a journalist. I write for the Rocky Point newspaper."

"Ah. Then why aren't you using your words?"

"I don't understand."

"You say he's tired and he has no fight left, but have you told him you love him, that you don't want him to leave you behind? He's taking your nephew, your heart, and you'll let him go?"

She spoke to the tabletop. "I can't make him stay. Not if he doesn't want to."

"Sometimes, Autumn, men need their women to stand up for them, not only the other way around. How do you think he felt, walking away and you didn't call out? Didn't stop him? Do you think, maybe a little, his heart was broken? You're a strong woman, yet you don't use your power to open your mouth and speak. That has been the problem between you all along, hasn't it? You have a degree in communication, yet you do not communicate your wants and needs."

"Summer—"

"Is an excuse. What are you really afraid of?"

"I don't know."

"Yes, you do. You fear what all humans fear. Rejection. You won't offer him your heart because you're afraid he'll tell you he doesn't want it. You think that's what he did when he married your sister, but you put another man's ring on your hand." Placing a finger under her chin, he asked her her look at him. "It was easier, accepting the sure thing, even when it wasn't right. Admit your mistakes and tell this man you love him."

"What if I'm too late?"

"It *will* be too late if you never say anything."

She'd let Cole walk away in the newspaper offices and she hadn't made a single sound. She'd waited for him to ask her to go to Denver, yet, she hadn't told him she wanted to go, either.

"How did you get to be so wise?"

"I'm not much older than you, and I have two ex-wives.

You're not the only one who doesn't know how to say how they feel."

She pressed her lips to his. "I'm sorry."

"No apologies are necessary. Just a foolish man's mistakes. Now tell me what you do at the paper. I have contacts in a few of the larger cities in Canada if you're open to freelance work. Perhaps some traveling, as well, if things between you and Cole don't work out."

She briefly described the pieces she'd been writing for the *Journal*. The small-town paper didn't add much to her résumé and instead, she focused on the more important articles she wrote for the *Herald* during her years in Decatur.

They passed another half an hour in a pleasant haze of professional conversation. As a thank you for her company, he said their martinis were complimentary, and she promised him a glowing writeup in the *Journal*'s Lifestyles section.

"Thank you, for being so honest with me," she said, sliding out of the banquette. "It isn't pleasant, sometimes, hearing the truth."

"You'll call me, if you and Cole don't mend things? I could provide some distraction, if needed," he said, a teasing sparkle in his eye. He handed her a business card. "My personal cell phone number's on the back. Use it anytime."

"I will. Thank you."

He walked her to the staircase and kissed her cheek goodbye.

She found her friends on the dance floor and they pulled her into their circle. She caught Phillip's eye as he watched her from the upper deck of the club, and she waved.

He lifted a hand in return and then walked away, a slight slump to his shoulders.

She wouldn't let Cole leave, not without a fight. If she wanted him and Ty in her life, she needed to be brave and tell him. Even if it meant she'd waited too long and he didn't want her anymore.

It was all she could do, and she prayed it would be enough, that she wasn't too late.

CHAPTER FIVE

Autumn woke to a persistent buzzing.

She'd set her alarm to go off nine intending to get a few hours in at the office despite the late night and drinks. Plus, she wanted to gather a few articles she was most proud of, send them to Phillip, and ask if he'd pass them on to his contacts. If she found a friend in all this mess, that would be a benefit she hadn't expected. She could use the professional networking whether she and Cole came to a truce or not.

Weak white light trickled in through her windows, but it felt like the middle of the night. They hadn't gotten home until three in the morning. When Marnie found out Phillip waived their tab, she demanded to meet him and Jules directed them to his office. He'd been gracious, and even though they hadn't paid for their drinks, Marnie insisted on tipping the bartender and the waitress who'd served them.

That endeared her to Phillip, and he'd said a sincere goodnight to her friends.

They retrieved their jackets and stepped into the

parking lot, and Phillip had kissed her cheek one last time and wished her luck.

Leah waited outside the door, leaning against the brick wall looking like a high-class hooker. Autumn didn't think she'd appreciate the comparison, but she smiled anyway.

"He's smitten," Leah said.

"I wish I could be. I think we would have been a good match."

"Good looking."

"A man needs more than looks."

"Don't I know it," she said, but without a trace of bitterness.

"Jared has it going on," she said, unlocking her car and scrambling into the cold car. The stars were bright, the sky black velvet, and all she could think about was taking off her heels and crawling into bed.

"Hmmm. Something I haven't been able to appreciate because Rita's still at their house."

She hadn't given a thought to Rita since Marnie's dinner. "How's that going? She didn't show up at Ivy's thing. She was invited, wasn't she?"

Leah shook her head. "No, I didn't ask if she wanted to go. I saw the way she treated Ivy the night she came into town. I ran out of Marnie's dinner and Rita followed me to the bar, remember? Gloating. So smug, warning me she and Jared were getting back together. She didn't give Ivy one glance and I didn't think Ivy would want her there. Rita's been keeping to herself, spending time with Briar and trying to work from home. I've tried talking to her, but to be honest, my heart isn't in it. She's everything I don't want to be."

"She'll always be on the outskirts of your relationship

with him, though. She'll pop up at inconvenient times, like when Briar gets married."

"I know, but at least she's not my sister. How are you and Cole going to work that out? You've been seeing a lot of him. I'm sorry. We were going to talk about this tomorrow. You probably don't feel like getting into it now. It's been a long day."

It had been, but not for the reasons Leah thought. Leah didn't know what Cole said to her at the paper, or that Buck had slashed one of her tires. Her hand hurt and her skin was tight and hot, but when Leah asked about her bandage while they were getting ready to go, all she said was she'd hurt herself at work and it wasn't a big deal. Leah looked like she'd wanted to argue, and she was lucky Leah left it alone.

"Yeah, it has. It'll keep."

After the cold drive home, she'd dropped into bed, too tired to wash off her makeup, her feet screaming in relief.

She'd fallen asleep in that very position, her head spinning with Veuve Clicquot and Phillip's kiss.

Her phone nudged her to consciousness, dregs of a dream fading like mist as she woke up.

Thinking she was late for work, she sat up, sleepy fear slithering through her. She took a deep breath and reminded herself she couldn't be late unless she missed a staff meeting, and there wasn't one scheduled today.

She fell back on her pillow and grabbed her phone, Cole's name lighting up her screen. "Good morning," she said, her heart in her throat. Maybe he hadn't meant what he said to her yesterday and he was calling to apologize, to tell her he loved her and that he wasn't leaving.

"What the fuck, Autumn? I tell you I'm moving to Denver with Ty and you take him overnight without letting

Summer know? You could have asked. I'm driving to your house right now to pick him up." He lowered his voice. "We know Summer isn't going to win the Best Mom of the Year award, but she's freaking out."

Her mind did a slow slog through what he said, but she couldn't make sense of it. "Ty's not there?"

"Don't play innocent with me. I was going to encourage you to spend as much time with him as you wanted before we moved, but you didn't have to be so underhanded about it. Have him dressed and ready to go. I'd let Summer pick him up, but you and I are going to have it out. This is ridiculous and it's not going to happen again."

"What are you talking about? Are you saying Ty isn't at home?" She sat up again and clutched her throat.

He growled. "Jesus Christ. Haven't you been listening to me? No, he's not here. He's usually up by seven, you know that. When eight o'clock rolled around, Summer went to check on him. Yes, even Summer went to check on *our* son." He said 'our' like suddenly it was him and Summer against her, and she swallowed back a stomach full of vomit. "He wasn't in his crib and there's only one explanation. You went in and grabbed him. You don't have to feel like we would stop you from seeing him."

How conveniently he forgot that yes, Summer did stop her from seeing him. It was only when Summer needed a "break" that she was deemed acceptable enough to spend time with her nephew.

"Have you thought that maybe he's playing hide and seek? Did you search the house before you called to accuse me of being a filthy thief?"

He didn't say anything.

"I didn't think so. He's probably fucking tired of the frozen waffles Summer forces him to eat every goddamned morning. Don't you dare blame me. You know how Summer treats that poor little boy, and you have the audacity to yell at me? The house is huge and she lets him go wherever he wants without any thought to his safety. He needs friends, Cole, he's bored, but potty training him is too much fucking work. God forbid Summer gets off her ass." She sucked in a breath. "I was out until three in the morning. Marnie had her bachelorette party last night, and as soon as Leah and I got home, I went to bed. That's where I've been until you called. Look somewhere else to put your blame."

She disconnected, wishing she had Cole's old rotary dial. Slamming the receiver into the cradle would have felt good.

The nerve to blame her because Ty wasn't in his crib! It wasn't the first time he'd escaped, and soon enough they'd find him coloring or sleeping in a closet Summer didn't use.

Let them take care of it. Cole made it clear Ty wasn't her responsibility.

In a scalding shower, she washed off the crusted makeup and most of her anger. By the time she dressed, changed the bandage on her hand, and made coffee, the mad had worn down to irritation and a hint of worry.

Of course, after tearing into him, when they found Ty, she doubted he'd call to let her know or apologize.

So much for talking to him about how she felt.

She dropped Leah at the Supply Company and went to the office as planned. Cole wasn't sitting at his desk, but that didn't surprise her. He'd avoid her now. Good. She didn't want to see him, either.

While the details were fresh in her mind, she wrote up the review of the Starburst—a great name for a nightclub—and submitted it to her Lifestyles editor. The editor would find a photo of Phillip and his brother and any accompanying shots of the interior needed since Cole hadn't been there.

She compiled a list of articles and their links, composed a professional email to Phillip, and sent him the information.

She worked until lunch.

He replied saying he was happy to have met her and time permitting, he'd look over the articles she sent. He ended the email instructing her to have fun at the wedding, his generic electronic signature closing the correspondence.

She couldn't have expected more, and she shook off the slight disappointment she felt not receiving it.

Emotionally, she wasn't available, and he knew that, but it was nice to be wanted, especially since Cole didn't anymore.

Her cell rang as she blew out a sigh.

"Layla, are you cashing in on a lunch?" Whenever Layla gave her a scoop, she promised Layla a meal, but the detective never took her up on it.

"Hi, Autumn," Layla spoke low and fast. "I'm letting you know we got a call to your sister's place. Ty's missing."

She scoffed, but a sick wiggle started in her stomach. "Still? He's sleeping somewhere, or hiding. Cole called me this morning and accused me of taking him."

"Did you?" Layla asked bluntly.

"No! Marnie had her bachelorette party last night and we were out until three in the morning. I came home with Leah."

"Can she confirm you didn't leave your house?"

She stilled. She was speaking to a cop about her whereabouts last night, not to her friend. "Do I need an attorney?"

Layla paused. "No. We're on our way to your parents' house. I thought you'd want to know."

"Thanks. I'll drive over."

Fear crept into her chest and her heart thrummed. Her parents' house was a three-story monstrosity, but it wasn't so big that Ty could hide all morning. Nor would he want to. It was lunchtime. He'd be hungry and he wouldn't want to miss his TV shows.

The situation became even more of a reality when Layla and her partner arrived ahead of her and the unmarked police car sat in the snow-covered driveway.

Cole's car was parked in the driveway as well, and she parked on the street to avoid blocking anyone in.

The air was frozen, and shivering, she picked over the trampled walkway. Summer never shoveled the sidewalk.

The front door was unlocked and she let herself into the house. Her parents had given her a key, in case of an emergency, but Summer had thrown a tantrum and she never used it.

Never wanted to use it.

Never needed to use it.

She tapped the snow off her pumps, toed them off near the door, and hung up her purse and jacket. Voices carried through the living room, and the scents of stale coffee, fear, and anger permeated the air.

Layla and another detective Autumn recognized but couldn't name stood near the table, their boots dripping water onto the title.

"What the fuck are you doing here?" her sister screamed. "Why do you always have to stick your fucking nose into our goddamned business? *You are not part of this family.*"

Summer's curls were a mess, sticking up in every direction, and her eyes flashed wildly. Deep grooves lined her forehead and mouth, but they weren't there because Ty was missing. Misery was leaving its mark, and every time Autumn saw her, the unhappiness laid more apparent on her face.

Sometimes she truly wondered what Cole had saw in her. Summer resembled her, yes, but a sour and unsatisfied version. A reflection in a warped and scratched-up mirror. She hadn't always looked like that. It had started when Autumn left to go to school in Decatur. The sniping, the comments, the jealousy. It hadn't taken her long to learn to stay out of Summer's way.

She swallowed against the pain. She wasn't part of their family. Ty wasn't hers, nor was Cole. She had no right to be there.

Loving Ty didn't give her a place in their lives.

She found her voice. "You're right. I'll go."

"I asked her to be here," Layla said firmly. "We have a missing child and we need every person willing to help. Mrs. McClure, perhaps you don't realize how serious this is?" The detective raised her eyebrow, her lips set in a thin line. Her cop face. Her "don't fuck with me" face. Layla complained she didn't get to use it often enough. She would have every opportunity with Summer.

Mrs. McClure. Nausea rolled in her stomach. The constant reminder Cole married Summer and not her. She'd never changed her name after the divorce. Why would she? It was another way to twist the knife she had so neatly plunged into her back.

"Summer doesn't understand because she doesn't care. Let's lay that out right now. She never locks her doors, she never sets the alarm. Our parents asked her to housesit, but anything could be stolen at any second."

"You're so fucking perfect, aren't you?" Summer asked, inching into the living room, her eyes narrowed. "Little miss can do no wrong. Oh! But wait. She did make a mistake. She got engaged and then when Cole married me, it was all my fault."

Her sister stopped a foot away from her, rage and hate twisting her features.

Part of her anger was fear. It was her fault Ty was missing. Summer didn't have a college education, but she didn't need a degree to know she had royally fucked up.

"Summer," Cole said, touching her arm.

He wore a suit. Well, slacks, shirt, and a tie. His hair was disheveled, and already his face bore the strain of his little boy missing. How would he look in a day or two? A week? As a reporter, she'd seen the damage of what a missing child could do to loved ones.

She covered her mouth and forced the tears down into her chest. Now wasn't the time to cry.

"This isn't about us," he said. "It's about Ty. Autumn loves him, and she'll help us look. That's all that matters now."

"Have you called Beth?" she asked.

"No. Not yet."

She met Layla's eyes. "Do we have a plan? Has someone notified Missing Children Minnesota? Or the Association for Missing and Exploited Children? Is someone going to help us?"

"We haven't gotten that far. We need to sit down and go over what's already been done, if anything. We'll need a recent picture, a description of what he was wearing, and we'll canvass the neighborhood first. Cole, you've checked outside? The garage? Is there a doghouse in the backyard he could be playing in? Did you find any tracks?"

"I looked in the garage and Summer's vehicle. I didn't see any tracks besides the ones we leave coming and going.

There's a shed in the back that has a lawnmower and other tools in it, but it's locked. There's no way to get inside unless you have the padlock's key."

"Okay. Since the house doors weren't locked, it could be Ty let himself out and a well-meaning neighbor took him in and he's sleeping on her couch. That's the best case scenario. I'm not going to get into the worst case because we've never had a kidnapping in Rocky Point and I think we'll find a reasonable explanation for all of this, but we'll go over every possibility. Just because we haven't seen something in town doesn't mean there isn't a first time for everything."

Layla's words did little to soothe. Ty was adorable and she'd brought him around town many times. So had Cole. It wasn't but a few days ago he had lunch with her and Leah at the busy diner. Hundreds of tourists flooded Rocky Point every day. He could be munching on graham crackers in the back seat of a car halfway through Canada by now.

She moaned. "This is just like Madeline McCann."

"This is nothing like that case. She was left alone," Cole snapped.

"Ty was too," Autumn said, glaring at Summer.

Before she could process her sister's intent and protect herself, Summer slapped her, and the crack of flesh against flesh was the only sound in the room.

In shock, she held a trembling hand to her cheek and sank to her knees.

"Hey!" Layla barked. "That's enough or I'll charge you with assault."

She couldn't hear through the buzz of disbelief zipping through her skull. No matter how bad things grew between them, it had never come to blows.

Summer had won. There was no reason to lash out. Only gloat.

Layla held out a hand, and grateful for the support, she staggered to her feet.

She kept her eyes glued to the floor. She'd help find Ty and then she would leave. She didn't have to put up with this anymore. She'd been a fool staying in town after finding out Cole had married Summer. She should have cut her losses and left a long time ago. Why had she stayed and let Summer pour salt into her wounded heart?

She lowered onto a kitchen chair and the reason laid a hand on her thigh.

"Autumn."

"Don't talk to me now."

Sighing, Cole moved his hand and rested his elbows on the table.

The silent detective, Layla's partner, shrugged out of his heavy jacket and hung it on the back of a chair. "I'm Detective Williams."

His name clicked.

Autumn lifted her head. "Trevor."

"Hey, Autumn. Didn't know if you'd remember me."

"Yeah. You let the Biology frogs go."

Trevor chuckled. "Yep. Now I volunteer at the animal shelter three days a week."

"Okay," Layla took a place at the head of the table. "Can someone start at the beginning? I don't need to remind you time is precious and every second spent squabbling is a second we aren't searching for Ty." She glared around the table and met everyone's eyes to drive her point home.

She needed to put old hurts aside. Keep her mouth shut

and not spew out the fact that if Summer was a better mother none of this would have happened.

Under the shock, she knew that was unfair. Parents weren't always to blame. Children disappeared all the time. She didn't want to think about the number of children missing in the United States right now. How many of those children were taken by someone they knew and the minuscule chances of them surviving if they were taken by someone they didn't.

Cole cleared his throat. "I was on my way here to pick up Ty before work to bring him to my sister's for the day. I'm not going to pretend this isn't a broken family and a lot of Ty's care is piecemealed together among me, Summer, Autumn, and my sister, Beth. It's not the best. Kids need consistency and we've failed Ty on that level." A breath shuddered out of him. "Summer called my cell. She said Ty wasn't in his crib. I looked everywhere."

Layla and Trevor scribbled in their notebooks. "When I asked Autumn to come by, she said you accused her of taking him," she said.

Cole tensed. "It was my first thought."

"Has she taken him without permission in the past?"

"No," Summer said, cutting in, "but she's always been jealous of my family."

"Maybe if we leave sibling rivalry out of this, we'll make faster headway," Layla suggested calmly.

Summer lifted her chin. "Look into her. Ty's probably at her house right now. I bet that woman she has staying there is hiding him. My sister has always wanted Ty for herself. She's always thought I was a shitty mother."

Layla squeezed her hand. "Her whereabouts are accounted for, but would you mind if we sent a car? Just to be sure he's not there?" she asked apologetically. "Everyone knows your Ty's aunt. Maybe someone found him and dropped him off."

Summer's jaw tightened. Her sister didn't like she was familiar with the cops who drew the case, but that was too bad. If Summer did more than watch TV and sleep, she'd know more people around town, too.

"The house is locked. Leah went to work at the Supply Company and she has my spare. You'll have to have someone pick her up, and she'll let you in. Tell her I said it was okay."

"We appreciate your cooperation." Layla sent a message on her cell.

She didn't know when she'd turned into the bad guy, but she knew the drill. If she didn't cooperate, the cops would waste time looking at her. Better to prove right away she had nothing to hide.

She wished with all her heart she *did* have Ty. She wanted more than anything for him to be here, safe, watching TV, running around in a droopy diaper because Summer was too lazy to change him and get him dressed.

"Can you think of anyone who would abduct Ty? Someone who thought they were helping?"

She shook her head. Practically everyone knew about their situation, but no one interfered. No one called Child Protective Services, though she'd been tempted a few times. Cole did his best. The best he could do without getting in Summer's way. Calling CPS would only hurt him and invite scrutiny.

"My sister's never been happy with how we're raising Ty. She's spoken to me about it several times, but she'd never take him, same as my parents. You can check with them," Cole said.

Trevor nodded. "We will. We'll need their addresses.

It's better to do it without alerting them, if you know what I mean."

Cole tipped his head back and closed his eyes. "Yeah."

Layla tapped her pen against her notepad and pursed her lips. "Autumn, your parents are quite wealthy, aren't they?"

"I suppose they are. Summer manages to live off them just fine."

"Fuck you," Summer snarled, crossing her arms over her chest.

"You have such an impressive vocabulary." She looked at Layla. "You think this is a ransom kidnapping?"

The detective lifted her hands, palms up. "Maybe, but we'll look into friends and family first. Possibly someone who had good intentions . . . being Ty's home life is a bit . . . shaky."

Summer muttered under her breath.

Cole rubbed his hands over his face. "I'm going to make some fresh coffee. Layla, what should we be doing now?"

"I've been in contact with the department and we're setting up a hotline. The second that number's available, we'll print fliers and start searching the immediate area. You and Summer will stay here in case he wanders in or someone finds him and brings him home. He'll need to see a familiar face. It's important you don't act angry. None of this is his fault."

She left Cole and Summer to talk to Layla and Trevor about what they needed to do. She wasn't Ty's mom and she wouldn't be included in the details. She could help look, or she could go home.

She padded into her parents' room and dug through her mother's clothes. She didn't want to waste time running home but she couldn't help question neighbors wearing her pumps and dress pants. Her mother was a little heavier than she was, but she managed to find a pair of yoga pants that had a matching top. At any other time, she would have admired the cute cutouts, but she pulled an old black cardigan out of the back of the closet and wrapped herself in it, covering up the decorations.

She put on thick socks, and by the time she stepped into the kitchen, several more officers had gathered in the spacious area and a tall stack of fliers were piled on the table.

The picture of Ty's sweet face brought tears to her eyes. Cole had taken that shot at the boutique, and joy lit up his face. He'd had fun that night, dancing in a miniature tux like a little Elvis Presley.

Her tears fell on the top flier.

Layla wrapped an arm around her. "Your house checked out. The officer's bringing Leah here. She said she wants to help."

She sniffled. "She's a good friend."

Cole sat in the living room, his face ashen. She wanted to go to him and hold him tight, but she couldn't. They weren't a couple, hadn't been by any meaning of the definition. They'd never dated, not seriously, they'd never lived together. Sleeping together didn't make them a couple. It only made them pathetic because they were two grown adults who wouldn't admit how they felt.

"Listen up!" Layla shouted, her hands in the air, ending the chatter. "We have fliers that have the hotline, Ty's picture, and description on them. We'll have the local news stations flash Ty's picture and the number. Let's get people looking. US Customs and Border Protection has been notified. We don't know how long Ty's been missing and every second counts. We've got people driving in from

Decatur who've handled situations like this and are more experienced, but it will take time for them to get here. When they arrive, let's give them our full cooperation. Until then, we need to do all we can. Ty's life may depend on it."

She needed air.

She found a pair of her mother's boots in the foyer's closet and put on her jacket.

"Take these with you," Layla said, shoving a stack of fliers at her. "We're going to find him."

"I hope so."

Just as Autumn was about to open the door, it opened from the outside.

Leah and an officer stood on the porch, and Autumn fell into her arms and sobbed.

She and Leah trudged down the road, the cold seeping into her bones. They were walking through her parents' neighborhood, handing out fliers. It would have been warmer to drive, but it was faster to walk. Everyone was at work, and they stuck Ty's face between doors, hoping later someone would see it and know something that would make a difference.

Whenever they thought they could get away with it, they searched backyards and sheds, peered into frosty garage windows. She held out hope it was someone they knew who thought they were helping Ty.

Rocky Point had a dangerous side, one someone from the outside looking in would never suspect, and Summer fit right in. In her experience, it took a couple of days until a kidnapping investigation swung around to the parents. But it always did.

Cole wouldn't deserve it. He didn't have anything to do with Ty's disappearance. He had the resources to take Ty away from Summer legally and didn't need to resort to this.

Maybe Summer found out. Maybe he'd already been in contact with an attorney and this was Summer's way of retaliating. She had resources, too.

Someone waltzed right into the house and stole Ty out of his crib.

That someone had to know Summer didn't set the security alarm or lock the doors. That someone had to know Ty would be spending the night in his own room and not at her place, or Cole's, or Beth's.

That someone knew how their family worked . . . or was told.

"How are you holding up?" Leah asked.

She'd been silent, the perfect partner. They worked as if their minds were on the same wavelength, handing out fliers, knocking on doors. Shared looks agreeing to snoop when it appeared no one was home.

So far they hadn't found anything.

"I keep thinking Summer's to blame somehow. Like this is a bid for attention or to get back at Cole."

"Did you tell Layla?"

"No. She's a good cop, and she knows Summer. She'll check into it."

"You and Cole—"

"We're not going to make it. At the newspaper yesterday he told me he was suing Summer for full custody. He's moving to Denver with his sister and her family."

Leah stopped on the sidewalk, the fliers fluttering in her mittened hand. "Oh, Autumn. I'm so sorry."

She tried to smile but she couldn't force the corners of her lips to turn upward. "We both knew it was impossible. Summer never would have let us be together. She'd have kept Ty away from us, and she never would've left Cole alone. We would've had to move."

"But he didn't ask you to go to Denver."

"Nope. He encouraged me to put my time and energy into my career, find the dream job I put on hold to be here with him. Before Ty disappeared, I'd decided to do it."

"You changed your mind?"

They walked to another house. No one answered the door and they left a flier between the storm door and the doorjamb.

"I'm going to Italy to visit Mom and Dad. I need a break. Buck's driving me insane, and I can't be around Cole anymore. It hurts my heart too much. I can't stand Summer. I'll miss Ty. I'll feel like I'm abandoning him, but what else can I do? He doesn't belong to me."

"But you belong with Cole," Leah said.

She huffed. She loved Leah, but sometimes her rosy outlook grated on her nerves. She'd found happiness in Rocky Point. In Jared, in the Supply Company, even in her budding relationship with Briar.

Rocky Point didn't hold that happiness for her.

"I fucked that up. I didn't tell him how I felt about his decision to move here. I didn't tell him how I felt when he divorced Summer. I didn't tell him how I felt when he said he was taking Ty to Denver. I let him slip through my fingers when all I had to do was say something. Anything. I let him down, and now the best thing I can do is continue to keep my mouth shut and let him get the hell out of here."

She and Leah walked to a clearing that in the summer months was nothing but tall grass. Across the snow, a group of people were going door to door in a different section of the residential area. A dog sniffed the ground near the heels of a uniformed cop. She couldn't make out who it was.

"By midnight town will be turned upside down," Leah said, standing by her side, watching the group.

"Ty's already been missing for God knows how long. By the time Summer noticed he was gone, he could have been halfway across the state."

"Let's pray that's not true."

"I'm praying for a lot of things right now."

"We all are. Come on, let go check in. Maybe there's news."

Her eyes filled with tears. "Thank you for being here. For being my friend. It's easy to forget I'm not alone."

"You're not alone. We're all helping. Jared has searched the arena from top to bottom. Marnie and Callie are handing out fliers in Gail's neighborhood. Logan and Ivy are questioning people in her apartment building and in that area. Mitch said Desiree asked that all the rooms at the resort be searched. Everyone's cooperating without a warrant. We'll find him, Autumn. I know deep down we will."

"I wish I shared your conviction."

Leah nudged her shoulder, urging her in the direction of the house. "Let's go talk to Layla. Maybe the hotline has had a few hits and we can help follow up."

"What can we do?"

"You're an investigative reporter, aren't you? That means you investigate."

She wasn't sure what there was to investigate, but Leah's determination sparked a fire in her heart.

They would find Ty, and he would be all right.

He had to be.

Because under the hope and fear was a little wiggle of an emotion called guilt.

Cole hid in the study and cried his tears alone.

He had not one doubt this happened because of how he and Summer parented Ty. She was neglectful and he looked the other way. He claimed to be busy, but he didn't want to deal with her, and instead of protecting his son, he left him there.

Beth pushed the door open carrying a plate.

"When did you get here?" he asked.

"A while ago. It was a bit of a surprise when two cops showed up wanting to search the house for Ty. That's not the kind of news you hear from a stranger, Cole. Why didn't you call me?"

She set the plate on a the side table next to him, a thick ham sandwich floating in a sea of potato chips. The pink meat turned his stomach, but he nibbled on a chip. He didn't want to listen to his sister complain.

"They told me not to."

She sank onto the leather loveseat beside him. "I mean, before? When you found out he was missing."

"Because I honestly thought Autumn had him. It's something she would do. Not kidnap him, but, you know. I called her and bitched her out, but she has an alibi." He flinched. That made it sound like she was, or had been, a suspect, when she was the last person on earth who would hurt Ty. "She said she was at Marnie's bachelorette party last night, then she brought Leah home and they crashed. I believe her."

"Me too. A friend of Russ's said he saw Autumn getting cozy with a guy at the Starburst. He brought her up to the VIP lounge. Russ's friend made it sound pretty swanky. Grey Goose and Cristal."

He scoffed. "Then what was he doing there?" He knew the kinds of people Russ and Beth liked to hang out with. Teachers who thought Scrabble parties were a wild Friday night.

"He and his wife drove across to have a drink. She wanted to see it. Not a big deal. He said his wife thought the guy was hot. Dressed like he had money."

"Beth. Why are you telling me this? I feel shitty enough as it is."

"You told her you were leaving."

"Yeah, I did."

"How'd she take it?"

He thought back to the pain and tears in her eyes. Her pale skin. The tremors in her hands. "Fine. I said she should get out of Rocky Point and write the articles she wants to write. I don't know why she moved back here."

"Yes, you do." She paused. "What did she say?"

She asked what she should do if she was pregnant, and I told her to get rid of it.

"Nothing."

"You didn't ask her to go with you and Ty?"

"No, and she didn't ask if she could go, either. Not that I gave her the option. I was pretty clear we were done because you're right. If we were going to work, then we would have. We're no closer to each other than we were five years ago."

"I'm sorry."

"Yeah, well, my mistakes are always going to bite me in

the ass, and so are hers. That son of a bitch is probably watching the house right now. Where is she?"

"Out looking for Ty, same as everyone else."

"By herself?" Christ, that bastard hurting her is the last thing he needed.

"I don't know. Maybe. She might have wanted some time to think."

"Fuck." He blew out a breath. "Someone we know has him."

"That's what Layla's saying. Tips are starting to trickle in, but it will take time to follow up. All we can do is wait and let the police do their jobs."

"They want Summer and me to go on the air. Beg for information. I don't know if Summer and Autumn have told their parents. Maybe they can offer a reward. I don't know."

He covered his face with his hands and let the grief roll through him. He missed Ty so much, and he wished more than anything Autumn sat where Beth did, patting his back and telling him everything would be all right.

Instead, she was kissing other men and making career plans because he'd told her to.

Beth put her arm around him, and he cried into her shoulder.

While the woman he'd been in love with half his life looked for a little boy who wasn't hers.

"He's not doing well and needs you." Beth pounced on Autumn the moment she stepped inside the stifling foyer.

The house felt . . . not as full, but heat and fear weighed

down the air. A murmur of low voices carried to them from the kitchen.

It was dark now and too cold to search. The volunteers and extra uniforms called it a night to get some sleep and start fresh in the morning.

It seemed too early to quit, but searching after the sun set could waste time. Even if Ty, God forbid, was outside, somewhere, a search party could walk right past him in the inky black.

Flashlight beams only shined so far.

The dogs hadn't been helpful. One picked up Ty's scent in the driveway but then lost the trail.

People installed cameras in front of their homes to deter thieves from stealing packages off their porches as online shopping reached an all-time high. Her parents' house didn't have one. There had never been a need . . . until now.

"Hi, Beth, thank you for being here."

She hugged Cole's sister. They had an amicable relationship but never had any reason to nurture a friendship. They didn't have much in common besides Cole and Ty. And a shared dislike of Summer.

"I'm going to head out," Leah said, touching her shoulder. "I need to close the store. I am so sorry, but I'll come back when I'm done."

"Thank you, sweetie, but if you're tired, go back to the house. Get some sleep and we'll look tomorrow."

"Okay. Call if you need anything. I'll leave my phone's sound on." Leah slipped out the door, not giving her a chance to ask if she needed a ride or if she wanted to drive her car.

Beth stood waiting, biting her lower lip, her hands shoved into the back pockets of her jeans.

"I'm sorry. There's so much going on." She rubbed her hands over her face. Her palm hurt like hell.

"I know. I've been here to support Cole, but he doesn't want to talk to anyone. He's in the study. Summer disappeared, and I've been sitting with my parents."

"Dean and Bonnie are here?"

"Yeah. There's not much to do. We sit and listen to the cops talk. Tips are coming in, but following up on leads takes forever."

"I know. When I lived in Decatur, I wrote a few articles on kidnapping cases. It's a hurry up and wait situation. They always are."

"Will you go talk to him?"

She almost said no, but Beth's eyes filled with tears and she relented.

"Okay. Let me use the bathroom first, then I'll go find him."

Beth sighed. "Thank you. Cole made a mistake, and I might have been partly responsible, encouraging him to move with us, but please don't hold that against him. Blame me, if you want. I didn't think you—"

"It's not your fault. Ty's what's important now. We'll find him, I can feel it."

"I'm praying," Beth whispered.

"Make sure you eat. I don't know what kind of food Summer has around here, but help yourself to whatever you find. It's going to be a long night and I doubt anyone will be able to sleep."

She nodded and shuffled into the living room.

Autumn used the bathroom and studied the cut on her hand. She'd need a doctor to look at it. The gash oozed blood and pus. It wasn't healing, but she couldn't take the time to do anything except apply antibacterial ointment and cover it with a new bandage.

She found Cole sitting in the dark in her dad's study. He hadn't drawn the blinds, and a TV's flicker next door cast the room in an eerie blue tint.

He sat on one of the leather loveseats, his head tipped back. He still wore his suit, rumpled now, his tie loose and askew. A dried-out sandwich sat on the side table.

She couldn't blame him for not eating it. The thought of food churned her stomach, too.

Without saying a word, she stood in front of him, and he held out his arms. She curled in his lap and inhaled what felt like her first breath all day.

He began to cry, and she reversed their positions, straddling his thighs and wrapping her arms around his neck, giving him comfort instead of taking it.

"Shh, shh," she whispered into his ear.

He held on tighter.

Finally, he leaned away, sniffling.

She handed him a tissue, and he wiped his eyes.

"Sorry. I can't stop crying."

"It's better to let it out than keep it inside."

"Is there any news?"

"No."

She brushed her fingers over his stubble and met his eyes. She shouldn't be thinking how sexy he looked, but he did, and her heart ached.

He cupped her face in his hands. "I should have asked you to come with us. I was angry, hurt, and . . . guilty. Autumn, I'm guilty of so many things."

"No more than I am. I should have told you I wanted to go with you. Even if you were that angry you said no, at least I would have said it. At least you would have heard it.

The last time we made love, I told you I loved you, but I haven't been acting like I do. Love is more than a word, and I need to start showing you I mean it."

"I do, too. I can't tell you I love you then say I don't want you in my life. I didn't mean what I said at the office. I want you with me, sweetheart, forever."

She lowered her head and brushed her lips against his. They tasted of salt and sadness, but he slid his hands under her shirt and love radiated from his palms into her soul.

They would survive this.

She would survive it because he loved her.

"Marry me, Autumn. When this is over. Marry me. Give me more children, a place to call home."

The words she'd always wanted to hear. It didn't matter anymore if Summer heard them first. She would be Cole's last and that meant more than anything else.

"Yeah, I will."

He blew out a breath. "Thank God. I love you so much."

She held him close to her heart until a knock interrupted the silence.

Beth poked her head into the room. "I'm sorry, you guys. Layla's asking for you. A news crew is here to film Cole and Summer. Autumn, she's asking if you'll talk to her. She's not cooperating."

He stiffened.

"Don't," she said, laying a hand on his shoulder. "I'll talk to her. We won't get anywhere blaming her for this. I know I've done a lot of it, and I need to stop it, too. She won't do what we ask if she feels cornered."

"We need a second," he said, and Beth slipped out as silently as she came in.

He kissed her, hard and fast. "I'll never take another

second we're together for granted. I'll never take for granted time with you or Ty. I'll never let Summer get in the way of what we have. Not anymore."

She rested her forehead against his. "I let her come between us, not you. I've wasted so much time because you hurt me and I wouldn't let it go. I didn't want to admit I hurt you too, and I'm sorry. I take responsibility for my share of our problems."

"Can you forgive me?" he asked.

"If you can forgive me."

"Yeah, I can. Just don't accept any more proposals."

She smiled. "Just don't ask anyone else to marry you."

"Deal."

He kissed her, and she melted against his chest.

With a mixture of reluctance and urgency, she crawled off his lap. She wanted the time with him, needed it, but there were other things more important than their relationship.

"Your parents are here," she said, opening the door and stepping into the hall. "Go show them you're okay. I mean, as well as you can be."

He backed her against the wall and pressed into her. "Thank you. For what you just did. I'm a jackass, and I don't know if I would have done the same."

She smoothed his tie, too wrinkled for it to do much good. "Thank your sister. She asked me to talk to you, but I almost said no. She started crying and I couldn't. Otherwise, I would have stayed away, too."

"We're both stupid."

Leaning her head on his shoulder, she said, "Yeah. Now let me deal with Summer. She needs to be in front of that camera."

He rubbed her back and let her go.

She shuffled down the carpeted hallway and choked up when she stepped over a pile of cars on the floor.

That was just like Summer. Step over them rather than pick them up and put them away.

The room was pitch black and smelled of sweat.

"Summer?"

"Get the fuck out of here."

"The camera crew's here. They want to film you and Cole asking for information."

"I can't."

"Why?"

"I just can't."

"Can I come in?"

"Don't you do whatever the fuck you want whenever you want to?"

She left the door cracked. She needed the light to pick her way across the room.

Summer wasn't the cleanest person, and dirty clothes littered the floor hiding God knew what.

She sat on the bed, Summer's limp form under a pile of blankets.

"He's always loved you more," Summer muttered, scooting to the edge of the king-sized bed.

"Who?" Autumn asked cautiously. She was well aware her conversation with her sister resembled a minefield. One wrong word and she'd blow up.

"Take your pick. You've always been better, always been first."

"Cole married *you*," she said, the words scratching her throat. She'd have to set that aside if they were going to move on. Choices had been made and hearts had been broken. On both sides. Leave the past in the past.

"Only because he thought he was getting a watered-down version of you. Do you know how it feels to be second best? Not just with Cole, but Ty. Mom and Dad? You have your fancy degree, a million friends, you have Cole—"

"Summer—"

"Don't try to deny it. I see the way he looks at you. He's *never* looked at me that way."

She tried to think of what to say that wouldn't upset Summer even more than she already was. "Do you remember Moxie?"

"Our golden retriever, yeah. Why?"

"You were always saying she loved me more than you."

"Because it was true."

"It *was* true. I won't deny that, but you don't understand why she did. Ty isn't Moxie, but listen—"

Summer jerked a pillow over her head.

"No, *listen*. Moxie loved me because I loved her. I took her out for walks. I would ask you to go and you'd always say no. You'd rather look at magazines and listen to music or talk on the phone with your friends. Moxie needed to go out. She had to pee. She needed exercise and attention. Do you remember when she was spayed and you made fun of me for staying at the vet's office with her? I was there when she woke up. That's love, Summer. Ty isn't a puppy. He's more. He needs hugs and kisses. Someone to feed him healthy food. He needs clean clothes that fit." She paused to control her tears. "Cole might have convinced himself he loved you, but the truth is, you never gave him the chance, did you? Were you ever kind? Did you cook him meals? Did you watch movies together? Did you make love?"

Summer scoffed.

"No, not have sex, you obviously did. But did you make love?" Her voice dropped to a whisper. "Did you ever place your hand on his chest and feel his heart beat? Did you ever look into his eyes and say I love you without speaking? Love is a verb, Summer. You cannot expect someone to love you if you can't give it."

Summer rolled over, her complexion pallid and drawn. She winced.

Somehow in all this, she'd forgotten her sister was a human being.

"You've always had what I want," Summer said, the usual edge to her voice gone.

"Funny, because the minute you married Cole, you've had what I wanted."

"I did that to get back at you."

"I've never done anything to deserve that. All I've done is be a good person and do the right thing. That's not impossible. Summer, you can turn this around. After we find Ty, you can be his mother. You can take care of him and love him. Go to school and get a job you like. Stop living off Mom and Dad and make your own way. You'll feel better."

"What about Cole? I've tried to keep you from seeing each other, but that's not going to work anymore, is it?"

"Cole's mine, and he's off-limits to you and any more of your shit. We'll need to figure out how we're going to share Ty without hurting him. No one is blaming his disappearance on you, but you're going to have to own up to the way you've been parenting him."

"He doesn't love me."

"Yes, he does, but that's what I've been trying to tell you. Ty has needs that aren't being met and he'll gravitate toward the people who will give him those things. People can't survive without love. Ty loves you, but you have to do more than say you love him, you have to show it by taking care of him."

"This isn't my life, Autumn. This stupid town, the cold. I'm more than a mother."

She wanted to say she wasn't one at all, but she held her tongue.

"We need to find Ty. Cole loves him and wants more time with him. Renegotiate custody and you can do whatever you want. Stop using Ty to punish him because he doens't love you."

Summer sat up and wiped her cheeks. She wore her hair shorter than she did and colored it platinum grey. In her own way, she was pretty, but bitterness and unhappiness dug into her face and took that beauty away. Summer's blue eyes stood out, so much like hers, and for once they looked at her without the hate she'd come to expect . . . and receive.

"Go out there and tell whoever took Ty to bring him back."

"No. You and Cole do it. You're more convincing."

"You're his mother. How would that look? Ty's *missing*. Don't you get that? You should be down on your knees in front of that camera, begging, pleading, for whoever took Ty to bring him the fuck back."

"I don't feel like his mother, okay? I don't love him the way a mother should love her son. Something inside me is broken. I look at him and—" Summer jumped off the bed and clawed at her hair. She paced across the room, panting like she was having a panic attack, until suddenly she deflated and sagged against the large picture window that looked over the street. "I'll feel like a fraud, and I'm not stupid. That's what people will call me. They're probably already saying I had someone kidnap him to scam money out of Mom and Dad. Or they're saying I got in deep with a dealer and they took him because I couldn't pay. I'm not a druggie—"

She raised her eyebrows.

"I'm *not*. I've never done drugs. When I party, I drink, smoke a little weed, but that's it."

She thought Summer was too old to be doing any of that, but some people never grew up and bitching about it would be useless.

"I'd feel like a fool." Summer hugged herself, a shiver running through her.

"You're not a fool." She stood and held out her arms, and Summer walked into them. She didn't admit the same thoughts had gone through her head or that Layla was checking into the crowd Summer hung around with. "We're going to work this out. You're not alone."

"Then please, help me." Summer sounded like a little girl. "Don't make me go out there. I can't."

"Okay."

Summer kissed her cheek and crawled into bed, hiding her body under the comforter.

Their talk was over.

She met Layla in the kitchen. Cole was sitting on the couch in the living room, his hands clasped tightly in his mother's, and he glanced at her. Beth hovered looking out of place and helpless.

"Is she coming out?" Layla asked.

"You don't want her on camera. She's not in a good place and she'll do more harm than good. Cole should do it alone, or with his sister and parents."

A woman dressed in a suit and heels, even at this time of night, stepped forward, holding out her hand. "I'm Natasha Michaels. I work with Missing Children Minnesota. I happened to be at a convention in Marengo, and when I heard, I drove up as fast as I could. We can put a positive spin on your sister's mental state. She's worried sick. Distraught to the point of being unable to speak. Some people won't like that. They want to watch other people's misery and there will be complaints, but this isn't anyone's business but yours. It's an appeal to the kidnapper, to bring Ty home. We'll use other members of the family. Cole, his parents and sister. You. Show the kidnapper Ty has a loving family, a large one, and hope he or she feels guilty enough to bring him back. I'm sorry about Ty. The police department has been great, and they're doing all they can."

She shook Natasha's hand but let it go quickly. The woman was too efficient, too stoic, though she knew the woman had to turn off her emotions or that kind of job could tear a person to shreds. Natasha's work, unfortunately, would never end.

Natasha handed them notes that guided them on what to say. Perfectly scripted as to not reveal any information not necessary to Ty's disappearance.

A sitting area upstairs was the perfect place to film, and the lights, microphones, and cameras had already been set up.

Cole gripped her hand the entire time, crushing her fingers, the anguish in his voice difficult to listen to, and after they filmed, Beth, Cole, and their parents settled in the living room to wait.

The news crew packed up and left, as did a couple police officers saying they were going to the station to follow more leads.

Out of a need to do something, she tidied the house, picked up empty coffee mugs, threw away gum and mint wrappers and tissues the officers left behind. She poked around the kitchen, found two frozen pizzas in the freezer, and slid them into the oven. No one would eat them, at least, she wouldn't be able to swallow one bite, but it made her feel useful.

She'd have to go to the grocery store, or if she wrote out a list, maybe Beth could go. Or Leah. She couldn't face people now, and doing something as mundane as buying bread seemed like such a huge waste of time when she could be out searching for Ty, but if the search volunteers and officers were going to use the house as a home base, she wanted to offer more than black coffee and cardboard pizza.

She leaned against the sink and massaged her temples, hoping she could ward off a headache. A couple of ibuprofen wouldn't be a bad idea, either. Her hand hurt like fuck. She needed to change her bandage again and she turned around and reached to turn the faucet on, but Cole caught her arm.

"Thank you for doing that, and for letting me hold your hand. I need—" He cleared his throat. "I need human touch right now. It feels so inappropriate when Ty could be cold, or hungry. Maybe even . . ." he faded off, unable to say the word.

Dead.

"It's not wrong to need someone," she said. "Some families, they don't make it through something like this because they put their needs last, and it breaks them. Whatever you need that I can give you, ask."

He kissed the top of her head and sighed.

None of it went unnoticed by Layla who looked more haggard as the minutes clicked past but refused to go home to rest, or Natasha, who peered at them through her eyelashes while she pretended to stare at her laptop.

She turned the faucet on, let the water run warm, and peeled the flesh-colored bandage off her palm. "Besides, I needed to. He's out there, and if I can make a difference, I'll do whatever it takes."

"Jesus Christ, Autumn, what happened?" He grabbed her wrist and cradled her hand in his.

The gash was a violent red and pus oozed. The antibacterial ointment had done little.

"That's infected. What the fuck happened? This needs stitches, not a goddamned Band-Aid."

Layla glanced in their direction, frowning.

"Someone slashed my tire last night. They left the knife behind and when I pulled it out, I cut myself. It's not a big deal."

"What the hell do you mean it's not a big deal? Did you report it?"

"No. You said you were leaving and I wasn't thinking clearly. I threw it in a snowbank. I called a tow truck, but the driver swapped my tire with the spare instead, then I went home to change to go to Marnie's party. I didn't think it was this bad."

Layla made a call and asked whoever answered to search for a knife in the newspaper's parking lot.

"I parked near the frontage road, on the . . . south side."

Layla nodded and relayed the information.

The uniform tasked to do that wouldn't be very happy. The wind howled and sleet pelted the windows. She forced herself not to think that Ty could be out there.

Cole gripped her shoulders, his fingertips digging into her skin. "You know who did that, don't you? He's starting to do more than just watch you. He's acting out. We told you not to go anywhere alone. Why don't you listen?" His voice cracked and he crushed her to him.

"People are busy. You told me you were leaving and I was in shock. What did you want me to do?"

"Fuck," he whispered into her hair. "Fuck. I'm so sorry."

"It's okay."

"No, it's not. Nothing will be okay until this is over."

The timer beeped, and Layla slid the pizzas out of the oven. She left the door cracked open to let the warmth into the room. The scent of pepperoni and cheese permeated the air, and an officer who was speaking to Beth came in, hoping to nibble on a late-night snack.

"Who are you talking about?" Layla asked, moving out of the officer's way.

"Buck Drayton," Cole said over her head, his anger vibrating through his chest under her ear. "We've reported him several times. He's been stalking Autumn for months but no one will do anything."

"We'll look into his whereabouts," Layla said, holding her hand and studying the cut. "Cole's right. This needs stitches and you probably need antibiotics. You should go to the ER. Let Cole drive you. He can give blood at the hospital while he waits."

"Why would he do that?" Summer stood in the living room, deathly pale, dark shadows under her eyes.

"It's customary for parents to give blood in emergencies. I don't want to scare you, Mrs. McClure, but when we find Ty, he may need medical attention. They prefer family members to have given blood so they have a fresh supply on hand. If you feel up to it, you should go as well."

"But it's not necessary, right? The hospital has plenty of blood."

"I already need to go in and have my hand looked at," she said, swallowing her irritation. Everything involving Summer had to be a struggle. "I'll donate, too, if I'm not prescribed antibiotics. Beth will give blood, so will Dean and Bonnie. Why does it matter if we give blood or not?"

"Because I don't want anyone to know."

"Know what?" she snapped, tired of the resistance, tired of the fight.

Summer covered her mouth, but a moan escaped between her fingers.

Beth stepped forward.

Dean and Bonnie sat up straighter.

No one took their eyes off Summer, and the skin on the back of her neck prickled.

"Summer? What don't you want anyone to know? Do you know where Ty is?"

Summer shook her head, her eyes wide. "Cole can't give blood because he isn't Ty's daddy."

CHAPTER SIX

C ole's vision blurred.

A blinding white light shot through his skull and then he saw red. He leaned against the counter, still holding Autumn in his arms. He couldn't speak, his tongue glued to the roof of his mouth.

Ty wasn't his. After being at Summer's beck and call during her pregnancy, then three years of worrying about that little boy and paying her child support, Ty wasn't his son.

"Then who is?" Autumn asked, jerking out of his grasp.

He was glad she asked. He couldn't make his mouth work.

"I don't know."

"I don't understand. What do you mean, *you don't know*? You were sleeping around behind Cole's back and you *lost track*?"

Summer toed the carpet. Her feet were bare, her bright pink toe polish chipped. "We had sex for years without birth control and I didn't think anything of it. I didn't want rugrats crawling around anyway. He went to Decatur one weekend, and I partied. I might have hooked up with a couple of guys. I didn't use anything, didn't seem like I needed to. When he got back, he said he missed me and we fucked. Two months later I found out I was pregnant."

Cole remembered that like it was yesterday. The editor had asked him to take pictures of . . . whatever. A train derailment. When he'd come back, he'd forced himself to kiss her, to make love to her. He'd tried to put everything he had into his marriage, and it still hadn't been enough.

"Then Ty could still be mine," he said.

"I put your name on his birth certificate. I had to. You were there when he was born. Everyone thought you were his dad, maybe even me. At least, I convinced myself you were. But after years of screwing without protection, you couldn't knock me up? I didn't believe that suddenly you weren't shooting blanks."

Beside him, Autumn huffed.

He agreed. Summer's terminology could have been better.

"Honestly, I forgot about it. You left and barely saw Ty because you didn't want to see me. That's how it's been. It didn't matter."

"Jesus Christ. Of course it matters. Now what? A paternity test? Do you know how crappy this is, Summer? You don't know you who your son's father is? Do you know how fucking shitty this is for me? I love that little boy." His voice hitched and he pushed the heels of his hands into his eyes. God, he was so tired.

"This changes the investigation," Layla cut in. "We need names, Summer."

She was Summer now, not Mrs. McClure. He wondered if anyone else caught the shift.

"If some random man remembers he could have

fathered a child by you . . . your parents are very wealthy. It may be only a matter of time before we get a call demanding a ransom."

Summer paled.

"I need this looked at," Autumn said. "I can drive myself. I'm parked on the street."

"No, I'll go with you," Beth said, stepping into the kitchen. "You're too upset to drive."

"Hey," he said, touching her shoulder. "Do you want me to go?"

"No. You should stay here. Layla might need to talk to you."

He let his hand drop, and he would have sold his soul to know what she was thinking.

"I need some air." He couldn't stay in this room another minute. He couldn't look into Summer's eyes without wanting to slap her, and that wasn't anything this situation needed.

He put his jacket, shoes, and gloves on and let himself into the backyard. An old wooden bench swing sat abandoned on the porch and he brushed the snow off it.

The temperature was below zero, but the frozen air woke him up. What time was it? Midnight? After? And no news about Ty except he wasn't that little boy's dad and Summer didn't know who was.

He'd ask for a paternity test, or Layla might order one.

Some fuckhead could have Ty right now, some asshole hoping for a handout in exchange for the kid.

Layla had been looking into Summer's friends, but this put a new twist on whom she would investigate.

It could be the break they needed to find out who kidnapped Ty.

He sat in the cold and tried to sort out his feelings. It

had been a mistake to marry Summer, and God was determined to keep making him pay.

Beth's minivan purred despite the cold, but the easy-going engine didn't help the vents spit out heat. Autumn huddled in her seat, tried to snuggle into her jacket the best she could.

The silent minutes ticked by as Beth drove them through town.

"Just ask," she said, tired of the expectation. Beth had something on her mind and this wasn't the time for tact.

"Did you know?"

She gritted her teeth. It would be a secret one sister kept for another, and maybe in a different situation, she would have. If she hadn't been in love with Cole. If Summer had been a better mother.

"No. Ty not belonging to Cole would have made a big difference for me. I resented him giving my sister a baby. It was something I struggled with every day."

"Now you can be together without any of that between you."

Her jaw dropped. "Are you crazy? You don't think that this changes everything for Cole? He's going to want to get as far away from the Bennetts as possible. The minute we know what happened to Ty, the minute we find him and know he's safe, Cole's out of here. You're his sister and you don't know that?"

Beth shook her head and slowed to turn into the ER's parking lot. Lights lit up the small lot, and a smattering of cars, despite the late hour, were parked in a few of the spaces. Even in a small town like Rocky Point, someone was always sick.

She parked and said, "I don't believe it. Cole's the only daddy Ty knows and he'd never leave. He loves Ty. But . . ." She sighed. "The past few years have been hell, we all know that, and on the off-chance he did take off, Summer doesn't give a shit about that kid. Who would take care of Ty?"

Autumn didn't want to think poorly of Cole, didn't want to think he would abandon Ty, but there was only so much someone could tolerate. He was at his limit. And had been. Her shredded heart could prove it. "I will, if it comes to that."

"I would, too—"

"No. He's my nephew. I'll work with you, Beth, but I won't let you take him to Denver. If Cole doesn't want him, I do."

Beth killed the engine. "You're going to do this? Right now? I love Ty, too, you know. I've babysat him as often as you have. Maybe my time counts more because I'm always the last resort. 'Cole has to work. Autumn's at the paper. Summer's hungover and won't get out of bed. Beth works from home. Let's drop him at Beth's.' I have just as much right to that child as you do." She turned, blinking back tears.

"I'm sorry. You're right, but I don't know how to feel about you moving away with him. I want what's best for him, but I don't know what that is."

"Yes, you do. He needs a mom and dad who are together. Who love each other and him, and he would have that with you and Cole." She paused. "You were pretty cozy earlier. You made up."

She pushed out of the van. "We did. He asked me to marry him and I said yes. But that was before. If he rescinds his proposal because of what Summer did, what I want won't matter."

"He's not going to hold what Summer did against you. If he leaves, it will be because of all of it." Beth followed her through the sliding doors and into the emergency room's lobby.

Glancing at Beth, she said, "Yeah. All of it, and that includes me and the way I've let Summer come between us. It's my fault the past few years have been a nightmare. We blame Summer, but if Cole and I had been together, she wouldn't have had so much power over us, or Ty. I won't be surprised if when we get back to the house, he's gone. He's put up with me and my resentment, Summer's continuous crap, and he's paid child support for a baby that's not his. Tonight he was told it was all for nothing."

"For nothing?" Beth asked, her face crumpling. "Then maybe I should take Ty after all. A little boy isn't nothing, no matter who his biological parents are. I'll wait over here."

Shamed burned her cheeks. Ty wasn't for nothing. Dealing with Summer to make sure he was loved and cared for wasn't for nothing.

She hadn't done enough, and neither had Cole.

Maybe Beth *should* take Ty.

It was obvious she and Cole didn't deserve him.

Wanting to spill the whole story, she sat quietly as the doctor cleaned the gash and stitched the wound together, *tsking*, saying she should have come in the second she hurt herself. "I'll prescribe pain medication and antibiotics.

You'll need to make an appointment to have the stitches removed. Around two weeks, okay?"

"Thank you."

The emergency room staff knew what happened, had seen their plea on the news, and they all offered prayers and well wishes. A nurse poked her head into the exam room and said she'd been on duty one night when Ty had an ear infection. She didn't know about it. Middle-of-the-night ear infections belonged to mothers.

Without speaking, Beth drove her home.

"Thanks for the ride," she said, but Beth only nodded and hurried in the direction of the bathroom.

Layla sat at the table, squinting at her laptop's screen. The poor woman looked done in and she was about to suggest she find a place to lie down, but the detective said, "Come sit."

"Is there news?" she asked, tentatively perching on the edge of a kitchen chair.

"I asked Summer about that party. She couldn't remember many names . . . she was inebriated, and she said the party was dark."

"Dark? How do you mean?"

"There weren't any lights on. The party was held in an old barn a few miles out of town."

"But she knew some people there. Was she . . ." She couldn't bring herself to say the word.

"No. At least, she didn't think so. She said she had fun and couldn't remember any negative vibes. She went home and woke up hungover, but from what she could tell, uninjured. She gave us a couple of names, and uniforms are searching one of the houses right now. Without a warrant. That means they don't have anything to hide and probably don't have Ty, but we're checking into her other friends.

One of them is in jail at county. He might have buddies who would do it, but I marked him off the list. His alibi is pretty tight." Layla grimaced.

"But it's something to go on."

"It is, though I have to admit, these guys are druggies and more apt to deal or set up shop to make a quick buck than participate in a kidnapping."

"Kidnapping's too personal."

Layla nodded, an appreciative gleam in her eye. "Yes. Perhaps if one of these men had a vendetta against Summer, or by chance, if he thought he was Ty's father and resented her keeping Ty away from him . . . but this isn't what we're dealing with."

"It doesn't sound like it." She squeezed Layla's hand. "You should lie down and get some rest. Even a short catnap would help."

"You should do the same."

"I'll try. Did Summer go back to her room?"

"Yeah. I had to pry the information out of her, but she gave us a little to go on."

"Did you check into Buck?"

"We did. A traffic cam caught him driving out of town. We think he's gone."

She blew out a breath. "That's something."

"I'm sorry we didn't do more while he was bothering you."

"I understand the position you're in with that kind of thing, but then women like me who are being harassed don't have anyone who can help them. The paperwork travels so slowly through the system my restraining order hasn't even been processed yet, and with the little evidence I have of him stalking me, it would've taken a very understanding judge to award it."

"Well, he's gone now."

"But for how long?"

Layla lifted a shoulder in an "I don't know" gesture and turned her tired gaze back to her laptop.

She should check on Cole and find out if he'd talk to her after the bomb Summer dropped. She wanted Beth to be right. With every fiber of her being she wanted Beth to be right. That Cole wouldn't leave. That he wouldn't find her guilty by association. That he loved her and Ty enough to stay.

"Is Cole still here, or did he go? How's he handling the news?"

Layla tilted her head toward the French doors that let out into the backyard. "He's been outside since Beth drove you to the emergency room."

"Good Lord. It has to be five below out there. Nobody thought to make him come in?"

"He's grieving, Autumn. No one wants to interrupt that."

"He might be grieving, but he's in shock. I'm going out there," she said, rising off her chair.

"Let me."

Bonnie McClure stood from the sofa. The past few hours of worry and fear gouged deep grooves into her face.

"Are you sure? I can ask him to come in so you can talk instead."

Bonnie shook her head. "No. I could do with getting some air, too."

In the foyer, she put on her coat and boots and trudged tiredly across the floor toward the French doors.

Autumn rested her head in her arms.

And waited.

Cole couldn't feel the cold. The swing's chains creaked and his breath came out in a white stream.

Stars glittered, the moon gleamed, and bare tree branches rustled in the wind.

He'd lost track of the time, only knew that on any other night he'd be sleeping in his bed, alone.

Tonight he sat in the backyard of a stranger's home, of a woman he hadn't wanted to get to know, the people he loved most sitting in the kitchen or in the living room waiting for news of a little boy who'd lost a game adults liked to play.

"Cole, honey, are you coming in soon?"

His mother sat next to him, and the old swing squealed in protest.

"No. I need to be out here. If Ty's in the cold, I need to be, too. To know how it feels."

Bonnie held his hand, and he squeezed.

"What am I going to do, Mom? Ty's not mine. Summer hid it and she used him to keep Autumn and me apart. These past four years have been a lie."

"That's not true, and frankly, I'm ashamed to hear you say it. There are more ways than one to be a father. Summer . . . you need to take responsibility for that, young man. You married a woman you didn't love. Nothing good can come out of that, and nothing did. What did you think? Summer wouldn't know? She did and made you pay for it, and to be perfectly honest, I admire her."

"Mother."

"What? She shouldn't have married you, either. You

were both punishing Autumn. Her reasons, I don't know. That would be between them, but you were punishing Autumn too, for getting engaged, when all you had to do was tell her you loved her and didn't want her marrying someone else. I thought your father and I raised you to be better than that, but apparently, we failed."

"I'm trying to correct that now. I asked her to marry me, and she said yes."

Bonnie scoffed, and he gaped at her and the unladylike sound. "You're lucky she did, what with the way you've treated her. You're lucky that after she came back to town and discovered you married Summer she didn't hightail it right back out of here. You owe her the moon and stars for staying and helping raise Ty. Then Beth tells me you're taking him and moving to Denver. Why would you do that?"

"At the time it seemed like Autumn was never going to let us move past this. Why would I stick around if she wouldn't forgive me?"

"Because she did it for you. She stayed in this little town for you and Ty and worked at the paper wasting her talent writing about blizzards and church bazaars, and that's how you repay her. It's time you step up and admit you've treated her like absolute shit. What are you going to do to make it up to her?"

"I won't be giving her a baby. Summer's probably right. I'm sterile."

"Good. You couldn't take care of the one you have."

"Did you come out here to make me feel better? Because you're not doing a very good job."

"No. I came out here to make you open your eyes. You need to start doing better, Cole."

"What do you want me to do?"

"Talk to Summer. Tell her you don't blame her for what she did. Sleeping around behind your back . . . you weren't in a real marriage and you have to stop blaming her for knowing it. Then you tell Autumn you love her and after all this is over, you'll do whatever she wants, live wherever she wants to live, and you'll support whatever she chooses to do. It's time you start doing something for her because she's put her life on hold for you, and has nothing, absolutely nothing, to show for it."

"What if we don't get Ty back?" He voiced his worst fear.

"Then we cross that bridge when we come to it. Children go missing every day, and the fact is, some of them don't make it back to their families. We can't hide from it. We keep living, we keep praying, and we support each other. Even Summer. Her little boy's in trouble and that has to tear her apart, yet she's been in her room alone this whole time because she knows people blame her. It's not right. There's no blame here. You need to go talk to her. Bring her something to eat. Then ask her to sit in the living room with us so she can see we don't blame her, either."

"You're right. This is all my mess." He stood, so cold his joints ached. "Are you coming in?"

"No. Not yet. I need to have a few words with God."

"Say some for me, too."

"Say them yourself. He listens to everyone who prays."

"I will."

He walked around the house, the deep drifts past his knees. He stood on the porch and rested his hand on the doorknob. Someone had walked right up to this door, let himself in, found Ty's bedroom, scooped him out of his crib, and carried him away. If Ty had cried out, Summer hadn't heard him, but Ty slept hard and he'd been busy with him and Autumn doing wedding things. The possibility of Ty sleeping through the whole thing was a good one.

He stepped into the house.

Beth sat on the couch, holding their father's hand. Layla had finally gone, either home or found a place to sleep, and Autumn sat at the table with Natasha, the woman from Missing Children Minnesota.

Autumn looked over her shoulder at him, her eyes red.

He shuffled over the thick carpet, cuddled her to him, and kissed the top of her head. "I'm going to bring Summer a cup of coffee."

"I just made a fresh pot."

"Thanks."

Carrying a large mug of coffee fixed the way Summer liked it, he plodded tiredly to her room, stepping over a pile of Ty's cars. He knocked once and pushed the door open. "Summer? I brought you a cup of coffee."

She sat up, and using the edge of a sheet, wiped her eyes. "You're talking to me? Did you come in here to scream at me and tell me you want nothing to do with Ty?"

He sat on the edge of the bed and tucked a curl behind Summer's ear. She looked so much like Autumn. The eyes, the nose, the mouth. He should have known he couldn't replace Autumn with Summer. With anyone. He'd been a fool to try.

"No. I wanted to tell you I understand. When we got married . . . you knew it wasn't because I was in love with you. I tried to convince myself I was, and maybe if I would've tried hard enough, I could have, but that's not how two people should be together."

"Autumn said I didn't give you a chance, and that's true, too. I knew you wanted her, and I hated you for that."

"It's nothing I didn't deserve. I used you, and I'm sorry."

She sipped her coffee. "It felt good to have something she wanted. Instead of figuring out what would make me happy, I thought stealing something that belonged to her would work, too, but it didn't. All it did was damage our relationship even more."

"She loves you, and she loves Ty."

"I know she does, and I'm grateful for that."

"Summer, about Ty . . ."

"I'm sorry I let you think he was yours."

"That's what I came in here to say. He *is* still mine. I don't care I'm not his biological father. I've loved him from the minute the nurse laid him in my arms and that won't change, but I want to set this whole thing straight. Autumn and I are getting married and there's nothing you can say that will stop us. After we find Ty, we'll work out parenting arrangements because I still consider myself his dad and I want him. Besides, what you said scared me. We slept together for two years and I didn't get you pregnant. You weren't on anything?"

She shook her head. "No. Sorry."

"Then Ty might be the only child I'm going to have. I won't give him up."

She set her coffee mug on the nightstand and crawled into his arms. He hugged her and rested his lips on her temple.

"Let's go see if there's news."

She stiffened. "I can't go out there."

"Yes, you can. Don't hide in here anymore. Mom wants to see you."

"Your mom? Why?"

"She knows this shit is *everyone's* fault. We were so busy trying to hurt each other, but we ended up hurting Ty most of all. Come on."

He held Summer's hand and they walked into the living room.

Bonnie hurried in from the kitchen and wrapped her arms around Summer. That small amount of compassion was all it took, and Summer started sobbing.

He met his mother's eyes over Summer's shaking shoulder. No one should be alone at a time like this.

Autumn watched him warily, her face pinched in pain and fatigue.

Gently, he smoothed a hand through her curls. "Is there someplace private we can go? We need to talk."

"Yeah. Upstairs."

"How's your hand?" His feet dragged, and he stumbled. He was too exhausted to climb even a short set of stairs, but he knew if he tried, he'd never be able to sleep. Not while Ty was out there.

"Stings like a son of a bitch, but I should have went in sooner. I was . . . overwhelmed."

He stopped her at the landing. "I'm sorry. That was my fault, like everything else these days. After this is over, I seriously don't know how I'm going to make this up to you."

"Do you still?" She padded down the hallway and stopped at the end. A large mirror hung on the wall, and a decorative table that had a dying plant in the center was positioned beneath it.

"Do I still what?"

"Want to make it up to me? Beth asked me if I knew about Ty. If I kept it a secret."

She moved the mirror aside and pressed a button that blended into the wallpaper. Without a sound, the wall slid open and revealed a dark room. She flipped a switch to turn the light on and motioned him around the little table. "This is my mom's reading nook. She wanted a space no one knew about, and my dad indulged her when they had the house built. It's not even on the blueprints. He was quite proud of that, and my mom loved it."

The bedroom contained a queen-sized bed, a large window that had a cushioned seat full of pillows, and more books than he'd ever seen outside of a library. The stale air gave off notes of abandonment. No one had been in here for a while.

"This is crazy."

"It's my mom's pride and joy. No one will know to look for us here, so we can't stay long. I don't want to be cut off from any news that might trickle in."

"No one else knows about it? " He'd had no idea this room existed. "Summer?"

"No. Just me and Mom. Dad. Summer wouldn't care. She doesn't like to read. When I lived in Decatur, Mom would invite me over and we'd hide in here with a pot of coffee, cookies, and our favorite books. It has an en suite bathroom, so we didn't need to leave to do that, either."

"Wow. I'm rubbing elbows with the rich and famous. Do they know? About Ty?" He tried to keep the misery out of his voice.

"No, not yet. I suppose keeping it from them is stupid. If I try much longer they're going see it online, but I don't want them to panic and fly back. If something doesn't break soon, I'll let them know. I was hoping we'd get a ransom note or . . . It'd be easier to give them something concrete than to tell them what little we know."

She sank onto the bed, a light pink comforter covering the mattress. Huge pillows were propped against the headboard.

"Do you think they would . . . I mean . . ." He could talk

about this with Beth, but not Autumn. Asking her parents to give money to a kidnapper.

She held his hand and tugged him onto the mattress. "Of course they would, but let's hope it doesn't come to that. Let's hope that one of Summer's friends got it into their head they could take Ty, and, I don't know. Play a joke on her or something."

"Some sick joke."

"I know, but I prefer to believe he's okay than think other things."

He wrapped his arms around her, grateful she allowed it. His conversation with his mother had been a huge wake-up call. "I haven't been good to you, and I need to make up for that, somehow. You have every right not to be here, supporting me. Supporting Summer. After telling you I was leaving, and God, taking Ty with me, you could have given your notice and walked out the door. Never talked to me again."

"I couldn't do that." She held his face between her hands. "I couldn't leave you. I love you, and I hope you still love me, too. But it's difficult to think beyond finding Ty. Maybe you won't want . . . Maybe it will all just be too much." She paused. "Will you touch me?"

He kissed her, letting himself fall into her embrace. He understood what she was trying to say. The future seemed so uncertain now, but whatever he had to face, he knew without a doubt he wanted her by his side.

She nuzzled his mouth with hers, and he pushed away the guilt and the selfishness he felt stealing this precious time to be with her. They shouldn't be doing this now. They should be downstairs, waiting like everyone else, but the need to be close to her, to know she loved him despite every-thing, won over common sense and propriety.

He slipped his hand under her shirt, and he grazed his thumb over her nipple. She whimpered, desire and fatigue, and her mewls made him hard.

He needed the intimacy, the comfort of her body, her affection and her compassion.

As he eased the chunky cardigan off her shoulders, she unknotted his tie.

He pulled her t-shirt over her head.

Clumsily, she unbuttoned his dress shirt at the same time he devoured her mouth, his hand cupping the back of her head, trapping her to him and bruising her lips. She freed the last button and brushed her fingers over his chest. Reluctantly, he leaned away, cursing the seconds wasted to unbuckle his belt.

"Wait," she said. "Let me. Calm down."

He drew a deep breath of musty air into his lungs and counted to five. "I'm sorry."

"It's okay." She unzipped his pants wrapped her warm hand around his cock. "We need to enjoy this because . . ."

Not only may they not have another chance to be alone, but they also may not feel like sharing themselves ever again. The guilt and pain of losing a child, the not knowing and lack of closure, wore couples down until there was nothing left. If Ty was never found, their guilt and sorrow would linger for the rest of their lives.

He and Autumn would drift away from each other, if he let it happen.

"Not for us, Autumn. This isn't wrong. Comforting each other isn't wrong. I'm not letting you go again. No matter what." He unclasped her bra and drew it over her shoulders revealing her delicate breasts. Tenderly, he nudged her backward onto the bed and sucked one of her nipples into his mouth.

Moaning, she arched her back.

"Don't push me away when you hurt, don't grieve alone," he said, his breath feathering along her ribcage. He trailed kisses down her belly and slowly slid her stretchy pants over her ass, down her legs, and tossed them aside. "You're so beautiful, it hurts my heart to think how I've treated you."

"Don't think about that anymore," she whispered. "I hurt you, too."

"Yeah, but I think I started it." He hooked his fingers under the waistband of her ice blue panties and they joined the rest of her clothes on the floor.

Her legs trembled.

He kneeled on the carpet and breathed in her musk. On his knees, begging, as he should have been all along. He belonged to her in every way a human being could belong to another person, and he never wanted that to change.

Licking her sensitive skin, he gently pushed two fingers inside her. Her clit quivered under his tongue. "You taste so good, sweetheart." He gorged, feasting on the honey that dripped out of her. She was so wet, he craved every drop.

"Cole, I'm going to come." Tangling her fingers in his hair, she panted, the sharp breaths shaking her body.

"Not like that. I want to feel you." He stood and wiped his mouth with the back of his hand.

"Okay. Hurry."

He took off his shirt and kicked his dress pants across the floor.

He stared at her, fire and tears burning bright in her eyes.

Lowering his body on top of hers, he said, "I love you, Autumn."

"I love you, too." She tilted her hips and he pushed inside her.

He never felt this complete than when he laid in her arms, as close as two people could be. Consuming her, he vowed he would never let anything come between them again.

Not even Ty. Especially not Ty. They had to stay together because one day Ty would come back.

He'd never stop looking for his little boy.

Making love to Autumn wouldn't bring a baby into this world. He may not believe everything Summer said, but she didn't lie about this. He'd get tested, and when they had proof he truly was sterile, maybe Autumn would want a man who could give her the babies she deserved.

Desperately, he shoved that thought out of his mind and tried to convince himself she'd love him anyway.

It'd be a miracle.

They rocked, every breath shared until they could no longer hold on, and he hugged her even tighter as they came, her pussy gripping his cock.

Emptying inside her, he swallowed back tears. Knowing what he now knew, making love would always be bittersweet.

He settled his weight on top of her, sweat covering his skin.

She wrapped her arms around his neck and nibbled along his jaw. He didn't want to move, but she shivered. This room wasn't heated as warmly as the rest of the house.

Carefully, he pulled out, and she crawled between the sheets. He followed, and closing his eyes, tried to block out the darkness and pain.

"Don't fall asleep," she murmured.

They hadn't been gone for more than fifteen minutes, but it was longer than she wanted. She didn't want to miss any news about Ty.

She'd needed this, though, and she rested her head on Cole's chest. "We should go downstairs."

He rubbed her back, and she cuddled closer. "Maybe one of Summer's friends will pan out."

"I think that's what they're all hoping for. Cole," she said, propping herself up and looking into his eyes, "you'll always be Ty's dad."

"I know. When I was sitting outside, Mom came out to talk to me and she shared some pretty harsh truths. I haven't been a good father, or a good man. I avoided Summer because it was easier, but I should have been protecting Ty."

"She'll work with us now, but it shouldn't have taken something like this to make us stand up to her."

"I'm going to be dealing with the guilt for a long time."

"You're a good man, and I love you. It's why I'm here and not in New York." She scrubbed her fingers over his scruff.

He huffed and shook his head. "There's always room for improvement."

"For everyone. Even me." She sighed. "We've been gone long enough. They're going to know what we've been doing."

He rubbed the ends of her hair between his thumb and

fingers. "I don't care. If we're going to make it out of this in one piece, we need each other."

"I know, but just because we managed to fix things doesn't mean we can take the time. Ty needs us. The investigation needs us."

"Come here. Just another second."

He slanted his mouth over hers, her flavor on his tongue, and she wiggled into him, wishing she could be closer.

It would take a fine balancing act to do what needed to be done but also do what she needed to keep herself from falling apart.

She dressed in silence.

Cole put his pants and shirt on but shoved his tie into a pocket. "I need a minute," he said, and went into the bathroom.

She made the bed and fluffed the pillows. There was no reason to wash the sheets. She didn't know the next time anyone would be in this room.

When he finished, she let them into the hall, righted the mirror, and blew the dust off the plant.

She trotted down the stairs in front of him, his solid presence at her back comforting. They stepped into the quiet living room, and huddling beside Bonnie, Summer glowered but didn't say anything. She blushed.

"Beth went home to Russ and the kids," Bonnie said.

"Good. There's nothing she can do here," Cole said.

Trevor sat behind his laptop at the kitchen table and she nodded at him.

"Nothing new," he said apologetically. "We're checking into a handful of sex offenders who have moved into the area in the past few months. We're doing what we can at this hour in the cold."

"We appreciate it." She squeezed Cole's hand. "I'm

going to check my phone and log into the newspaper's website. I need to write a new blog post, and maybe someone has left a tip or two in the comments section."

Cole nodded, sank onto the couch, and rubbed at his face.

She should have told him to stay upstairs and rest. There was nothing to be gained by not sleeping a little. Maybe if they were quiet he could grab a few hours before search parties went out in the morning.

Holding in her tears, she looked for her purse, hoping she hadn't left it in Beth's minivan. Leah never came back, and she might have texted to tell her why. More than likely something had come up at the store or she was using the opportunity to spend time with Jared since her house was empty. She wouldn't be surprised if he was spending the night with her.

She found her purse in the foyer where she dropped it in front of the closet. She'd missed several calls and texts, many of them from her friends. Ivy messaged her and said they were helping search and to call if she needed anything.

There were over thirty voicemails, most from numbers she didn't recognize.

She was tempted to give her phone to Trevor and be done with it. She wasn't strong enough to listen to hate mail, and it never failed to come. No doubt there were people blaming Ty's kidnapping on her, but she didn't need to anyone to tell her that they were right.

The phone chimed in her hand, and she jumped. "Holy shit."

Trevor looked at her, his eyebrows raised.

"Sorry. It's my friend. She scared the crap out of me." She accepted the call and wandered down the hall. "Hey,

Marnie." She stopped in Ty's room and sank into the rocking chair near his crib.

The police had searched the nursery looking for anything they could use to locate Ty, but nothing had been disturbed or left behind. No boot prints in the carpet's piling, no stray glove. Whoever had taken Ty wrapped him in his *Paw Patrol* blanket and left no evidence for anyone to find.

"Autumn, I'm so sorry. I was going to leave another message. You're not sleeping?"

"No. I can't. I should because tomorrow we'll be out searching and there won't be time, but I can't. I was checking my phone to see if there was any news, and I'm going to update the blog and ask for information."

"We're doing what we can here, too, and we'll hand out more fliers in the morning. James and I were up talking about the wedding, and I wanted to call. Listen, Autumn, we're going to postpone the ceremony."

"Oh, Marnie—"

"No. We can't get married while this is going on. It's not right. Instead of going on our honeymoon, we'll help search for Ty."

She bent over, clutching the phone to her ear, and tried to keep the wails inside.

"I should be there," Marnie said, sounding like she was going to drive over right then.

"No. Please. Get some sleep. I don't know how to thank you—" She couldn't go on. Tears ran down her cheeks and soaked into her pants.

"You don't have to thank us. We're doing the right thing, that's all. I'll let you go. Try to sleep a little. You aren't doing yourself any favors and when Ty comes home, he's going to need you at your best."

"Thank you. You're a good friend."

"I love you, and we're here for you. If you need anything, and I mean anything, let us know. Never forget that."

"I won't. Bye, Marnie. Tell James thanks from us as well."

"I will. See you soon."

She disconnected the call and leaned back against the rocking chair. She never rocked Ty here. She didn't know if Summer had, either.

She let her sister flounder through Ty's first year because she didn't want to deal with Summer's attitude and well, she'd been jealous and hurt. She'd felt like an outsider looking in at Cole and Summer's not-so-happy family, and it had take a while for Ty to steal her heart.

If she hadn't been so self-centered, maybe Summer would've asked for help. She'd have to be honest and tell herself the truth. Would she have given Summer that help if she'd asked?

It had hurt to be around Ty. Still did.

But Ty wasn't Cole's.

It shamed her to admit she may have been more apt to help if she would have known.

She'd let petty jealousy, bitterness, and resentment keep her from a baby who needed her.

Well, she could help now. Appeal to the public and beg. Searching for a child required time and resources. She could set up a donation campaign like Callie's father had done for Mitch's parents. Even a few hundred would pay for more fliers, a billboard along the highway.

She'd take a leave of absence. They'd have to tell her parents.

They had plenty to do after the sun came up, but she wouldn't wait.

Cole dozed in a recliner, and his mom and dad slept on the couch. Summer had gone back to her room.

Layla sat at the table sipping a cup of coffee. "Another of Summer's friends cleared. He has a solid alibi."

She tilted her head in question.

"He was at work. There are witnesses and he punched in. That can only be done in person."

Her shoulders drooped in disappointment. "Okay. I'm going to write a new blog post. Is there anything you think I should include?" she asked, setting her iPad on the table.

Layla shook her head, but it was Natasha who said, "We've been doing all we can."

"All right." She woke up her device and poured a cup of coffee. She needed the caffeine and breathed in the soothing aroma.

Her editor had emailed her and his message stood out in all caps. STOP BLOGGING AND WRITE THE FUCKING ARTICLE. THIS IS FRONT PAGE NEWS. DON'T DROP THE GODDAMNED BALL. RUN WITH THIS, AUTUMN.

Jim's faith in her buoyed her spirits, but she also knew he wouldn't want to miss the inside scoop on a news piece like this. Tragedy sold copies, and she'd make that work in their favor. She'd write the article, but the paper had gone to bed hours ago. At this time of the morning, they were being stacked into trucks and carriers were just waking up to bundle themselves against the cold and make their deliveries.

Despite what Jim said, she could still blog, and she signed into the backend of the site. She asked that if anyone had any leads or thought they had seen Ty *anywhere* to call the hotline and added new pictures of him.

She skimmed comments left on the previous blog post looking for clues, an odd sentence that would stand out against the rest. There was nothing but the usual thoughts and prayers and the nasty anonymous people who said they were getting what they deserved. Cowards. The least they could do was tell her to her face.

Her phone chimed again, flashing a number she didn't know.

Tempted to let it go to voicemail, she stared until Layla said, "It could be crank, but it could be news."

She couldn't shy away. Anything to help Ty.

"Hello?" she rasped, her throat raw.

"Autumn."

She sprang to her feet, hot and cold washing over her skin. Layla straightened, and Cole sat up in the chair, his gaze locking with hers.

"Buck."

Layla motioned to her, and she lifted her shoulders in question. The detective scribbled *Speaker* on a pad so hastily she could barely read it.

She moved the phone away from her ear and pressed Speaker.

Buck's gravelly voice was the only sound in the entire house. "Are you missing your little boy yet?"

"Do you have Ty?" she asked, trying to remain calm.

"Yes, yes I do. He's a good boy, but you know that, don't you? He was supposed to be ours. When I asked you to marry me, we talked about having kids. We would have two. A girl who looked like you, and a boy who would take after me. We had it all planned out."

Layla motioned for her to keep him talking, but it was

like Buck knew their intentions. "Don't think you can trace my cell. It's an old burner phone and the GPS is disabled. I'll get rid of it after we make our plans."

We can still ping the cell towers, Layla scratched onto the pad.

Keeping their conversation on track, she said, "Buck, we'd like Ty back, please."

"Well, that's gonna be a problem," he said, and the floorboards creaked in the background as he paced.

"What do you mean? You said he was okay."

Cole rested a trembling hand on her shoulder.

"He's fine, he's fine," Buck snapped, annoyed. "But I won't give him up so fast. I want something in exchange."

"Money? Are you talking about money?"

"No!" Buck exploded.

She flinched and almost dropped her phone.

"I don't want your fucking money. I want something more precious to me."

She swallowed around a lump of dread. She knew what he was going to say.

She stiffened her spine.

She'd do it for Ty.

"I want you."

CHAPTER SEVEN

Cole raked his fingers through his hair, his heart hammering so hard he felt like he was on the verge of a heart attack.

"No!" he mouthed, spit flying. "No, no, no!"

Layla stood between him and Autumn, her hand braced against his chest, blocking him from ripping the phone out of Autumn's hand and telling that sick fucking bastard to go straight to hell.

The call, the demand, they were good things. Ty's kidnapper was reaching out. This was what they'd been praying for. Layla kept him from ruining it, but there had to be a better way.

Buck was fucking crazy. The things he'd do to Autumn if he got a chance to put his filthy hands on her twisted his gut.

"Do you hear me, Autumn? A trade. Before sunrise."

Summer shuffled into the living room, her eyes wide.

He rushed to her, covered her mouth with his hand, and whispered in her ear, "Stay quiet. Autumn's stalker has Ty."

"We swap," Buck was saying. "I'll give you the kid and

you can put him in your car. Then we'll take off. Pack a bag. You won't be going back."

Autumn licked her lips, a dead look in her eyes. She would do this for Ty no matter what he said, and he tensed, Summer's hand clutching his arm, her fingernails digging into his skin.

Layla nodded, encouraging Autumn to speak.

"Okay. But . . . we need proof Ty's okay."

"You should trust me, Autumn," Buck said, and the asshole's voice sent shivers down his spine. There wasn't an ounce of love in his tone. She wouldn't be safe with him. Cole knew that in the very depths of his soul. "I've taken care of him like I'll take care of you. We'll move, somewhere warm. By the ocean, like we talked about, and we'll be happy."

A tear rolled down her cheek. "I remember."

He swallowed, bile rising in his throat. He was going to throw up.

Her phone chimed, indicating she had a new text message, and shaking, she opened it. He let go of Summer and looked over Autumn's shoulder.

Ty slept on a ratty couch, his *Paw Patrol* blanket wrapped around him. He seemed unhurt.

"Are you satisfied?" Buck growled.

"Yes. Where do you want to do this?" Autumn asked.

Layla scribbled notes as they spoke.

"The newspaper parking lot. *Alone*, Autumn. Not your fucking boyfriend. Not the cops. Not either of those women who've been sitting with you, sticking their noses into family business."

Her eyes widened.

He bit back some of the nastiest words that had ever wanted to leave his mouth.

Buck had been watching them the whole time.

"Forty-five minutes. That's all you get, and that's all you need. Say your goodbyes."

Autumn's cell beeped, and the screen went dark.

Moaning, she sank to her knees, her phone tumbling onto the floor. She covered her face with her hands. Her shoulders quaked.

He glared at Layla. "This is insane. She's not going."

"Try to calm down," Layla said. "We'll do the swap, and then we'll follow them. They won't get far."

"No. It's too dangerous. Do you know his location? Send a SWAT team to wherever the hell they are."

He was talking stupid. Rocky Point didn't have a SWAT team, only a handful of officers who'd never encountered something like this before, who may never have discharged their weapons in the line of duty.

"It's best for Ty," Autumn said, wiping her face with the sleeves of her sweater. "That's all that matters now. I'll find a bag."

He pulled her aside and did his best to turn his fear into anger. "I'm not letting you do this. I can't lose you."

"It's best for Ty," she repeated, jerking her arm out of his grasp. "Buck hasn't hurt him, yet."

"He's going to hurt *you*," he said, his voice cracking. "What am I going to do if something happens to you?"

She stood on her toes and brushed a kiss over his cheek. "Then you and Summer parent Ty the way you should have. This is all my fault. I brought Buck into our lives and it's my responsibility to fix it." She turned to Summer. "I'm sorry. I'll make this right."

She walked slowly down the hallway.

He stood in a daze, listening to Layla call the department and request backup. Autumn would meet Buck, secure Ty in her car, and then she'd go with him and do what he said until the police could reach her.

What would Buck do to her once he and Autumn were alone? He wouldn't need any time at all to hurt her.

Desperately, he appealed to Layla. "There has to be a better way."

"I wish there was. We're working with the cell phone companies to target his location, but pinging the towers will only give us a radius. During the swap we could ambush them, but to what end? Buck could be armed. He could shoot them both in the blink of an eye. Let Autumn draw him away from Ty. Cole, Autumn's strong, you know she reported on some dicey situations in Decatur. Plus she has a history with this guy. In his deranged way, he loves her, and we need to take advantage of that."

"I'm ready."

She wore the same clothes, but she carried a plain black backpack that God only knew what inside. Maybe nothing.

Maybe everything.

Maybe everything she needed to be on the road with this slimeball for a while.

She wouldn't look at him.

"We don't have time to put a wire on you. I don't have the equipment here, and he did that deliberately. We can still track your phone, and a car will be on your tail the minute we have Ty."

"Okay."

Something inside her had shut off, and needing to see a glimmer of light in her eyes, he pulled her to him and pressed a hard kiss to her mouth. A kiss she didn't return.

"We're going to get through this," he said roughly, shaking her.

She turned away. "Let's go."

"We'll follow from a safe distance. Remember that, Autumn," Layla said firmly. "Even if you can't see us, we'll be there. You won't be alone."

"I'm going with you," he said, and Summer gasped.

She clung to him, and it took every bit of willpower not to push her away in irritation. "Stay with me," she whispered.

"No. My parents will be here, and Ty will need to see a familiar face."

Autumn shoved boots onto her feet, put on a winter jacket and gloves. Grabbing the backpack by a strap, she slipped out the door without looking back.

Layla barked orders into her phone, and Natasha, whom he hadn't noticed until now, made her own phone calls.

"We'll have Ty checked out before bringing him home. It's been twenty-four hours and he may be hungry or thirsty."

They would examine him for more than that, but he was grateful Layla didn't say it.

He put his jacket on and followed her and Trevor outside.

Caught up in his worry for Autumn and Ty, he didn't spare Summer a single glance.

"Autumn." He caught up with her before she could get into her car, the driver's side door hanging open.

"Don't tell me not to do this." She threw the backpack into the passenger's seat. "Buck probably had this planned all along. He's been watching us for months and knew our every move."

She leaned against the car, her expression so sad and weary it broke his heart.

"We're going to get him back, and after this is over, we're going to be a family. You need to be careful. I love you. I've been living without you, and I can't do that anymore." He trapped her between his body and the car and cried into her hair.

God, he was so tired. Tired of the way things had been since Ty's birth, tired of the years before that when they hadn't been together because neither of them would admit their feelings. Now he faced losing her to a psychopath who thought she belonged to him.

"Cole, it's going to be okay. We'll get Ty back, I promise. Kiss me, for good luck."

He cuddled her to him and brushed his lips over hers, softly, gently. "Be careful."

"I will."

She sat behind the wheel and he slammed the door shut. She idled near the curb, waiting for Layla's go-ahead who would be following as closely as possible while staying out of sight.

"Are you okay?" Layla asked, standing beside him.

"Yeah. When we know Ty's safe, I want to go with you. I need to be there."

She pursed her lips and shook her head. "Absolutely not. We don't need civilians getting in the way. Cole, we may not be able to help Autumn, not immediately. You understand that, don't you? We can't turn this into a high-speed chase on slippery highways. We'll follow and approach at our first opportunity. We need to endanger as few lives as possible. Including Autumn's."

He knew that, but . . . "The more time we give him, the more time he has to hurt her."

"She's smart, and she knows this guy. Give her some credit, okay?"

He blew out breath. "Okay." Autumn was strong, and she was smart, and he had to trust she wouldn't take any unnecessary risks.

"Then let's go get your little boy and bring him home."

Layla waved Autumn on, and she drove down the empty, snowy street.

Her taillights glowed blood-red in the dark.

By rote, Autumn drove to the newspaper offices. Though she considered it morning, the sun wasn't even thinking about rising, but a hazy glow floated above town, the lights reflecting off the snow.

She didn't see anyone behind her, and she wondered if Layla convinced Cole to stay behind. Doubtful. Thinking of him and Layla arguing almost brought a smile to her lips.

This would all be over soon. Ty would be safe, and she'd go with Buck. Let him do what he wanted to her. It would be a small price to pay for Ty's safety.

She parked in the newspaper's deserted parking lot. No one was there, even the janitor had finished his work hours ago.

She let the car idle to keep the inside warm for Ty.

Headlights lit up her rearview mirror, and she stepped out of the car and leaned against the trunk.

Buck's old truck rolled to a stop behind her. There was

nothing to prevent a quick getaway. No snowdrifts, not a car left overnight. It was the perfect place for the exchange.

Her ex-fiancé opened his door and climbed out.

He didn't look much different than he had years ago when they'd been engaged. He kept his hair longer and combed it away from his face. He wore a five o'clock shadow just as sexily as any handsome Hollywood star, and he hadn't lost his hard physique.

They'd made a good match. An attractive couple. Everyone thought so. They could've been happy, if she could have loved him.

"Autumn," he said, pulling one of his gloves off. He brushed her hair off her cheek and it took everything she had not to flinch.

"Hey, Buck."

"You're not looking so good."

She huffed a laugh, disguising the desperate need to ask about Ty. She had a part to play and she had to play it well. Their lives depended on it. "These last few years have been rough."

He rested his hand on the back of her neck, and her stomach lurched. He nuzzled her lips with his, his whiskers scratching her skin, so much like Cole's had when they'd made love earlier. "It's going to be okay, baby. We're together now. I'll take care of you."

"Thanks. I need you to," she said, appealing to his over-inflated sense of importance in her life.

"I'm glad you see that. It will make things easier." He unzipped her jacket and caressed her breast. "When we get back to the cabin, we'll make love. The way we used to. Before you left me." A hard edge found its way into his voice.

"Please," she whispered, leaning into him, distracting him. His anger made him dangerous. "I want to."

Tracing his finger over her lips, he said, "Patience. When we're alone I'll give you a good fucking. One you'll never forget. You'll be begging for more by the time I'm done."

She licked his finger, hoping she wasn't playing it up too much.

"Naughty. I like it. I suppose you want the kid. A deal's a deal."

She tried to regulate her breathing, sucking the frozen air deep into her lungs. She hated being so close to him and the flavor of his skin on her tongue churned her stomach.

Buck opened the truck's passenger door and lifted the sleeping little boy out of the cab. "I took care of him. He likes macaroni and cheese, and we played cars. He doesn't talk." He frowned. "We'll have babies, you and me, and they'll be smarter than this one."

She ignored him, her gaze greedily roaming over Ty's body. He appeared unscathed, but they wouldn't know for sure until a doctor checked him over.

Still holding Ty, Buck paused. "Don't do anything stupid."

"I won't. I promise."

"Your promises don't mean much to me. Trust is earned. You'll have to earn mine back."

"I will," she said. Anything to encourage him to give Ty to her.

Buck laid him in her arms, and she clutched him to her, desperately inhaling his sweet baby smell and the strong scent of urine.

She opened the door of the backseat and gently put him down, keeping his blanket wrapped around him. He didn't stir, and that worried her. Ty was a heavy sleeper, but by now he'd be frightened, missing Summer and Cole, and he wouldn't want to go to sleep. Heat permeated the car. He wouldn't be cold while the police evaluated the right time to approach.

She closed the door. The soft click sounded so final, her fate slithering down her back in a shiver of fear and sweat.

"Come on. You packed a bag like I told you?"

"Yes."

"Then get it. I want to be long gone by the time the cops come."

She retrieved her bag out of the front seat and glanced at Ty, saying a silent goodbye. She shut the door and squared her shoulders. "I'm ready."

Buck boosted her into his beat-up truck.

She crammed the bag onto the floorboard by her feet and fastened her seatbelt. She had no idea what would happen now, but she had her phone in her bag and her GPS enabled. Unless he thought to throw her phone out the window, the police would at least know where they were headed. That gave her a small degree of comfort, but it was very tiny.

He settled behind the wheel, turned up the heat, and buckled his seatbelt. He opened the glove box and wrapped his hand around a black handgun, his finger on the trigger.

He rested the cold barrel against her cheek.

She couldn't stop herself, didn't want him to know she was scared of him, but she blanched.

"Don't do anything stupid. You're mine now. Not that motherfucker's whore, do you understand?"

"Yes," she whispered.

"Good."

Sitting still as stone, she said nothing as he drove out of

the parking lot, down the frontage road, and turned onto the highway that pointed them southbound out of town. Adrenaline battled with fatigue, and she fought against closing her eyes even though her blood sizzled. She needed to be on guard every second. She couldn't let exhaustion slow her down.

The side mirror was frosted over but she didn't need it to know that no one was behind them.

They parked behind the building near rusted dumpsters and recycle bins, snowbanks taller than he was creating a shield. Layla and Trevor stood outside and peered around the corner of the building, guns drawn, watching the exchange. The second they could no longer see Buck's truck, a plain black sedan that had its headlights turned off eased onto the frontage road to follow them, and Layla and Trevor holstered their weapons and ran across the lot to Autumn's car.

He scrambled out of Layla's vehicle, the radio droning.

An ambulance's sirens sliced through the quiet morning.

Breathing shallowly, his pink lips parted, Ty laid on the seat, his *Paw Patrol* blanket tucked around him. Layla carefully picked him up and offered his little boy to him as the ambulance sped into the lot.

Snuggling his son to his chest, he searched for any sign of injury. He stank of urine and something rotten, but his face was serene and he looked unhurt. He knew sleep could be deceiving. Ty could have been drugged, and when the

EMS approached him, he handed his son to the medic without hesitation.

He and his partner secured Ty to a gurney and lifted him into the back of the ambulance.

"Go with Ty," Layla demanded.

He stood his ground. "No, I need to know Autumn's okay." Now that he knew Ty was safe and unharmed, the thought of her with Buck and what he was doing to her scared him more than anything.

Sighing, she relented. "Fine, but they better not have my badge for this. All my instincts are telling me this is a bad idea. You have no business going, but I'll call Summer and let her know she should head over to the ER. Come on."

Relieved he wouldn't have to fight with her, he murmured a "Thank you" she didn't hear as he strode to her car.

He sat in the passenger seat, his hands clenched into fists, his leg jiggling in agitation.

"Target vehicle located southbound on 51. All units be advised this is a hostage situation. Subject may be armed," a stoic voice on the radio said.

"Hostage?" he asked, tense.

Layla lifted an eyebrow. "She didn't go willingly."

"Hostage has blonde hair, blue eyes, five-four, and approximately one hundred and twenty pounds. Injury status, unknown at this time," the dispatch continued.

"How far ahead are they?" he asked, scanning uselessly out the windshield. He didn't see a speck of light . . . anywhere.

"About three quarters of a mile. We don't know where Buck's taking her."

They weren't driving toward Marengo. Trees, as opposed to farmland, covered this part of the state, and evergreens, their branches weighed down by snow, crowded the highway. There was nothing in this direction except woods, and the next little town was an hour away.

"What will you do if they keep going?"

"Pass the situation on to the county sheriff. Cutting them off would be impossible. There's too much black ice. It'd be different if there was a way we could get ahead of them, but if he tries to outrun us . . . we won't have this stretch of highway to ourselves much longer. We can't take the chance."

"I understand."

Autumn had already been in one car accident because of this guy. He didn't want her in another. One that she couldn't walk away from.

He sat, his stomach twisting, and while the dispatch's voice buzzed in his ears, he prayed.

"Where are we going?" Autumn asked, staring dully out the window. Not one vehicle drove behind them, and it was difficult not to feel abandoned. They had Ty. Cole wouldn't be thinking about her now.

Her mind told her that wasn't true . . . but her heart whispered all he cared about was his son.

They were probably at the emergency room with Ty. Cole and Summer. Maybe they would try again. For Ty.

She rested her head against the cracked Naugahyde and tried not to cry.

Buck glanced at her. "Don't be sad. You're with me now, where you belong."

"I'm tired. I've been up all night."

"We'll rest before we keep going, but not for too long. We'll go to California and cross the border into Mexico. Then it will be just you and me, and we'll teach our kids Spanish and let them play on the beach." He rubbed her thigh, his gun still gripped in his hand. "It'll work out."

He slowed and turned down a path that was barely visible in the dark. The wheels spun in the drifts until they found the tracks already dredged through the snow.

The vehicle bumped along the ruts as he drove deeper into the woods.

No one saw them turn off the road and a vehicle going only slightly faster than Buck would cruise right by. Especially since it would be another two hours before the sun rose.

In defeat, she hunched into her jacket.

They'd been too cautious and now they wouldn't be able to find her.

Buck followed the trail for what seemed like miles, but finally, a small hunting shack came into view. Abandoned, the porch sagged and the walls leaned. It didn't look safe to step into let alone live in.

"Have you been staying here all this time?"

"It hasn't been pleasant, but it paid off." He unlatched her seatbelt and yanked her to him, steadying her head with his hand, the butt of his gun biting into her skin. He kissed her, his slimy tongue slithering between her lips. "Let's go inside and warm up. The bed's not half bad, and I bought some bread and peanut butter. Got a few beers, too. I'll let you get a couple hours, then we need to head out."

She opened the truck's door and snaked her arm through the backpack's straps. Her boots sank into the snow.

He led her into the cabin, opening the door and

gesturing her inside. A fire in a stone fireplace blazed brightly, the flames the only light in the room.

Staring at her, his eyes hard, Buck tucked his handgun into the waistband of his jeans. He made it impossible for her to reach it. "Don't even think about it. If you do, I'll put a bullet in your knee. Now, gimme your bag. What do you have in there?"

She forced herself to give it to him. "Some clothes. Feminine things."

"You won't need that when I knock you up. Sooner the better. What else?" He dumped the contents onto a scarred table. He snagged her phone as it clattered onto the wood, her Lock Screen glowing. Her wallpaper was a picture of Cole and Ty sleeping in a recliner in Cole's living room, and Buck growled.

"I'd like to check to see if they found Ty," she said, reaching out her hand.

"No. What happens to that little brat doesn't concern you anymore. That life's behind you, Autumn. I'm all you need."

He popped the phone out of its case, dropped it on the floor, and smashed it under his boot. The screen cracked and the phone went dark. He stomped on it again and kicked it under a metal stove.

Tears filled her eyes.

"Don't fucking cry. Are you hungry?" he asked, taking his jacket off.

She shook her head, unable to speak.

"Then let's go to bed. Didn't you miss me?" he asked. "I missed you."

"I . . . I did."

"Show me." He covered her mouth with his, and she tried not to panic. He shoved his hand down her pants, his fingertips digging into her belly. "This is where our baby will grow. Take your coat off. I'll keep you warm if you get cold. We can make love in front of the fire."

She wiggled out of her jacket, and gooseflesh covered her skin. She toed off her boots, grateful she wore thick socks. A coat of grime covered the wooden floor, and even in her socks, the cold seeped into her feet.

"That's more like it," he said, grabbing her hand and forcing her to feel his erection. "I've been dreaming about this for months. Dreaming of your tight pussy wrapped around my cock. Seeing you around town, cozying up to your lover, that hurt me, Autumn, it really hurt me."

"I'm sorry."

"You need to make it up to me." He turned her around and bent her over the rickety table, her head pushed into the pile of clothes that had fallen out of her backpack. His cock snug against her butt, he gripped her hips. "Like this."

Tears soaked into the sweatshirt she'd taken out of her mother's closet. Her perfume lingered in the cotton.

He tugged at the waistband of her yoga pants, his intent clear.

She couldn't let him do this. She couldn't let him do this to her when she and Cole had made love barely four hours ago. His cum was still inside her. Buck would know.

"Wait. I'm hungry after all. Do you mind? It's been such a stressful day I forgot to eat."

He yanked her pants down and spanked her. Pain zipped down her legs.

She bit back a cry. She couldn't afford to make him angrier.

"Fine. You can have a sandwich and a beer. Maybe it will loosen you up. I don't remember you being so frigid."

Impatiently, he pulled her pants up, and she whimpered in relief.

She had to get out of here. If Layla and Trevor weren't going rescue her, if Cole had already forgotten about her, then she needed to get herself out of this mess.

"Come on, then," he said, tangling his fingers in her hair and jerking her away from the table. "Go sit on the couch."

She yelped. She couldn't help it. Her scalp burned.

"Were you always this stupid? Did that motherfucker fuck all your brains out or what?"

"I'm sorry. I haven't had any sleep."

"I hope that's all it is. The mother of my children won't be a useless bitch. You're going to have to earn your keep."

"I'll try," she said, hoping to appease him.

"You'll do more than try."

She walked around what would be considered a living room. Dusty pictures hung on the walls and a bookshelf still had books on it. A bedroom was to the right and Buck's clothes laid in heap on the old mattress. A back door let out into the woods. Unless the bedroom had an exit of some kind, that door and the front door were her only means of escape. She looked for a weapon, something she could use to defend herself, but there was nothing except Buck's gun.

"Here," he said, shoving a cold bottle of beer into her hands. "Drink this and loosen the fuck up. This is the start of a new life for us, the way we should have been."

He took a long swig of his beer.

"I said drink it." He set his bottle on a coffee table made of cinder blocks and particleboard.

"I will." She stepped back.

"Do it now." He grabbed the back of her neck and lifted the bottle to her lips. He tipped it too far too fast, and beer ran down her chin. "God, you're so stupid. You can't even swallow. That's not looking good for you when I want my cock in your mouth."

She choked and coughed as the carbonated liquid went down the wrong way. The fizz burned her nose and she wheezed, doubled over. The last thing she wanted was Buck out of her line of vision, but she had no choice as she tried to breathe.

He smacked the back of her head. "I need to piss, then we'll sleep. I have a pair of cuffs. I don't need you trying to get away while I catch a couple hours. Don't think you can run from me. I'll always find you. Always."

She wiped her eyes. "I believe you." She did. She'd never be free of him unless he was dead or in prison.

"Good."

Undoing the button of his jeans, he walked across the living room, the boards creaking under his feet, and stood in the bathroom off the small living room. Needing the light, he left the door cracked, and he looked over his shoulder, his gun on the sink, taunting her. His pants drooped over his ass.

She tried to smile, reassure him she would do exactly what he said.

Satisfied, he turned around.

This would be her only chance. Once he shackled her to the bed, he could do whatever he wanted and she wouldn't be able to defend herself. Layla should have been here by now. They'd lost Buck's trail, and she didn't think tracking her phone would work if it was broken.

She hurried to the front door and shoved her boots on her feet. Her hands shook as she put her jacket on. She wouldn't last long in the cold if she wasn't dressed properly, and her best bet would be to hide in the woods.

First, she had to give herself a head start. There was no way she could outrun him in the dark.

Buck zipped up his pants.

She grabbed a beer bottle off the coffee table and stood outside the bathroom. She held her breath as he opened the door, and with all her might, she swung the bottle at his head. Beer poured onto the floor.

"I could hear you, you stupid bitch," he roared, knocking the bottle out of her hand and slamming her into the wall. "What did you think? I'd just let you bash my brains in?"

Her head bounced off the wooden paneling and she cowered against the wall, waiting for him to hit her.

Instead, he caressed her cheek, his gaze softening. "I love you, Autumn. We had so many plans. Let's try again, baby. The two of us. There's no need to be violent. Come with me. I'll give you everything I promised."

She let him brush his lips over hers. Wrapping her arms around his neck, she kissed him back, hate and fear roiling in her heart.

He pulled her to him, his hands kneading her butt, and when she felt him relax into their kiss, she bit his bottom lip as hard as she could. The coppery taste of blood filled her mouth, and she gagged. He tore away from her, grappling at his face.

"You fucking bitch!"

She hit his nose with the heel of her hand like she saw in a movie, and a sickening crunch met her ears. A river of blood flowed down his mouth and his chin and he howled, dropping to his knees. She ran out the back door, over a slippery porch, and into the frozen maze of trees.

A gunshot rang out, and a window exploded.

Buck screamed behind her, but she didn't stop.

"We lost them," Layla said, coasting to the side of the road.

Cole slapped the dash. "No! Keep looking. They went this way, I know they did."

"I know they did, too, but it's like they went up in a puff of smoke. Where could they have gone?"

"What about her phone? You said you were tracking her phone."

"They were in this area when the signal died. Trevor said that was ten minutes ago. Chances are good Buck broke it to stop her from calling for help. We're close. That's the best we can do."

"That's bullshit. This is all woods, Layla. There has to be somewhere to hide."

"This would be easier if it was light out. We could check for . . . I don't know. A trail, a path, something. Smoke. My dad used to hunt deer in these woods. Maybe Buck's been staying in a hunting shack near here." She spoke into her radio's mouthpiece. "Is there a path, a trail, something off-road? ATV tracks? Snowmobile? Anything that could lead to a cabin?"

"We got something," a voice said over the radio. "Up here. Tracks look fresh, but the snow's too deep. We'll need to go in on foot."

Layla closed her eyes. "We didn't go far enough. Praise Jesus, we didn't go far enough."

The relief in the vehicle was palpable.

Looking in the rearview mirror, she checked that the road was clear and slowly drove off the shoulder.

He figured they hadn't gone more than half a mile when

they came upon another unmarked sedan and an RPPD cruiser parked on the side of the road, their lights out. Trevor leaned against the back fender. Sweating, he got out of the car. He needed news. Now.

"We've got tracks," Trevor said. "Thank Merritt later. He has eyes like a hawk. Don't know how far they go in."

"You need to stay here," Layla said, checking her gun.

He stiffened. Fuck that. "No. I said I'm not leaving her alone. I've let her down too many times these past few years. I have to be there."

"You can be there by staying here. We don't know if this guy's armed, we don't know what he's capable of. We don't need you in the way."

"Fine." If he couldn't go in with them, he'd follow them.

Layla pinned him with a hard stare. His agreement had been too quick to fool her. "Don't do anything stupid, Cole. Getting yourself killed isn't going to help anyone, least of all Autumn. He knows who you are. Did you think about that? He kidnapped Ty to get at you because he knows you and Autumn are a couple. He'll take you out in a heartbeat, if anything, to punish her even more for leaving him. Don't tempt this guy."

He paused in mid-denial, then clamped his mouth shut.

"What?" she asked.

Trevor and two other cops gathered around them.

"I may have baited him a few times," he admitted. "I couldn't stand him hanging around."

"Then it's not just Summer to blame, is it?" She shook her head and holstered her weapon. "Poking an injured bear is never a good idea." Raising her voice, she said, "We've got a white male, mid- to late-thirties, about six foot, brown hair. Potentially armed, very dangerous."

He hunched his shoulders.

The group started down the trail following tire tracks that had already been carved into the snow.

They could be on a wild goose chase. This might not be the trail, this might not be the place. They could be entirely off the mark. He didn't know what they'd do if they were.

His fingertips numb, he called Summer.

"They're checking Ty," she whispered, voices murmuring in the background. "He hasn't woken up yet. They think he was given something to sleep through it all. He was in his diaper for too long and has a bad rash."

He blew out a breath. "But otherwise they think he's okay?"

"I don't know. His bloodwork hasn't come back yet. I'm with him. My little boy." She started crying.

"It'll be okay. You have a second chance to be a better mother. We have a second chance to be better parents."

"Yeah, I know. I've been thinking about that." She paused. "How . . . how's my sister? Is she okay? Where are you? At the house?"

"No. The cops lost the trail, but they think they found something and went to check it out. We're about twenty miles out of town."

"I thought they were gonna get her out right away!" Summer cried.

"That was the plan but the highway was empty and a car on his tail would have been too easy to spot. We'll get her back. Text me news about Ty," he said, torn. He wanted to wait with Summer on the phone for Ty's test results but his voice sounded louder than a stampede of elephants in the silent breaking dawn. Always torn between Ty and Autumn. Always torn between his son and the woman he loved. "I need to hang up and wait."

"Oh, God," Summer said, panting. "This is never going to end."

"Shh. Shh. Ty needs you, okay? Be there when he wakes up. He'll be scared."

"Okay, okay. I'm sorry, Cole. I'm so sorry."

"You aren't the only one who made mistakes. Summer . . . I'm sorry, for all of this."

He disconnected and slipped his phone into the pocket of his jacket. Putting his gloves on, he leaned against the police cruiser. He could wait inside Layla's vehicle, but he wanted to be able to hear, wanted to be able to reach Autumn as quickly as possible if she needed him.

He should follow them, but what Layla said made too much sense. Buck could have twenty guns, and by the look of him, he knew how to use anything someone put in his hand.

The only thing he could shoot was his camera.

A gunshot echoed through the trees, and without thinking, he set out at a dead run.

The first thing Autumn did was trip over a branch buried in the snow and belly-flop onto the ground. The wind knocked out of her and snow covered her face. Quickly, she wiped it out of her eyes and scrambled to her feet.

Behind her, Buck bellowed in fury and pain, and she took off, not wasting a second to see how close he was. A path of sorts had been chopped through the trees, but she veered off. Maybe he'd think she followed the trail.

The sky had softened from black to grey, but it did little

to help her. Clouds hid the moon, and while she cursed the lack of light, the shadows would help her hide.

Her breath streamed out of her mouth as she huffed. Dried-out sticks cracked under her feet, and reluctantly, she slowed to lessen the noise.

"Autumn, it doesn't have to be this way," Buck pleaded, his voice thin and reedy.

She'd gotten him good, but it hadn't slowed him down.

Trying to be as quiet as possible, she crouched behind a huge oak tree. Every sound echoed through the air, and the rustling she made might as well have been a homing beacon to Buck's ears.

"You can't run, you know," he said, branches snapping under his feet. It helped her keep a bead on him, but what helped her, helped him, too. "We're at least twenty miles out of town. Probably more. Where are you gonna go? You're not gonna make it before you get frostbit. How are you gonna type without any fingers, honey?"

She hadn't thought about the cold, not while sweat and fear trickled down her back, but he was right. It wouldn't be long before she got cold. Real cold. Serious cold. It was five below or more.

He fired a shot, maybe hoping to draw her out, and the explosion sent pain and adrenaline through every nerve-ending in her body. She forced herself to remain calm.

As quietly as she could, she inched to a different tree. He was moving too close to her.

"Autumn, I can see you."

She believed him, and she bolted.

He fired again and a tree trunk burst into splinters.

Too close, he was too close. A couple of feet to the left and he would have gotten her right in the middle of her back.

A fallen tree, a huge one, blocked her, and she scrambled over it, the bark tearing at her palms. Under the bandage, her stitches ripped, and pressing her lips together, she stifled a cry. She couldn't stop moving, and lying on her belly, she wormed her way along its length, her fingers digging into the snow, numb.

Buck's footfalls grew louder, branches cracking under his boots. "I know where you are. It's no good hiding. Come out, and I won't hurt you . . . much. You might even like it."

She crawled on her hands and knees, giving up the safety of the log to take shelter under a huge bough of an evergreen. Snow fell into her jacket and melted on her neck.

Maybe he was only bluffing. Maybe he had no idea where she was.

If he did, she was a sitting duck. All he had to do was shoot up this tree and she'd be done.

Tears dripped down her cheeks. She couldn't feel her hands and she tucked them into the sleeves of her jacket.

Another gunshot rent the air and she hid her face in her arms. She couldn't scream.

"Over here!"

She whipped her head in the direction of the voice. Layla's voice.

"Buck Drayton! Drop your weapon. Drop your weapon, now! We have you surrounded."

"Like hell you do!" Buck screamed at her.

Wide beams of light flickered back and forth, and she caught flashes through the tree's branches. She didn't want to risk trying to see Layla or if she had backup like she claimed.

"Buck Drayton, you're under arrest for the abduction of Tyler McClure and Autumn Bennett. You have the right to remain silent."

"Fuck that," Buck snarled, and another shot blasted through the early morning air.

Shots were fired in quick succession, and trapping a whine in her throat, she curled into a ball. It was like listening to an old radio program. She could hear the story but had to imagine what was happening, and everything she pictured ended with Buck still standing and coming after her.

A quiet filled the woods, and she forced herself to breathe, to wait.

Finally, Layla's voice called, "Autumn! Are you out here? He's down, Autumn. Buck's dead."

Dead?

"Autumn! It's safe to come out, I promise."

Sticks snapped as her friend stepped through the woods, and beams of light swished back and forth.

Tentatively, she crawled out from under the branches.

"Autumn. God, you're okay."

Layla stood near a tree, holding a flashlight. She ran over the snow and forest debris and fell into Layla's arms, sobbing uncontrollably.

"Shh, it's going to be okay. It's all over. He's dead. He's never going to hurt you again." Layla dropped the flashlight and held her.

"Ty?" she asked, trying to control her sobs long enough to ask. "Did you find him?"

"Yeah. We were parked behind the newspaper building and had an ambulance on standby. They brought him to the ER. I haven't heard any updates since we've been looking for you. We were too cautious, and I thought we lost you more than once. Don't look over there. I don't want you to see the bod- him." A hand to her back, Layla urged her to toward the cabin. "He shot at me, and I took him out. I had no choice. I'm sorry, Autumn."

She let Layla turn her away. Buck had been standing there, alive, only moments ago, threatening her life. Now that he was dead, all she could feel was relief. "No, I'm fine. I don't want to see him. Knowing he won't bother me anymore is enough. I just want to—"

"Autumn!"

Cole ran toward her, his figure materializing out of the shadows, worry and fear haunting his face.

She couldn't do anything but let him sweep her off her feet.

CHAPTER EIGHT

Gunshots had him running down what there was of a path, his feet slipping and sliding. He lost his balance more than once, went down hard on one knee, but it didn't stop him. He didn't care if he was running into the gunfire. He needed it to be him instead of her, needed to pay for the things that he'd put her through. If that meant taking a bullet, he would, dammit, but as he ran around the dilapidated cabin, Layla and Autumn were walking toward him, and Autumn had never looked more beautiful than she had at that moment.

Alive. Weary, but alive.

Holding her had never felt more right. "Christ, I was so scared when I heard those shots," he mumbled into her hair. He squeezed, afraid it was too much, but she hung on, her feet dangling over the ground.

"He's dead." Her voice shook. "Layla said he's dead."

"I won't say I'm sorry about it. He's put you through hell for months, and tonight . . . I almost lost you. Forever."

"Ty, did you see Ty?" she asked, and he reluctantly put her down to answer her. "Layla said he was okay, but—"

"They're doing bloodwork. He's sleeping, and they think Buck gave him something. Summer's there waiting for the results."

She stepped back. "Of course she is."

"Autumn." He didn't like her tone, or after everything that had just happened, that she pulled away from him. His heart ached, and she pulled away.

Goddammit.

"No, she has every right to be there. More than me. You should be there, too. Be there when he wakes up." She walked toward the cabin.

"Where the fuck are you going?"

"My backpack—"

He knew what she was doing. Trying to change the subject. He wouldn't let her. "Forget your backpack. You didn't pack anything you couldn't lose. I love you, and Buck scared the fuck out of me tonight. He could have killed you."

"I know. He scared the hell out of me, too, and it made me see some things. Clearer, you know? Ty's going to need you two. Together. I think you and Summer should try again. This will change her. It will make her grow up."

"No! Haven't you heard anything I've said? I love you. This parenting thing, we'll work it out. Ty loves you, too. That's what counts. Don't do this."

"Hey, let's get you two into town," Layla said, standing to the side, listening to them argue.

The back of his neck burned in embarrassment. He'd have to get used to airing his dirty laundry in public, at least until Ty's kidnapping cycled out of the news, and only God knew how long that would take.

Everyone would be talking for weeks, if not months,

possibly years, about the kidnapping and who was responsible.

"You're not thinking clearly," he said, putting his hand on her shoulder. "You need to get some sleep. Let's bring you to the hospital and they can look you over, give you something to help you rest. Okay? For me? It's colder than fuck out here."

She met his eyes and nodded, but said, "Drop me off at my parents' place. Leah and Jared might be at my house and I don't want to go to the hospital. My hands are okay, I think. My stitches . . . but there's time for that. All I need is a hot shower, a pain pill, and some sleep."

It was the only compromise she'd give him, but it was enough. "Okay. Thank you."

He cuddled her in the back of the cruiser, his lips pressed to the top of her head.

A coldness had come over her, though not the chill that saturated her clothing. Something else, and it scared him just as much as hearing the shots shatter the silence in the woods.

He hung on tighter, though it did little against the fear hammering in his heart.

He was losing her all over again.

The cop turned the cruiser into Autumn's parents' driveway. His parents were still at the house, but besides his car, everyone else was gone. He parked and opened the back door, and Cole slid out of the car behind Autumn.

He should go inside, tell them that Ty was okay and that they could go home, but he wanted to go to the hospital to see Ty and he had something else he needed to do while he was there.

"I'll see you later, okay?" he asked.

She scrubbed her fingers over his jaw. "Give Ty a kiss for me," she said.

"I will."

The tired officer scooped her up into a bear hug. "We're glad you're okay."

"Thanks, I am too." She kissed his cheek and trudged up the porch, her shoulders hunched.

Tears blurring his vision, he watched her disappear inside the house. The door shut, and he turned to the officer. "You Merritt?"

"Yeah."

He stuck out his hand. "You probably saved Autumn's life. I don't know how to thank you."

"When I was a kid, my dad taught me how to track moose. Not so different. He got what he deserved and won't hurt Autumn or your boy ever again."

"I appreciate that more than I'll ever be able to say. Drive carefully."

"Will do."

Officer Merritt backed out of the driveway and drove down the quiet street.

He pulled his keys out of his jacket pocket and sat heavily behind the wheel of his car. He wanted more than anything to follow Autumn into the house, take a shower with her and then sleep, his body curled around hers, but even though Ty was safe and Buck was dead, this was far from over. His engine growling in displeasure, he backed out of the Bennett's driveway and headed toward the hospital.

He parked in visitor parking and plodded across the lot. He could barely pick up his feet.

The automatic doors chugged open, and he quirked his lips. He could relate.

At the lobby's reception desk, he asked where Ty was, if he was still in the ER, and a kind woman told him Ty was in his own room and directed him to the pediatric wing.

Walking down the empty corridor, he thought he should feel something for Buck, but he didn't. He imagined Autumn's terror at being hunted like a deer during open season. Not knowing if she'd live to see Ty again, or him, or her family and friends.

He'd wanted to stay with her. He wanted to be with Ty. He wanted to speak to his parents and call Beth. He'd never felt pulled in so many directions.

One thing at a time.

He stepped into Ty's room.

Summer dozed in a chair next to Ty's bed. An IV was attached to his slender arm, but the little boy slept peacefully under a white blanket, a fluffy pillow under his head.

Gently, he shook her awake. "Hey. How is he?"

Summer's eyes fluttered open. "Cole. Hey."

He dragged a chair close to hers and sagged into it. "Hi."

"Is my sister all right?"

"She's shaken up, but she's okay. She's back at the house. My mom and dad were still there. Buck's dead. Layla shot him in self-defense. He won't be bothering anyone anymore."

She sighed. "Thank God."

"Yeah. How's Ty doing? Have you talked to a doctor?"

"He's okay. They took some blood and did a toxin screen. That woke him up a little bit. He didn't like it much." She tried to smile, and he huffed a quiet laugh.

"I don't suppose he did."

"He has a pretty bad diaper rash and they found antihistamine in his system. They think Buck gave him Benadryl to knock him out, but it wasn't enough to do any damage. At least, that's what the doctor said. He'll sleep it off. He's dehydrated and low on some vitamins and minerals." Her cheeks colored. "They want to keep an eye on him for a few more hours, but a child psychologist talked to me and said we should get back to our normal routine as fast as we can."

"*Paw Patrol,*" he said, squeezing her hand.

"Yeah."

"I meant what I said, Summer. Ty being okay doesn't change how I feel. I'm not going to let us go back to the way things were. I'm always going to be his dad because I love him, and we're going to have to work together to do better than what we've been doing."

Like hell he'd try a relationship with Summer again. Ty's kidnapping had softened her to a degree, but it wouldn't be long before she was back to her old self. A person he couldn't tolerate.

"I know. I have a plan."

"We'll talk about it later, when things settle down. For now, I'd like to wait here, until he's discharged, if that's okay."

"Yeah. It is." She crawled into his lap.

He wrapped his arms around her. There were a lot of feelings he'd have to work through. He wanted to hate Summer for cheating on him, for having someone else's baby, but he couldn't. They hadn't had a real marriage and he couldn't fault her for wanting the affection he hadn't given her.

Ty was the best thing that came out of their relationship, and he'd value that.

Summer fell asleep in his arms, and he dozed, too, until
midmorning when a little voice said, "Daddy."

It was the sweetest thing he'd heard in a long time.

The doctor gave them the okay to take Ty home, and
Summer held Ty in the lobby as he parked her SUV under
the canopy.

It killed him to let her take Ty, but he agreed with the
child psychologist. Ty needed normalcy as soon as possible,
and that included some Cheerios in a *Paw Patrol* bowl and
his favorite show. He stood at the doors until Summer drove
away, Ty buckled into his car seat.

He stopped at the registration desk. "Where would I go
to have sperm tested?"

The woman raised her eyebrows but clicked a few keys
on her keyboard. "Do you have an appointment?"

"No. It's actually kind of urgent."

"We had a cancellation and have an appointment in
family medicine in ten minutes. Are you a patient here?"

"Not recently, but I should be in your system." He gave
the woman his insurance card and date of birth. Somehow
through this whole thing, his wallet had stayed in the pocket
of the slacks he'd been wearing for the past twenty-four hours.

He shuffled down the hallway and rode the elevator to
the second floor. He didn't need to have this appointment
now, not when he could be doing a million other things, but
he put all that on hold. He'd be talking to Autumn tonight,

and he wanted all the pieces. He needed to paint her a clear picture of their future, and he couldn't do that with the allegation he was sterile hanging over them.

He checked in, but he was called back before he could sit down. In a cold exam room, the nurse took his blood pressure—through the roof—and his temperature. She noted his chart. "The doctor will be in momentarily," she said and stepped out of the room.

He slouched in the chair and prepared to wait, but a minute later someone knocked faintly on the door. He sat up straight and a young redhead stepped into the room wearing heels, a dress, and a white coat. A stethoscope hung around her neck. She looked barely older than him. Sitting on a stool near him, she said, "My name is Renee Carlson and I'm a physician's assistant. What are we doing for you today?"

He told her the story. His two years with Summer, that he was in a new relationship now and they wanted to talk about family planning. "I'd like to find out the results today, if that's possible."

She frowned. "Usually we send our lab work to Marengo, or complicated tests to Decatur, but circumstances being what they are, I'll put in a special request. We've all been watching the news and we're so happy Ty's okay. Several of us stopped by his room to wish him and his mother well."

"Thank you. It's a big relief."

"I'll need to get you a cup. Just a moment." She returned holding a sample cup that had a sticker on the side that had his name and date of birth printed on it. "This isn't a fertility clinic, so we don't have anything to help you . . ." She cleared her throat.

"It's okay. I'll take matters into my own hands, so to speak."

She smiled. "You can use the restroom down the hall. Place the cup in the metal box when you're finished, and it will be collected and sent to the lab."

"How long until I know the results?" he asked, standing. "I was hoping not to wait too long. As you can imagine, I have a lot to do."

"We'll do our best to be quick. I don't know how back-logged the lab is. It may take a couple of hours, but I'll let them know we need the results ASAP."

"I'll wait, if you don't mind."

"That's up to you. We'll let you know as soon as we can."

Giving a sample took less time than he thought considering how exhausted he was. He imagined ravaging Autumn in the back of a police cruiser after they rescued her from Buck. In his fantasy, she was grateful to be alive, and to thank him for the part he played in saving her, she'd give him whatever he wanted . . .

That was all it took to get the job done.

He placed the cup in the collection box, washed his hands, and settled his aching body into a cushioned chair in the waiting room. He propped his feet on a coffee table littered with drug brochures and tissue boxes. An aquarium gurgled on the other side of the room, and a local news program played on the TV. A coffee cart beckoned, but a hit of caffeine wasn't what he needed. He needed sleep, information, and Autumn, not necessarily in that order.

His cell phone vibrated in his pocket. In retrospect, he realized his cell had buzzed every five seconds since Ty went missing, but it had so often he tuned it out. Now while the TV hummed and the water bubbled, he noticed it and pulled it out of his pocket.

Beth texted, asking where he was, and he typed out a quick response.

I'll be there in ten minutes.

Okay.

He scanned texts and social media messages to see if he'd missed any recent news. There was nothing but well-wishes and exclamations of relief and joy that Ty had been found safe.

Beth bustled into the waiting room, plopped into the chair beside him, and gave him a hug. "What the hell are you doing here? Are you okay? Are you hurt?"

"No. I'm tired, but I'm okay. I wanted to be tested. You know."

"No, I . . . oh. To see if Summer's right?"

"Yeah."

She clutched her purse to her stomach. "What if she is?"

"Then that's one more thing Autumn and I are going to have to deal with, if, after all this, she still wants me. She has some stupid idea in her head that Summer and I need to get back together and parent Ty as a family."

"She said that?"

"Yeah, she did. She was . . . distant on the way to her parents' house. I know bad things are floating around in her head."

Slapping his arm, she said, "She'd just been through a horrible ordeal and she was probably in shock. Stop thinking about yourself."

"That's hard to do when she's my whole life," he snapped. He closed his eyes. "Sorry. My nerves are shot."

"This is stupid. You're exhausted. Let me drive you home. You need a shower and twelve hours of sleep."

"I can't. When the results come back, I need to check on Ty and Autumn. We've wasted so much time."

"Another few hours won't hurt anything. You won't be any good to anyone if you're so tired you can't function. You said Autumn's at the house. Ty will be okay and you know it."

He shook his head.

She sighed and took her jacket off. She leaned into her chair and tucked one foot under her thigh.

"Needless to say, I don't think Ty and I are going to Denver with you."

Beth bit her bottom lip. "Russ and I talked about that. We went back and forth for a long time, and we decided not to go. After everything that happened, I wouldn't feel right moving away."

"Don't be stupid. Russ is turning down a fantastic opportunity. Don't do that for us. To be honest, I don't know what's going to happen now. I don't know how we can give Ty a stable environment without hurting Autumn."

"She'll understand. She knows that we all need to do better, and she'll be on board with whatever you decide."

He scoffed. If that was true, they wouldn't be in this mess. "We can't have a relationship if Summer's between us and she always will be because of Ty, but his needs are non-negotiable. I don't see any way around that."

"You should give Summer some credit. I think after this she'll grow up a lot, and having a relationship with Autumn will be easier than you think."

"I hope so. Or Summer will change for a while and then things will go back to the way they were. She's not happy being Ty's mom, and her reputation as a crappy mother will make it worse. Throwing Autumn in her face will eventually make her explode, and Autumn isn't going to want to deal with that anymore. God, Mom was so right. She's given me everything, and all I've given her is shit."

"Cole," a nurse holding a tablet called into the waiting room.

"And it looks like I'm going to hand her some more."

He pushed out of his chair and grabbed his jacket. "You might as well come with me. What she's going to say won't be a surprise, but I need to know what I'm dealing with."

The nurse asked him to confirm his last name and birthdate as they followed her into a different examination room.

Only one chair occupied the small space besides a black stool that sat in front of a desk. Beth sat in the chair, and he hopped onto the exam table, the thin paper crinkling under his ass.

They sat in silence until Renee poked her head into the room.

"This is my sister, Beth," he said. "It's okay she's here."

"Nice to meet you," she said, shaking Beth's hand. She sat on the stool and opened the file. "You have some viable swimmers, but you do have a very low sperm count, and they're low in motility as well. You aren't sterile, but these issues can cause problems, as you know. There are things you can do to increase your odds such as wearing boxers instead of briefs, altering your diet, and not drinking alcohol. There are other tests we'd like to run, to determine if other factors are causing this. How long did you say you were trying to get pregnant?"

Cole blew out a breath. He wasn't sterile. That was something, anyway. "We weren't trying, exactly, but we were having unprotected sex for two years, and nothing happened."

"You didn't think to get tested then?"

"Children weren't on our radar, so when it didn't

happen we didn't think anything of it. I've . . . met someone, like I said, and I wanted to get my facts straight. We need to decide . . . I mean, so *she* can decide, if she wants a future with me."

Beth leaned over and patted his knee.

"You can try the natural way." Renee paused and scanned the paper laying on the desk. "But I feel your best bet, when you're ready, is a procedure called IUI, or intrauterine insemination. We collect a concentrated number of sperm, and when your partner is ovulating, we insert the sperm directly into her uterus. That increases the egg's chance of fertilization. The fertility clinic in Decatur has a wonderful success rate with IVF and IUI."

It sounded complicated. And expensive. He rubbed his face. "Do you have any good news?"

Renee lifted her hands. "I don't think I've told you any bad news. If you're looking for a silver lining, you have sperm. That's the bottom line. You can have biological children, though it may take a little work. Some men can't say the same."

"What do those men do?"

"Some choose to use donor sperm. Some decide to foster or adopt. Some decide not to have children. It's a very personal decision. Insurance coverage varies by companies and plans, and a lot of couples can't always do what they want."

"There're options, at least." As bleak as they sounded.

She stood and opened the door to the exam room and ushered them into the hallway. "There are options. I'll have a nurse email you an information packet, and you can do your own research online. There are natural things you can try first. It could just be you weren't having sex at the right time, or your body's chemistry wasn't a good match with hers."

He scoffed. "That doesn't make me feel better. They're sisters."

Renee cleared her throat. "That's . . . none . . . I mean, that's out of my scope, but if you need to talk to someone . . ."

"No. That won't be necessary, but thank you. Thanks for your time." He shook her hand.

"You're welcome. Have a nice day."

"See, it's not as bad as you thought," Beth said as they walked to the elevator.

"No, but it still sounds like a hell of a production, and she didn't give me any guarantees."

"There are no guarantees, about anything, and Autumn could have problems, too. Remember I had two miscarriages between the girls. If you love each other and support each other, then these things don't seem so heavy."

He felt like he had a boulder sitting on his chest, and his ribs cracked under the pressure. He didn't think his sister's description was that far off. Heavy was a good word. "What time is it?"

"A little after two. Will you go home now and get some sleep? Please? You shouldn't talk to Autumn when you're jacked up like this. Just a few hours. Then go back to the house and talk to her."

He didn't want to wait, but Beth was right. He needed a shower and a meal. Ty and Autumn were safe and he could rest without worrying about anyone. "Okay." He kissed her cheek. "Thank you."

"You're welcome. Let me know if you need anything."

"I will."

He leaned against his car and sucked in a lungful of air.

He'd go home, get a little sleep. What he'd learned at the clinic wasn't life or death. Maybe Autumn would work with him, if she'd given up on the crazy idea he and Summer belonged together.

He hoped she wouldn't do anything stupid. Like contact that guy she met at Marnie's bachelorette party. Or pack up and disappear before he had a chance to explain. To convince her that he couldn't live without her anymore.

Pausing, his hand on the cold door handle, he considered driving to the Bennett's house no matter how tired he was, but in the end, he slid behind the wheel, started his car, and drove to his house.

He took a hot shower and leaned against the wall in the steam, tired and drained. He could still feel it. The cold, standing outside that rundown cabin, the frozen fear. The gunshots. Autumn, staring at him, her eyes blank. Yeah, she'd been in shock. He didn't know what Buck had done to her, and he'd wanted to be there for her, terribly, but as always, Ty and Summer had come between them.

He turned the water off. The only thing that could thaw him out now was Autumn telling him she still loved him.

Needing to fill his queasy stomach, he chugged a glass of Ty's chocolate milk, and naked, he fell into bed. He set the alarm on his phone and stared at the ceiling.

Please, Autumn. Don't do anything stupid. I love you. Please wait for me.

That was the best he could do before his mind blanked out.

Autumn trudged into the house, heartsick, tired, and sore. With Cole on his way to the hospital and Summer already there, she felt out of place. She shouldn't be here, not when she had her own house to go back to, but she couldn't lose the connection to Ty or separate herself from the tragedy. To return to her own home would be admitting this was over, and even though that was true, she didn't want to go back to the way things had been.

So she kicked off her mom's boots and slid off her jacket covered in snow, pine needles, and dirt. Her palm burned, the stitches tearing at her skin under the filthy bandage. She'd need to cover her hand somehow, tape a plastic bag over it or something because she desperately needed a shower. Buck's scent lingered on her skin, along with the cheap beer he'd forced down her throat.

Cole's parents sat in the living room. His father slept in a huge recliner near the electric fireplace, but Bonnie stood from the couch, the past twenty-four hours carved into her already aging face.

"Oh, Bonnie," she said, dismayed. They'd been sitting here by themselves. Even Natasha was gone. "You and Dean should go home."

"Autumn," Bonnie said, holding out her hands. "Thank God you're okay."

She grasped them and asked, "Have you heard anything about Ty?"

Bonnie shook her head. "We haven't heard anything from anyone."

"I'm sorry. He's okay, but he's at the hospital getting a checkup. Summer's there, and Cole's driving over." She didn't know what to do. Sitting still seemed wrong and she started cleaning the living room, picking up plates and dirty coffee cups. The cleaner the house, the less Summer would have to do when she brought Ty home.

She carried them into the kitchen and dumped everything into the sink.

"What happened? Can you slow down and tell me?" Bonnie asked, lowering into a kitchen chair.

She rinsed out the carafe and started a fresh pot of coffee. "Sorry. I need to keep my hands busy or I might have an anxiety attack." She told Bonnie everything that happened since Buck's call. "I wanted to see Ty, but I didn't feel it was right to be there . . . and I need to get some sleep."

She leaned against the counter and peeled the bandage off her hand. The stitches were a bloody mess, and she dampened a paper towel and wiped her palm. She'd forgotten to take her antibiotics too, and she glanced around the kitchen, hoping to spot the pill bottle.

It sat near the toaster, though she couldn't remember putting it there. Maybe Beth had, or she'd given it to Cole, and she thanked whoever had been thinking about her. She poured the first two inches of coffee that dripped into a mug and added milk. Hoping the medication wouldn't upset her empty stomach, she swallowed a dose.

A wave of dizziness washed over her, and she swayed on her feet.

"You should go to bed, sweetheart," Bonnie said, jumping up off the chair to steady her. "You've been through so much, and you need rest." Cole's mother hugged her, and she melted into the woman's embrace.

"I will, but I need a shower. I'll sleep better if I'm clean."

Bonnie rubbed her back. "I understand." She paused. "Autumn, I know we haven't been close, but I feel I need to say this."

She poured more coffee into her mug and sipped, savoring the warm liquid as it moved through her. She still couldn't shake the cold out of her bones.

"What is it?" She didn't need to be told that Cole and Summer belonged together and the best thing would be for her to step aside. She already knew that. She wouldn't be surprised if Cole moved into the house. Even if he and Summer didn't share a bedroom, Ty having access to both his parents on a regular basis would be a positive change for the little boy.

"Cole loves you, very much," Bonnie started, and she fumbled her mug.

"What?" she asked, stunned. That was the last thing she expected Bonnie to say.

"Cole loves you, and he's going to beat himself up about his . . . condition. He's felt guilty for, well." She sighed. "For many reasons, but knowing Ty isn't his won't change anything. All it will do is shift that guilt because now he knows he can't father a child. My brother has a low sperm count, and so did my mother's brothers. It seems this is something I've passed on to Cole, but all these years we thought Ty was his and I never gave it a second thought."

She lifted a shoulder. "The news was a shock to all of us, but Cole will always be Ty's dad and I've come to terms with that. He and Summer will do better. I don't have a place here, and I've come to terms with that, too. Families are successfully blended all the time—"

Bonnie parted her lips but she lifted a finger, silencing the older woman. "But this is more than me being Ty's stepmother. Summer and I have always been at odds. She's always wanted the upper hand, and her pregnancy gave that to her. Ty's kidnapping has given her even more to hang over Cole's head, and don't think she won't use it saying it's what's best for Ty. When Cole threatened to take Ty to Denver with Beth and her family, he was going about it the wrong way but he was on the right track. It's better for everyone if I find my own path. Wanting what Cole gave Summer has done nothing but waste years I could have been working on my career and moving on in my personal life. Buck almost killed me tonight and I need space or I'm going to have a nervous breakdown. It's best for all of us, Bonnie. Stop shaking your head. You know it's true."

"No, I don't. Cole needs you. He's been handed a few hard blows these past twenty-four hours. I'm afraid he can't take anymore." Bonnie gripped her injured hand, and she winced.

"We had several chances to make a relationship work, and we both blew it. I think it's best to know when to throw in the towel." She pulled her hand away. "Cole has his phone. You should call and ask how Ty is. He'll be at the hospital now. I need to sleep . . . and pack. Be careful driving home." She kissed Bonnie's cheek. She appreciated the woman's presence when her own mother was halfway across the world. "I understand what you're saying, I really do, and it means a lot to me, but Ty was kidnapped. By a man I used to be engaged to. That's nothing I can push aside, either. A little bit of time will do all of us some good. The holidays are coming. Let's put the bad behind us."

"Don't give Cole a broken heart for Christmas," Bonnie said, stepping away. "He loves you. He said he asked you to marry him, and you said yes. He's going to hold you to that, and so am I. You don't want to turn me into a scary mother-in-law." She tried to joke, but her exhaustion made it fall flat. "We'll give you some peace. I'm feeling good enough to drive us home a few blocks. Sleep well."

Bonnie walked into the living room and roused her sleeping husband.

She set her mug on the counter and padded down to one of the guest bedrooms. She'd have to raid her mother's closet again, but all she needed was some comfy things to sleep in after a long shower.

She ended up in her mom's reading room. The sheets were still scented with hers and Cole's lovemaking, but the bedding permeated more than sex. She could smell fear, desperation, and hopelessness. Ty had been found and would likely fully recover from his terrible experience, but the scents pinged something deep in her heart.

This wasn't over.

More would come.

But she didn't want to be here when it did.

CHAPTER NINE

When Autumn woke, everything slammed back into her mind. Her mouth had dried, her eyes had crusted over, and her body ached, but she bolted out of bed and rushed down the hallway. She didn't want to miss any news.

A huge bouquet of flowers sat on the kitchen table.

God answers prayers, the card said, and it was signed by the pastor of the church she and Summer used to attend as children. Maybe that was another thing Cole could do for Ty. Start bringing him to church. A little bit of God could go a long way.

She dug through the kitchen and looked for something to eat. No one had thought to go shopping, but she didn't have the emotional strength to do something so mundane. Besides, this wasn't her house, and it wasn't her responsibility to put food in the fridge.

In the back of a cabinet, she found a dusty can of chicken noodle soup. The expiration date read two months before, but she opened it anyway. Rather than heat it in the microwave, she dumped the contents into a pot and set it on the stove to warm.

While it heated, she cleaned up the remains of the crusty pizza, a little surprised Bonnie hadn't done it, but it kept her busy. She scrubbed down the counter, wiped the table, and poked through what food there was to write a grocery list. She realized she could make a batch of chocolate chip muffins and a loaf of banana bread using a bunch of brown bananas that had been overlooked.

The baked goods would give Ty comfort food to nibble on after he came home.

She planned to leave after the muffins and bread were done, and part of her wished that would happen before Summer brought Ty home. She wanted to see for herself that he was okay, but the longer she lingered in the house that Summer had lived in for the past five years, the more she felt like an intruder.

Standing by the sink, she sipped her soup, hoping it would calm her stomach. She rinsed her bowl and put it in the dishwasher. It was almost full, mostly plates and coffee cups, and she shoved a pod into the detergent slot and turned it on. The noise felt homey, if that made any sense, like a family lived there, ate meals there, but she hadn't been part of the family that lived in this house. Her parents built it when she lived in Decatur and she didn't have a bedroom there. She ran the vacuum over the first floor, picking up Ty's cars and dropping them into his toy box, and when everything was set to rights, the rooms appeared like nothing had happened.

The house was too quiet, and to drown out the silence, she turned on the TV. The children's network Ty loved popped on. The goofy program brought tears to her eyes.

The timer dinged, and she pulled the tin of muffins out

of the oven. She adjusted the temperature and slid in the bread pan.

She'd just taken the oven gloves off when the front door burst open and Ty barreled into the house shouting "Auntie A! Auntie A!"

She rushed into the living room, lowered to her knees, and holding back her tears, wrapped her arms around Ty. She couldn't cry in front of him. He'd been through so much and things needed to return to normal. That included leaning away and ruffling his hair. "Hey, buddy." Her voice quavered, and she cleared her throat. "You're so cold!"

She clamped her mouth shut. That could have been taken as a recrimination, but Summer stepped into the room behind him and shrugged ruefully. "In all this mess, I forgot to bring his jacket to the hospital. I tried to wrap him in mine, but he got a kick out being outside in his pajamas."

"I understand. I'm sorry I'm still here. I cleaned and—"

"No. I'm glad you're here, and so is Ty. He was asking about you."

A smile trembled on her lips. "Thank you."

"It smells awesome in here, doesn't it, Ty?"

He nodded, but the TV distracted him and he drifted slowly toward it, wiggling his butt to the theme song of a program just beginning.

"Do you want a chocolate chip muffin?" she asked Ty. He nodded, but she blanched. "Can he have a muffin?" she asked her sister.

"He had lunch at the hospital. I don't know what Buck fed him . . ."

"I'll give him a muffin and some apple juice. He can pick at it if he's hungry. You'll have to—" She stopped. She wasn't in any position to tell Summer what to do.

Summer tilted her head. "What were you going to say?"

She moved into the kitchen and slid a small plate out of the cabinet. "I was going to say you'll have to go shopping soon, you're out of almost everything. Maybe Cole—"

Pressing her lips together, she pried a muffin out of the muffin tin and poured apple juice into a sippy cup.

She set them in front of Ty and kissed the top of his head. "I want you to know I won't be in your way. I promise. You and Cole will work it out. You definitely don't need me around. In fact, I've decided to take a vacation. The past few hours have been terrifying, and I can't do this."

Crestfallen, Summer asked, "Where are you going?"

"Maybe visit Mom and Dad. I don't know. I can't be here. That's all."

"But what about—" Summer stopped and poured a cup of coffee. She used the rest of the milk, and now the fridge was even emptier. She sipped and poked a butter knife at a muffin.

"What about what?" she asked.

"What about you and Cole?"

She tamped down her anger. "There isn't a 'me and Cole.' What I thought we could have was nothing but a joke. You can wish all you want for something, but that doesn't make it happen. I'll leave you to it. The banana bread has another forty-five minutes. If you could take it out when the timer goes off, that would be great," she said, turning away.

"Wait. Please," Summer said. "I wanted to talk to you."

"I don't think there's anything left to say. After all these years, you've won. You won, and I'm tired and I'm sore and I just want to go home." Too bad she didn't know where that was.

Summer reached out her hand. "How are you? Did Buck . . . ?"

"Hurt me? Not really. But I took a nap and dreamed he was hunting me down in the woods. I kept trying to scream, but I couldn't. I kept trying to call for help, but nothing came out of my mouth."

A psychologist didn't need to interpret her nightmare. She'd felt unheard in her dream. Like she did in real life whenever Ty came up, or Cole. It didn't matter what she wanted because she had no say.

"I'm sorry. It'll take time for everything to go back to normal."

She didn't want everything to go back to normal. Normal meant spending her days wanting something she couldn't have because her sister already did.

"Yeah. Anyway, I'll get out of your face." She blew out a sigh. Fuck. Her car was still at the newspaper. A taxi then. Or she'd walk.

"Will you sit and have a muffin? Since you went through the trouble? You always were better at it than me."

Summer pushed a piece of hair behind her ear. She needed a shower too, and the least Autumn could do was offer to watch Ty so she didn't have to hurry.

"Better at what?" She slid two more plates out of the cabinet and placed a large muffin on each one. She split them open and smeared butter on the halves.

"Making a home. Doing domestic stuff. Cooking."

"That doesn't mean I'm better than you. It just means I like to bake and don't mind doing chores."

Summer sat at the table and lifted a fork. "It makes me feel like you are. Always had friends, always did better in whatever we tried. I had nothing of my own. Mom said I've always been scared of my own shadow but you'd make friends with yours and invite it to tea. These past two weeks I've been insanely jealous. You're so busy doing stuff for

Marnie's wedding and some weird woman comes to town and the next thing you know, you're best friends and she's staying at your house. I've never had that."

"Leah isn't weird."

Summer laughed. "Who works for free?"

"Who asks to be paid to help?" she countered. "You need to change your mindset. That's why you don't have friends, and that's why Cole left you. Because you've only been in it for yourself. It's why you were with Cole in the first place. To get back at me, and for what? Wanting to go to school? And it's why you had Ty. To get back at Cole." She stabbed a fork into her muffin.

"He was in love with you."

"Then you had no business marrying him!" she shouted. She deflated and pushed her plate away. "This is why I can't stay here. You tied Cole to you forever the minute you put his name on Ty's birth certificate. Before that. When you let him believe Ty was his."

"You're right. Because you've always had everything. When we were kids you had our dog, friends, a position on the school's newspaper. I wanted something too."

She scoffed. It wasn't a newspaper. It had been little more than a glorified brochure and the school board cut funding for it several years ago.

"You've always known your place."

"Not always," she whispered. "When Cole moved back here . . . I was so lost and confused. Torn between wanting an exciting career and what I could have with him. He never said anything, never put into words how he felt."

"He showed you though," Summer said.

"Yeah, he did. Every look, every touch, every movie we went to as 'friends.' His actions told me he was in love with me, but I'm a reporter, for Christ's sake. I write articles for a newspaper. I blog to pay my bills. I needed the words. He never said them, I never took the hint, and he left. Buck . . . he knew how to talk and swept me off my feet. So, no, Summer, I haven't always known my place, and by the time I figured it out, it was too late."

Summer leaned forward, her eyes gleaming. "I don't want it to be too late for me. I've been reading about ocean pollution. Do you know hundreds of thousands of marine animals die every year due to pollution?"

She opened her mouth to defend herself, or explain something, *again*, because Summer never, *ever* understood what she tried to say, but she gaped instead, her brain slowly processing the change of subject. "Ummm, no? Do you mean the lake? Because there have been reports—"

"No, no, the oceans. The Gulf of Mexico. We're losing hundreds of thousands of animals every year, not to mention our coral reefs are dying at an alarming rate."

Summer rattled off statistics and her head spun. Her sister sounded like a documentary.

"Why the sudden interest in the plight of our oceans?"

"Because I've been thinking really hard about what I want to do. I'm not getting any younger. Half my life's gone, and all I've done is party."

And gave birth to a beautiful little boy.

"I want to do something for myself. Do something I'm passionate about. I talked to Mom—"

"What? When?"

"This morning, before Cole came to the hospital. I caught her by the pool and I told her what happened. She's not mad we didn't say anything, but she wants to talk to you. She said as soon as possible, and she might have said fuck a couple times."

She grimaced. Their mother never swore. "Thanks a lot."

"You're not the only one who's had her whole world turned upside down."

"I know. I'm sorry."

"It's okay. Anyway, I was talking to Mom, and I told her this whole thing changed how I want to live the rest of my life. She was so happy, Autumn. It made her cry. I didn't know how much me drifting through life had affected everyone."

"We all wanted better for you, but you took that as an insult. You twisted it, accused us of saying you weren't enough and that wasn't true, for a long time, but after you had Ty, who you were and what you were doing *wasn't* enough. You had a little boy who needed you, and you let him down."

"I know. I can't do that anymore, and the best way to take care of him is to take care of myself. Mom and Dad talked, and they okayed it. I'm moving to Florida. I'm going to enroll at the University of Florida and major in Marine Sciences. It's going to be a lot of work. I don't have any college, but it'll be worth it. Mom and Dad said as long as I keep my grades up, they'll pay my tuition."

Her eyes flew to Ty. Muffin crumbs covered his mouth, and he danced holding his sippy cup. "That's . . . great." She could barely push the words out of her mouth.

Summer was taking Ty away.

Well, wasn't the outcome just the same as Cole moving Ty to Denver, or her going to Italy to visit her parents? It seemed she was destined to live without her nephew.

But this was a new Summer. Passion sparkled in her eyes, and she couldn't resent her sister finally finding her path.

Sun, the beach, swimming with sharks . . . that fit her sister to a T.

She couldn't even worry about Ty. She was sure her parents said they would pay for Ty's daycare while Summer was in school, and with her parents' help, she wouldn't have to work. Ty's life might see a fair amount of improvement, going to a good daycare and having a happier mother.

"What did Cole say?"

"I haven't talked to him yet." Summer bit her lip.

"I don't think he's going to be happy. You'll have to figure out custody arrangements." She sighed. "Sorry. That's between you and him. Well, I'm happy for you. I really am." She nudged Summer's shoulder. "Took you long enough."

"Yeah, it did. I hurt a lot of people because I was jealous and lazy. I hope you can forgive me."

"It's not my forgiveness you have to ask for. It's Cole's. Ty's too young to remember any of this, but it's been hard on him too, being shuffled around to whoever can take him because you didn't want to get out of bed."

Summer's cheeks pinked. "I know. I haven't been a good mom. That's why I needed to talk to you."

"What? Haven't you said all there is to say?" She didn't know how she could help Summer be a better mother. All she knew of being a mom was spending time with Ty when Summer permitted it and the example their own mother set while they were growing up.

She'd blown her chance to have kids when she let Cole move back to Rocky Point without telling him how she felt. If they could ever find their way back to each other, she'd want to focus on their relationship, not throw a baby into the mix.

She was stupid hoping he'd get her pregnant the few

times they'd made love, and now knowing about his fertility issues, she didn't have to worry about that after all.

Cole might decide to follow Summer to Florida. It's not like what he did here he couldn't do anywhere.

She bit back another sigh.

Italy was looking better and better.

Ty bolted across the living room and launched himself into her lap.

He straddled her thighs, his arms wrapped around her neck, and she held him close. Breathed in the scents of love and apple juice.

Her little boy. She'd miss him.

"I . . . Ty, can you go into the living room for a little bit longer? I need to talk to Auntie A."

She growled and munched into his neck, and he laughed. "It's okay, baby. I'll be there in a few minutes and I'll watch TV with you."

Her heart hurt, watching him scamper off without argument. Ty was used to being shoved aside.

"I don't want to bring him to Florida with me," Summer said, and a tear rolled down her cheek. "I want to give school my full attention." She looked away. "That's not all true. I've been a shitty mom, but not only because I've been lazy and jealous. Autumn, I need to say something, and you can't judge me, okay? Let me say it, just accept it, and tell me that you won't take it out on Ty."

Her heart pounded with dread. She'd heard enough bad news to last a lifetime. "I promise."

"I don't want to be a mom. I've treated Ty like crap because I resented having him. I had him to get back at you and Cole, and I never should have done that."

"No, you shouldn't have. You hated us for no reason,

and for years, we paid for that. Cole will take him. You don't have to worry."

"No, you don't understand. I don't want to be his mother anymore. At all. Like, legally. I want to give up my rights."

"You can't do that! Ty won't have a mother. He's already going to be confused after you leave. You share blood, and he'll miss you. He doesn't understand that you've treated him poorly. All he knows is what he knows. What the hell is wrong with you?" She stood from the table and raked her fingers through her hair.

Summer crossed her arms. "You said you wouldn't judge."

"I didn't think something so idiotic would come out of your mouth. Just because you're going to school doesn't mean you have to give up your rights. Cole will take him. If you're worried about him having a female presence in his life, Beth will be there, so will Bonnie, and I'll . . . do what I can. When I come back from . . ." Wherever the hell she was going.

"I want you to do more than 'what you can.' I want you to have him. You've always loved him more than I have. He loves you, too."

"Jesus Christ. You can't just give me a child like I asked to borrow a pair of heels. And Cole needs a say in this. You need to tell him."

Summer rolled her eyes. "Like he's going to give a fuck," she whispered. "I'm giving you what you both want. I'm leaving and you can get married, be a family. You'll have a couple more kids, or you'll adopt, or whatever, if Cole's really sterile."

"Is that why you're doing this? Because you think this is what we want? Be a pretend family with your kid? What we want is for you to step up and be Ty's mom. You don't have to go to Florida to go to school. You can do two years at the community college then transfer to Decatur."

"Yeah, because there are so many oceans there. Marine Science is what I want, and having Ty with me would be impossible. I'll be out on a boat, sometimes for days at a time."

"You don't have to terminate your rights."

"I don't, but it's what I need to do. Ty needs a mother, a real one. You share his blood, too, you know. You love him, and you'll do right by him."

"Did you tell Mom this, too?" she asked.

"No, not that I'm giving up my rights. She doesn't know Ty isn't Cole's, either. We can keep it a secret, or you can tell her, or you can wait and just tell Ty when he's old enough to understand. I don't know who his father is, and not one guy I screwed bothered to ask. No one will be sniffing around to challenge Cole's paternity." She wiped her cheeks. "I need you to do this. Take Ty. Please."

She sagged against the counter and held her head in her hands. She didn't want a baby, not like this. Not as a consolation prize because her stupid sister didn't understand what she was giving away.

Summer stood and grabbed her shoulders. "You've always been better."

"What about the house? Are Mom and Dad going to sell it?" she asked, shaking her sister off.

"Ty needs stability. That's what the child psychologist at the hospital said. I know he has a bedroom at your house, and at Cole's, but if you move in here, he can stay in his own room."

"Then what will we do when Mom and Dad come back? They're coming home eventually, aren't they? I'm not living with them when I'm thirty-six years old. It's better if we move him to my—scratch that. It's better that he lives with Cole."

"Mom and Dad aren't coming back. They have a million places they want to go."

"What? They aren't coming home?"

"They want to visit because of everything that happened and to see you and Ty, but no. They don't have any interest in living in Rocky Point anymore. You and Cole can have the house. Mom said she'd write the deed over to you as a wedding gift. Ty can stay in his room and you won't have to worry about two mortgage payments."

She swore under her breath. "You and Mom have my life all worked out."

"She wanted me to feel good about leaving, and I do. Ty will be in good hands. He'll have a mom and dad who love him. How can that be wrong?"

"What if I don't want him?" Saying it made her want to throw up. It was far from true, but what Summer was doing sucked. She'd always used her love for Ty to twist things to get her way.

"You love him. You want him. I can see it on your face. You're like a dog looking at a big bone that's too good to be true, but there're no strings, Autumn."

"If I do this, you will never be able to take it back. I will fight you to the death if you ever decide to try to take him back. That little boy—" Her voice cracked. "He'll be mine. He'll be mine and you won't ever have him back. Don't do this if you think you'll change your mind. I won't allow it."

"And that's why I never would. Ty needs that fire, that passion. He needs a mother who will protect him. He needs a mother who will put him first."

Summer hugged her, and her sister still smelled of the

hospital's sharp antiseptic.

"I'll be his mom," she murmured. She wouldn't be, not really. To Ty, she'll probably always be Auntie A, but in her heart, she'd be his mother the minute Summer walked out the door.

"Yeah, you will, and there's no one who can do it better than you."

She stepped back. "I don't know how to go about this."

"I do. I called James at the resort. He's waiting for you to text him and give him the okay to drive over. He's been printing off the paperwork we need to fill out and sign."

"Christ, Summer, when?"

"In the car, on the way home from the hospital. I've been thinking about this for months. It's not a decision I'm making lightly."

"Months? I don't believe you." She shook her head. There was no way in hell Summer had been planning this for months.

"I don't blame you, but I have. I've known for a long time this was the right thing to do, but I didn't know how to go about it or what you would say. Ty's kidnapping just kind of opened the door, and I'm walking through."

She scoffed. Yeah, it was easy for Summer to take advantage of opportunities when she knew people would be there to clean up the mess behind her. But it was a mess she wanted and if leaving made Summer a bad person, then she was a bad person, too.

"I don't like doing this behind Cole's back."

"He might be mad at first, that we didn't tell him, but I don't want to see the look in his eyes. I've given him plenty of reasons to hate me. Let me go in peace. Please."

She still didn't like it, but it was Summer's choice. "Okay. If that's what you want."

"It is."

"Then I'll stop asking and message James. I need to find my iPad because Buck broke my phone."

"Will you explain to Ty while I pack?"

"What do you want me to say?"

"Whatever you think is best." Summer squeezed her in the tightest hug she could remember her sister ever giving her. "Thank you."

She rushed through the living room, a smile lighting her face.

Autumn found her iPad in her work bag and messaged James. He replied he'd been waiting for her text and had everything they needed.

She sat on the living room floor and Ty crawled into her lap. "I have something to tell you. Mommy's going on vacation, and you're going to stay with Daddy and me for a long time."

"This is only the start," James warned, sliding a thin stack of papers across the table, "and Autumn has to be in place to move forward with adoption proceedings. Of course, if Cole disagrees, he could stop everything. He should be here, and I'm not being held accountable because he's not."

Summer stiffened. "We're doing what's best."

"Whether that's true or not isn't up to me. You asked me to help you, and as Autumn's friend, and that's what I'm doing. You'll need to attend a court hearing."

"What if I don't? Or can't? I'm leaving today. As soon as I can."

"That may move things faster," he said, collecting the

papers Summer signed. "Abandonment is a viable cause to terminate rights, but you need to be sure this is what you want."

"It is. Autumn and I have gone over this many times."

"Okay. Autumn, I can give you names of a couple of family law attorneys in Marengo and Decatur. This is a complicated process, but it helps you've been taking care of Ty in some capacity since he was born."

"Thank you. It means a lot you're taking the time to do this."

They stood from the table and Summer shook James's hand. "Thanks. I need to finish packing."

"Good luck, Summer." She hurried toward her room and he turned to Autumn. "I'll keep these and fax them to the attorney you choose." He slid the papers into his brief-case and closed it. "This must have been unexpected."

"It really was. On top of Buck kidnapping Ty, and then Layla shooting . . . it's been an overwhelming couple of days."

"I'm sure it has been, and I wish I had time to talk to you about it."

She blanched, and he chuckled.

"Okay, maybe you're tired of talking, but unfortunately I have something else to discuss with you. Listen, Marnie felt like crap asking me to bring this up, but our rehearsal's tonight—"

"Oh, shit, it is." She groaned. "Summer's leaving and Cole doesn't know anything. He's probably still sleeping off last night. God. I don't think I can— Maybe Cole's sister—"

James gripped her shoulder. "Hey, it's okay. She canceled everything, but the minute Ty was found and she knew you were okay, she asked if everything could be put back on. It all worked out except that the ceremony at the church will be a little later than planned, but that's a good thing, I think. Will you be able to be in the ceremony tomorrow evening?"

"Yeah, I will. And Ty seems like he's fine. We were encouraged to keep things normal, and he loved his tux. I think he should still be able to be the ring bearer, too, since Marnie went through the trouble of renting it."

His face smoothed out. "Thank you. We both feel shitty asking—"

"Don't. It's okay, and I think a big party after all this is exactly what we need."

"We were hoping you would feel that way." He brushed a kiss over her cheek. "Marnie canceled our photographer, and she booked another gig. Do you think you could ask Cole if he'd mind taking a few pictures? Set up a video camera in the back of the church? We'll pay him. Whatever his rates are will be fine."

"I'll ask, but I can't guarantee anything. I told Summer she needed to talk to him about this, but she didn't want to face him. I don't know if she's taking the coward's way out or if she has her own reasons, but Cole will be angry, there's no doubt about that. I'll let you know as soon as I can."

"Thanks. I appreciate it."

"Good luck tonight. I'm sorry I can't be there."

"After all this, we're just grateful everyone's safe and we can still get married the way we want. It's been a helluva two weeks." He shook his head in amazement. "Marnie will text you the details. The new time to meet at the church tomorrow and all that."

"Okay. I'll look for it."

James left and she leaned against the door, her head spinning. Ty ran up to her, and she boosted him into her arms. Soon he'd be too heavy carry. For now, he needed a bath and fresh clothes. Something to eat for dinner. God. They didn't have any food.

Summer rolled a suitcase down the hallway and stopped in the foyer.

She sparkled, and the joy that radiated from her took Autumn aback. Never had she seen her sister look so happy. She had to be careful her sister's happiness didn't twist her heart. Summer was only happy because she was finally doing her own thing and leaving Ty behind.

Her sister's loss was her gain, and she'd always remember that.

"I'm taking off."

"I suppose it makes sense to drive," she said over Ty's shoulder.

"Yeah, I'm going to need a car. Mom said she wired me some money so I have cash for the road and to find a place to live. She wants to talk to you about Ty . . ."

"I can afford what he needs. Things might be a little tight, but Cole will help, too. When your rights are terminated, he won't be paying child support anymore."

"That's right. See? Things will be better for both of you. Well, I'm gonna go. With any luck, I can make it out of Minnesota before I get too tired to keep going. I don't know what route I'm taking yet, but I'm looking forward to some time alone. Come here and give me a hug goodbye, Ty."

Reluctantly, she handed Ty to her. He gave Summer a smacking kiss on the mouth but then reached for her.

That lightened her heart.

What made her hum was the fact that Summer gave him back without an ounce of hesitation.

"Are you sure you don't want to wait until after Christmas?" she asked.

"No. I haven't even decorated." She waved a hand at the

living room. "I haven't put up a tree or anything. You always loved the holidays more than I ever did. I know you'll make this year special for Ty . . . and Cole."

She blew out a breath, relieved her sister insisted on leaving. "Be careful driving, then. And let me know when you reach . . . wherever it is you're going." She didn't know in which city the University of Florida was located.

"I will." She paused. "You don't have to, but it would be nice . . . I don't know how to ask." Summer's hand tightened on the handle of her suitcase.

She knew what her sister wanted. "I'll send you pictures. He's going to be in James and Marnie's wedding tomorrow night. I'll text them to you."

"Thanks. Okay. Goodbye, and thank you. I don't deserve you taking Ty." Summer leaned in and she hugged her briefly. It might be the last hug she'd give her sister. Once Summer reached Florida, like her parents, she may never come back to this cold little town.

"Probably not, but he deserves a home."

"Yeah. I never gave him one. I know. Bye."

"Bye," she said softly, closing the door behind her.

Still holding Ty, she watched Summer back her SUV out of the garage and turn onto the street.

Summer waved. She tried to show Ty, but he wouldn't lift his head off her shoulder. Maybe the little boy knew what was going on after all.

She stood at the window waiting for Summer to come back and tell her it was all a mistake.

Her sister never did.

Cole woke to a black sky, and he jackknifed out of bed. He needed to check on Ty, see how Autumn was doing. Talk to Summer about how all this was going to shake out. He'd wrestle an agreement out of her while this nightmare was fresh, while he had her fear on his side.

He grabbed his phone off the nightstand and relaxed. His alarm was set to go ring in ten minutes. He'd slept so deeply, it felt like a million hours had gone by, when, in fact, he'd only allowed himself five, and that's all he'd slept.

Several well wishes clogged his Messages app, and he accidentally scrolled by Autumn's text. She asked him to pick up a few things at the grocery store, including a list of staples Summer always ran out of and didn't restock, forcing him to do it for her. Bringing groceries to her house was a weekly occurrence, but that would stop too. Part of being Ty's mother was feeding him nutritious meals, and they would start that sooner rather than later. If she didn't want people giving her nasty looks, instead of avoiding the store, she'd have to do better, that's all.

He threw on some clothes and told Autumn he'd pick up what she asked, but she didn't say anything more than "Thanks" and that worried him. He wanted to ask if she was all right, if she needed to be checked over after all and wanted a ride to the ER, but everything said would sound better in person.

He stopped at Rocky Point's only grocery store, strangers stopping him in the aisles saying how happy they were Ty and Autumn were okay, and on impulse, threw four steaks into the cart. They could fry steaks and nuke potatoes and have a decent meal while they talked about how things would be from now on. The three of them at the dinner table. Jesus Christ. Too bad grocery stores in Minnesota didn't sell booze. A couple of shots of whiskey would go down real good before dealing with Summer and Autumn at the same time.

The lights were on in the Bennett house and it looked cozy and warm. Like a real family lived there. No one standing on the street would know how horrific the past thirty-six hours had been, or how long a road they had to travel to find some normalcy.

Even just a few rocks of common ground seemed more than he could hope for these days.

Autumn threw the door open before he could knock and relieved him of the bags and gallons of milk he juggled. "Thank you so much. The lack of food in this house has been eating at me, pardon the pun, but I couldn't bring myself to go to the grocery store. The errand seemed so monumental somehow."

"I understand." He kicked off his boots.

"Daddy!" Ty flew across the living wearing only a *Paw Patrol* t-shirt.

Cole knelt and hugged him, a little longer and a little harder than he had in the past. "What's all this nakey-butt?" he asked, laughing, ruffling Ty's hair.

Autumn blushed. "I called the ask-a-nurse hotline about Ty's diaper rash. I gave him a bath earlier, and the water hurt him. The nurse said the best thing would be to give his skin air, if we could deal with the accidents, so here we are."

His throat burned. He did not deserve this woman in his life. "Thank you." He paused. "Where's Summer? I bought some steaks and potatoes. I thought we'd eat a grown-up meal while we talked about what we'd be doing moving forward."

"She's . . . not here."

He took his jacket off, suddenly too hot, but it wasn't his winter coat that made him sweat. "Why am I surprised? Did she go party again?" Anger sizzled under the surface. After Ty's kidnapping, she had the audacity to go out.

"No. Will you calm down and come into the kitchen? You'll have to decide if it's bad news or not. I'm . . . not sure it is. Bad news, I mean."

Clenching his teeth, he carried grocery bags and gallons of milk and followed her into the kitchen. He set them in front of the fridge and wearily lowered into a chair at the table. She handed him a bottle of beer he didn't want, but the cool glass anchored him and he uncapped the bottle and sipped to wet his mouth.

She put the groceries away in the efficient manner he'd always admired about her. No lost movements, everything in its place.

Did he fit into her life anymore?

He wanted to ask, but he didn't dare.

She opened a can of mandarin oranges she'd asked him to buy, drained them, and dumped them into a bowl. She shoved a spoon into them and offered them to Ty. He looked puzzled, and Cole shook his head. The poor kid had never seen fruit before. His fault, he reminded himself. That was his fault, too.

"Oranges are good," she said, fitting one onto the spoon. Ty opened his mouth because he did everything Autumn wanted him to do, just like everyone else, and his face lit up. "See? They're good. We'll eat supper soon." She walked back into the kitchen. "Four steaks are too many. Ty and I can share, and Summer isn't here."

"Will you tell me where she is? You said she's not out partying."

"No. She's not." She sank into the seat next to him and rubbed his thigh. The contact soothed him. It gave him a small idea of where her thoughts were. She sipped his beer. "She's gone."

"Gone where? Summer never leaves the house unless it's to party. Get some D." He didn't mean drugs, and Autumn knew it, too.

She wrinkled her nose. "I know, but apparently, while Ty was missing, she had an epiphany, and with our parents' blessing, she left. She's driving to Florida even as we speak."

"She's what?"

"She's driving to Florida. She's going to study Marine Sciences and the U of F."

"What the fuck? When did this happen?"

"Earlier this afternoon. She didn't want to tell you."

He tried to curb his anger and failed. "You're goddamned right she didn't want to tell me because there's no way in hell I would've let her go. After all this, she's abandoning Ty. For some fucked up idea she's going to school. Jesus Christ." In disgust, he flopped back in his chair. Summer was the most selfish person he knew.

Autumn's face smoothed into a mask, and while Summer's taking off lit a fire of indignation under him, her impassive features chilled him right to the bone.

"You would have kept her here. What about Denver?"

"That was different. That was before Buck kidnapped Ty, that was before when I thought having a full-time dad was better for him than two part-time parents. Things have changed, and I realize now that he needs two full-time parents, not all this piecemeal bullshit of who can watch him when. He needs a solid family, and that's shot to shit because she up and left."

"Then where was I going to fit into all this?"

Where *had* he fit Autumn into their lives? While he grappled to find an explanation, she unwrapped two steaks and tossed them into a frying pan. She sprinkled salt and pepper over them and turned on the heat.

Finally, he said, "I still want to marry you, if you'll have me."

She scoffed. "And then what? The three of us were going to live here as one big happy family? For Ty?"

That sounded like hell. They'd be anything but happy. "I hadn't gotten that far. I've been a little worried about my son being missing."

"You asked me to marry you and I said yes. You must have been thinking something. Were you going to live here with Summer and Ty, and I would . . . stay at my house?"

"No, but I don't want Ty shuffled around anymore."

"Broken families shuffle, Cole. You started that marrying my sister when you knew it wouldn't last."

"I didn't marry her intending to get a divorce."

"*Pfft*. Well, you did. Now you have to deal with the consequences. That means shuffling and piece-mealing care because we both work."

"Families do the daycare thing and hold down jobs. We don't need to be different."

"Well, we are," she said, jabbing a fork viciously into a potato. "You have an extra woman in your scenario, and because I'm not Ty's mother, that extra woman is me."

He stepped behind her and placed his hands over hers. They trembled, gripping a fork and a potato.

This woman, who, while arguing about her sister having a place in their lives because of his stupid mistake, was cooking a meal for him and a little boy who belonged to neither of them but both of them and it humbled and shamed him to his very core.

"What do you want me to do? Admit that I'm glad she's

gone? I can't do that, even if I am, because she's Ty's mother. He loves her, and he needs her."

"She isn't. Not anymore. At least, she won't be after the paperwork goes through."

His hands tightened over hers. "What do you mean?"

"She called James this morning, and he brought over the paperwork we need to file after I find a family law attorney. She signed her rights away. She didn't want to be Ty's mother anymore, and after the paperwork goes through and the judge signs off on it, she won't be. I will."

"She abandoned him," he whispered, his body still molded to Autumn's, his hands still resting on hers.

"She didn't abandon him so much as decided it was better if he was ours while she finally did what she wanted to do with her life." She turned in his embrace and spread her hands over his chest.

Shadows rested beneath her eyes, and tired lines crossed her face. Despite that, she looked beautiful, and he tightened his arms around her. "Do you want him, Autumn?"

"More than anything."

"Do you still want me?" Not a fair question since he hadn't told her his news yet, but he wanted an answer, even if that made him an asshole.

She paused, and he died a million little deaths until she answered.

"More than anything."

"God." He lifted her onto the counter beside the potatoes and covered her mouth with his. Their tongues tangled together and he grabbed at her shirt, eager to find bare skin. He unhooked her bra and held her breasts in his hands.

The steaks sizzled in the pan, and the heat matched the blood in his veins.

She whimpered and pulled at his hair.

He licked at her mouth, and she wrapped her legs around his waist. "We can't," he said, as much as he wanted to. "Ty's in the living room."

"I know. Can you . . ."

He slid his hand into her sweatpants and rubbed her clit. Squeezing one of her nipples, he murmured against her lips, "Come on, baby, let it out."

He wanted nothing more than to shove his cock inside her and find his own release, but this was her way of finding peace after Buck hunting her down. This was her way of connecting with him after the horrors of last night, and he'd give that to her. It would be the start of him giving her whatever she needed, whenever she needed it.

She increased the pressure against his hand, and he coaxed the orgasm out of her, his mouth muffling her cries.

He pulled his hand out of her pants and steadied her on the counter's ledge as she sobbed into his shoulder. "Shh, shh." Several minutes went by until her whimpers faded, and she lifted her head and wiped her tears.

"Can you turn the steaks?" she asked, her breath watery. He did, but he didn't let her go.

"Thanks for that," she said. "I mean, you know. Not for turning the steaks."

He nibbled her jaw. "You don't have to thank me. I've been an asshole. You had a horrible experience and it looks like you didn't get much sleep."

"I didn't. I was worried about Ty, and the nightmares . . ."

He sighed. "We'll both have them for a while."

"Yeah."

He helped her down to the floor.

She fastened her bra and finished poking holes in the potatoes. She put them in the microwave and set the cook time.

He washed his hands and looked in on Ty. "Oops, it looks like we have an accident underway."

She laughed. "I figured it would happen, but there's not much we can do. Summer doesn't have a potty training chair, so we can't start doing that while he's naked. There's carpet cleaner under the sink."

"Gotcha." He kissed Autumn's cheek. "I love you."

She tilted her head and his lips met hers. "I love you, too."

He cleaned the carpet and cuddled on Ty while he watched TV and ate the rest of his oranges. This felt right. This felt how it should, and guilt ate at him.

He didn't miss Summer at all.

"Supper will be ready in a couple of minutes, okay, buddy?" he asked Ty, getting up off the couch.

Ty nodded, happy, and snuggled into his blanket to watch his show.

Drying his palms on his jeans, he walked into the kitchen and said, "Hey. Sit down, will you? I need to tell you something."

Lies of omission were still lies, and he needed to tell Autumn about his clinic visit, or any decisions they came to in the next few days about raising Ty, getting married, and building a life together would be for nothing.

CHAPTER TEN

Autumn's heart leapt into her throat.

He'd already hurt her, wanting Summer to stay in Rocky Point, even though the years he'd been married to her had been hell, and Ty, for the most part, had been neglected while her sister played at being a grownup.

She could understand his point, barely, but it wasn't like they ran Summer out of town with pitchforks and torches. She left of her own accord. She'd hurt Ty, and he would be better off without her. Hell, even their own mother gave Summer permission to leave knowing she'd be there to pick up the pieces. There were plenty.

"I think I'd rather stand. There's only so much more bad news I can take."

"I love you, and you love me. That means we can make it, right?"

She'd never heard him sound so vulnerable. Maybe because what he said was full of shit, and he knew it.

"Not necessarily. We've loved each other for years, but we're only now getting around to admitting it and doing something about it. We're lucky something else didn't happen. Like one of us finding a real partner. Then what? We would have been stuck living half-lives because we were too stupid to say something."

He took a long drink of his beer.

She needed one too, and she pulled a bottle out of the fridge.

"You're right. We need to start being honest, start voicing our feelings, or this is never going to work." He paused. "I went to the clinic after Summer brought Ty home. I had my sperm checked to see if what she said was true . . . and it is."

She lowered the bottle onto the table. "Oh, Cole."

"I'm not completely sterile, which is good news. It means there are things I can try by myself, and things we can do as a couple if we ever decide we want biological children. But the bad news is those procedures can get costly, and well, there would be more work in it for you than there would be for me." He lifted a shoulder. "On the bright side, Ty won't be a wedge between us anymore because you can't hang on to the resentment that I gave Summer a baby. I didn't, and you can . . . I mean, *we* can let that go."

"It was a valid reason. That hurt me. A lot."

"I know it was. I'm not saying it wasn't, and I'm not saying it didn't. You looked at Ty and saw the family I didn't give you. I completely understand that, but it's going to be different looking at him now. You can see your nephew, and I—"

She straddled his legs and forced him to look at her. "Can see your son. That's all you need to see. That little boy represents a lot of feelings and emotions, bad ones as well as good ones, but that's not his fault. I'm going to adopt him. He's going to have a mom and a dad, and we're going to get married, and we're going to love him."

"You don't care about what they told me at the clinic?"

"I care about it for you, if you want biological children. Giving Ty a sibling would be nice, but he'll need to adjust to not having Summer around, to preschool, to things he should have had but didn't. That's going to take a lot out of him, and for now, I was thinking . . . a puppy."

He rested his forehead on hers and rubbed her arms. "You're too good to me."

She feathered her fingers over his smooth jaw. He'd shaved recently, and she missed his whiskers. She loved this man, had for many years, and Summer wasn't in her way any longer. "No, I'm not. I love you. But we *do* need to start treating each other better. I'll start by not burning our dinner."

"I'll help you."

He took the potatoes out of the microwave and she lowered the heat under the steaks.

A wave of peace settled over her.

Things felt like they would be okay.

After dinner, while Autumn changed Ty's crib sheets and tucked him into bed, he called Summer. He needed to hear for himself what she decided. He trusted Autumn, but their problems as sisters went back further than his history with either of them, and as the mother of his child, he wanted to make sure she was okay.

She didn't answer right away, and he paced.

"Hello?" she finally said, her voice warbly and distorted.

"Summer?"

"Hold on."

He waited, and the noise faded until it was only her voice and the hum of tires against pavement. "Cole?"

"Yeah. Hey."

"Is Ty okay?" she asked, and the question made his heart a little lighter. She still cared. Or maybe she'd always cared, and that's why she'd done what she did.

"Yeah, he's fine. Well, the rash is still pretty bad, but Autumn gave him some air-time, and . . ." He faded off. He didn't know how to talk to Summer about motherly things. About anything.

"Cole."

She said his name so gently he sagged against the wall. Somehow, he'd wandered into the basement, and the paint cooled his skin.

"Yeah?"

"You're calling to ask if I think I did the right thing, and I know I did. You and Autumn will do a better job than I would ever do. Wanted to do. I had Ty for all the wrong reasons. I wanted to keep you, punish you. But I didn't get to keep you and I punished everyone, not just you."

"I wasn't calling to ask you if you thought you made the right choice, not exactly. I called to make sure that Autumn and I didn't push you into this. You can come home and go to school here. You can still be Ty's mom."

"You'd lose Autumn, you know that, don't you?"

His heart sank. "What do you mean?"

"If I came back and wanted to parent Ty with you. With her. She'd leave because that's not her way. She'd leave and let us be Ty's parents. She was already talking about leaving town before I told her I wanted to go to school. She was talking about going to Italy, or, I don't know. She said something about a vacation, but I didn't listen because all I could hear was the fact that if she left, I couldn't."

"She never said anything about that." He wasn't surprised to hear it, though. He'd known she'd been thinking thoughts, bad thoughts, on the way home from the shack. She'd been planning to leave, planning to give him and Summer room to be Ty's parents.

"Of course she wouldn't," Summer said. "Saint Autumn doing what she thinks is best for everyone and never thinking about herself. What's best for you, what's best for Ty. She never considered that what's best for you and Ty is her. I finally saw it, and I stepped aside. The right person finally stepped aside. Let me have that, at least."

"We didn't push you out. I'm going to build a life with our son and your sister and I need to believe that so I can be happy."

Summer let out a long breath he knew so well. Annoyance and not a little bit of impatience. "You didn't push me out. What happened to Ty and Autumn made me open my eyes. Not only to how I was treating Ty, but how I was treating myself. I spent all my life wanting what my sister had, but I found out that once I had it, I didn't want it after all. I'm doing something for me now. Maybe that would be really shitty if Ty wasn't being loved and cared for, but he is, so I need to let it go. So do you."

"Are you happy?"

"There will always be a part of me that will wonder. I can't lie about that, not even after all the lies I've told you. There will always be a part of me that will wonder how Ty would've turned out had I stayed, but I'm happy. I'm following *my* heart, *my* dreams. And I'm sorry, Cole, for everything I did to you."

"I want to say it doesn't matter because we have Ty, but it does. I would have given it a shot."

"Yeah. That's what Autumn said. Because you're like that. You two really are meant for each other, you know?"

The floorboards creaked above him and he straightened. Autumn must have gotten Ty to sleep. "I do know that. I love her very much, and I'll treat her well. I promise."

"You're a good guy and a good dad. Now let me drive. I have a couple more hours before I stop for the night. Good luck."

"Goodbye, Summer," he said, but she'd already disconnected.

Things had a strange way of working out.

He bounded up the steps to give his son a goodnight kiss.

And to ask Autumn to show him how to set the alarm.

Nothing was going to take the people he loved away from him ever again.

He stood in the middle of the living room, uncertain. Autumn clanked dishes in the kitchen, cleaning up after their meal. He'd offered to help, but she declined, telling him to relax, but he couldn't. There was still so much that needed to be said, but he didn't know where to start.

He wanted to jump into his new life with Autumn and Ty right now, right at this minute, but there wasn't anything he could do. The urgency made his nerves twitch.

"Are you okay? Do you want anything?" Autumn asked, stepping into the room.

Her cheeks were flushed, her curls a frizzy halo around

her head, and he thought she was the most beautiful woman in the world. Summer called her Saint Autumn, but really, she was an angel disguised in human clothing. What other explanation could there be for who she was? For who she'd taught him he could be?

"I'm fine. Do you want me to go? I mean, I don't . . ." He rubbed the back of his neck in agitation. The last thing he wanted was to spend the night alone without his family.

She held his hand and tugged him down to sit on the couch. "I guess we're not done talking."

He rested his elbows on his knees and laced his fingers. "No, we're not."

"Well, first things first, I guess. When James was here, he said that he and Marnie put the wedding back on. We missed the rehearsal tonight. He said they understood, but he's hoping we'll be at the wedding tomorrow."

"Fuck," he muttered. "I forgot all about that."

"Me too. But I'd still like to be in it. Ty enjoyed wearing his tux, but if you think it's too soon for him to be doing something like that, then he won't be in the ceremony. Marnie will understand."

"Why are you asking me?" he asked, confused. It wasn't up to him if Ty was in the wedding or not.

"Because you're his dad, and if you think he can't handle being in the wedding, we'll tell Marnie and James we want to keep his days quiet for a while."

"I don't know."

She wrapped her body around his, and he leaned into her. There would be so much to get used to. Freedom to be with her. Summer gone. Nothing between him and Autumn. No animosity. No resentment.

"I don't know, either, but we can give it a try and if he seems overwhelmed, we can take him home."

"Yeah. That sounds good. We can bring him to Beth's, or my parents."

She shook her head. "No. We can take him home. We. Can. Take. Him. Home."

The meaning of her words finally sank in. No more shoving Ty onto whoever. They were his parents now.

He squeezed her hand. "That sounds perfect."

"Good. I talked to Mom earlier, after Summer left. I wanted to make sure Summer wasn't feeding me a line of crap, but everything she said was true. Mom encouraged her to leave and go to school and live her life."

"Marine Sciences. God." He had to laugh. He couldn't picture Summer on a boat.

"I know, but Mom was more interested in talking about you and Ty. About what happened. I told her everything, and she invited us to visit them, whenever we think Ty can handle a trip like that. I told her we'd have to play it by ear, but she said she and Dad aren't coming back to Rocky Point. They don't want to deal with the cold and the boredom. They go out dancing every night. They've made friends there, and Mom's learning Italian."

He didn't know where this was going, and he raised his eyebrows to keep her talking.

"They're giving us the house. Since they're paying Summer's tuition and her room and board because she won't be working while she's in school, she said it's the least they could do. Dad yelled in the background to consider it a wedding present."

He rubbed his thumb over her cheek. "You told them we're getting married."

"Yeah. Well, Summer did, but I told her it was true. I said I love you with all my heart. She only laughed and said she already knew. I guess I should have asked you first, but I said we accept the house. They'll sign the deed over to us in the next couple of weeks. We don't have to live here, we can try to sell it, but I don't know how long it would take. Maybe someone in Marengo or Decatur would want it as a summer house. The lake isn't that far."

"I like this house, and so does Ty." The driveway would be a bitch to shovel, but they'd make good use of the huge backyard.

"Me too, and he'll be able to stay in his room. I think that's important. He'll need a safe and familiar place if what Buck did affects him somehow, or if he misses Summer and doesn't understand why she's not here."

"Yeah. Autumn . . ." He tried to speak, but nothing came out. Turning his feelings into words should have been easy, but Autumn sitting there, in flesh and blood, alive and telling him she loved him, made his heart seize and he choked.

"You don't have to say anything."

"There's too much to say, and I don't know how to say it." He'd been dropped into this perfect family and he didn't know if he deserved any of it. A spectacular house, a woman who'd waited for him, a little boy who loved him and called him Daddy when he'd done nothing to earn it. "What Buck did to you . . . when I heard the gunshots. I thought, in those seconds, my entire life was gone. You're my everything, and in the blink of an eye you could've been gone."

The past couple of days caught up with him, and he let the tears fall.

She cuddled him to her, and he cried out the terror and fear.

"All that's over now," she murmured into his hair. "Tonight, let's start our new lives. The three of us."

Nothing sounded better.

But.

"What about your dream job? I thought you wanted to do more than just write blog posts for the *Journal*? I can't ask you to give up your career."

"You're not. I'll do what I can from here. I haven't been trying, and I blamed my lack of motivation on Summer, you, this town. I'll dig deeper into freelance jobs. Leah's going to commute to Marengo a couple times a week to supplement her income headhunting and visiting her grandma. Maybe I can go with her and write an article here and there for the *Marengo Gazette*. If my career's been stagnant, that's no one's fault but mine. When we get Ty settled, we'll both have more time to focus on our professional lives. What I'm giving up traveling the world, I'm gaining by making a home for you and Ty. That's what I want."

"Are you sure? I don't want you to stay if you don't want to be here . . . like Summer."

"I'll never be like my sister, and we already promised that we wouldn't lie to each other anymore. What I just told you, I mean it, but I'm going to need your support. Both of us working won't be easy."

Cole searched her eyes, but he saw nothing but sincerity. "Okay. I know things will get sticky, but you have my promise."

"What about you?" she asked, looking away. "You were the one who was excited about opportunities in Denver. That didn't suddenly just disappear."

"No, you're right, but there are things I can do with my photography. I've been dragging my heels too, but the opportunities are here, and like you, I have to search for them and take advantage when I find them. I'm not saying that one day we won't want to do something else or try different things . . ." He gripped her chin and met her eyes.

"But if we ever start to feel restless or unsatisfied, we need to let each other know, okay? So we can work it out together."

"Okay."

"Tell me you love me," he said, picking her up off the sofa.

She squealed. "I love you. I think you know that by now." She leaned up and brushed her lips over his.

"It'll take a lot of work if we want our own babies." He had to warn her, one last time.

She only laughed and wrapped her arms around his neck. "I'm not worried about it, and we'll have fun trying."

Pausing in the middle of the hallway, he had to ask which room they were going to sleep in. In the coming months he was going to have to ask a lot of questions and look to Autumn to lead the way, but they were on the right path to being a family.

As they should have been all along.

CHAPTER ELEVEN

Cole set up his tripod at the back of the sanctuary to film the ceremony. An organist played while people milled about. Joyful energy filled the church.

Poinsettias sparkled, and candles flickered.

The air lent a note of vanilla.

Because the ceremony was being held later than originally planned, the sunset glowed through the stained glass windows, and he thought Marnie and James lucked out with the timing.

They'd been at the church for a while now, Autumn helping her friends and changing into her own bridesmaid dress.

Ty was excited he could wear his tux again.

Several people asked him about Ty' kidnapping, about Autumn and what happened that horrifying night in the woods. The story about Buck, and his death, had slowly made its way around Rocky Point, and she couldn't walk five steps without someone hugging her and thanking God she was okay.

Just as he finished taking candid photos of the wedding

guests, anticipation settled over the church. The organist drifted into the first strains of the "Wedding March" and people turned in the pews to watch the wedding party walk down the aisle.

He took wide shots as Marnie's bridesmaids and James's groomsmen shuffled down the white runner sprinkled with rose petals. Callie and Logan walked together, as did Leah and Jared.

When it was Autumn's turn, he snapped more of her than the others. He'd save them and put them in his private collection. She held on to Ty's little hand, and he did his Elvis Presley dance as he walked, the lights in his *Paw Patrol* tennis shoes flashing. Everyone laughed.

He took pictures of the wedding party standing at the altar, James waiting for his bride and the pastor holding his Bible, before Marnie began her march.

"How do I look?" she asked, gliding up next to him, sucking in a deep breath.

He couldn't guess how long she'd needed to dress, but she glowed. She glanced at James looking just as nervous as she did, and tears filled her eyes.

"Beautiful, but terrified," he said, laughing.

She grinned. "Then I'm ready."

Hugh walked her down the aisle, and Cole shuffled around the church taking as many pictures as possible and trying to stay out of everyone's way while doing it.

Her father handed her off to James, who shook Hugh's hand, and she gave Callie her bouquet to hold. Cole paused near the front of the sanctuary and zeroed in on the faces of the wedding party and the audience.

The pastor started the ceremony and Callie smiled at Mitch.

It wouldn't be long before they did this song and dance.

Through the lens of his camera, Cole found Mitch in the congregation. The man couldn't take his eyes off her. Meeting Callie had changed Mitch's life for the better. He never would have attended a function like this before her, or been accepted.

He snapped a few pictures so he could tease Mitch with them later and focused on Leah. She couldn't stop staring at Jared, who couldn't wipe the grin off his face, but every time Leah looked his way, Jared was already looking at her.

He took a few pictures of them mooning at each other. He didn't know Jared well, and Leah not at all, but she'd turned into Autumn's best friend. It would be nice if the four of them could double date once in a while.

Shifting his focus, he paused on Logan. The man couldn't stop twisting his own wedding ring around his finger as Marnie and James said their vows. Ivy sat next to Mitch, and Cole took a few pictures of her, too. She looked serene, listening to the promises being spoken, having said hers just a few days ago. Logan met her eyes, and she blew him a kiss, her wedding band glinting in the sun. Mitch nudged her, and she hid a giggle behind her hand.

Lingering on Autumn, he couldn't tear his eyes away from her. She glowed, happy and content, listening to the ceremony. She held Ty, and the little boy rested his head on her shoulder, scanning the crowd, knowing in her arms, he was safe.

A couple of clicks captured them forever. They were his life, those two perfect creatures who belonged to him.

"By the power vested in me, I now pronounce you husband and wife. James, kiss this woman," the pastor demanded, and the guests laughed.

"I don't need to be told twice," James said, pulling Marnie into his arms, and he kissed her long and hard.

Everyone stood and clapped.

"May I present Mr. and Mrs. James Fox."

The pastor had to raise his voice to be heard above the cheering, and the hooting and hollering continued as Marnie wiggled her hips and pranced down the aisle. James shook hands and accepted kisses.

He stopped her to dip her and give her a deep kiss, and she played along, raising a leg and a scarlet stiletto high into the air.

Cole captured their joy.

James and Marnie had a lot to be grateful for.

They all did.

Their wedding brought a lot of people together.

And it was time to celebrate.

THE ROCKY POINT DAILY JOURNAL BLOG

BY AUTUMN BENNETT

A wedding to start off the holidays!

The residents of Rocky Point are excited to have old and new faces in town to celebrate the nuptials of Marnie Zimmerman and James Fox.

Marnie and James grew up in Rocky Point and graduated with the class of 2001.

I'll dig into all the activities and keep you up to date on the comings and goings of the bride, groom, and their guests.

Along with general reporting of the event, I'll be interviewing the wedding party.

Pictures, of course, will be included, taken by staff photographer, Cole McClure.

I hope you enjoy this fun, in-depth look into the Zimmerman/Fox wedding. I'll certainly enjoy bringing you the latest. If you have any questions, leave them in the comments and I'll do my best to answer them.

This is Autumn Bennett for the *Rocky Point Daily Journal.*

Small-town news delivered with big-city style.

An Interview with the Bride and Groom, Marnie Zimmerman and James Fox

Autumn: Marnie and James graduated from Rocky Point High School in 2001. After graduation, James moved to Decatur to go to school, but Marnie, you stayed here and went to school at Rocky Point Community College before transferring to the University of Decatur. Was that a hard decision for you?

Marnie: Well, you have to remember that James and I weren't together back then. We might have dated on and off, but him moving to Decatur with Logan wasn't a concern at the time.

Autumn: James, you and Logan Draper shared a dorm on campus. Was it nice to have a friend with you?

James: It was. Anytime you're not alone it helps a lot, but it didn't stop the homesickness.

Autumn: I understand that. It's been eighteen years since high school graduation. Did you think, James, you and Marnie would hook up in Decatur?

James: Not really. Law school's difficult and it's lot of work, especially if you want to graduate at the top of your class like I was aiming to do. One night Logan said there was a party in some housing off campus and did I want to go? I wasn't much of a partier, and he wasn't either, but I went along to blow off some steam. That was, what, babe? When you were a junior?

Marnie: Yeah.

James: That's how I found out she was in town.

Autumn: But you two didn't start dating right away, did you?

Marnie: Nah. It's cool to see people from your home-town, you know? But it was like bumping into someone you know at the grocery store. I didn't think much of it.

Autumn: How did you two meet up then? And how did you know it was for good?

James: It was a few years ago now, but we were both invited to a dinner party. He went into law like I did, and his wife was friends with Marnie. They met taking human resources classes, right, babe?

Marnie: Right. I have a BS in Human Resource Management, but Fran has a business degree with a concentration in HR. We were partners in a Union 101 class.

James: She was dating someone.

Marnie: *blushing* We were talking about getting married, but something didn't feel right. When I bumped into James that night, that's when I knew he'd been in the back of my mind.

James: I didn't like the way he hung on you.

Marnie: Pete's a nice guy. He's engaged now, too.

James: You never told me that.

Marnie: *swatting his arm* It was in the paper. Don't be getting all jealous.

James: Good. Stay away from him. You're mine now.

Autumn: *smiling* What made you decide to have your wedding in Rocky Point instead of Decatur?

Marnie: Besides it being tradition the bride marries in her hometown, James and I love the atmosphere. Plus we wanted our wedding guests to feel like they could relax, have some fun. Rocky Point gives off an easy-going vibe we wouldn't get in Decatur.

Autumn: How far in advance did you have to plan this for everything to work out?

James: I wanted to elope as soon as I realized I was in love with her, but she deserves a real wedding, so we started planning the summer before last. We've been working with Desiree, the manager of the resort, for a long time.

Autumn: Has everything gone smoothly?

Marnie: Besides a couple of snags, things are going great! Everyone who's spending the full two weeks here should be arriving later today. I have a few group activities planned, but mostly the guests will be on their own to relax and enjoy the resort. I have a list of activities for you, too.

Autumn: *laughing* That's right. I should say for the record I'm a bridesmaid, and I'm honored you asked me.

Marnie: You're one of my dearest friends, and I love you were asking all those questions like you didn't know I rushed to your apartment the night I met James at that dinner party, my stomach all twisted up because I didn't know what to do.

Autumn: Living in Decatur seems like a lifetime ago. Anyway, this interview is about you two, not me. Is there anything else you'd like to add before we wrap it up?

James: Just looking forward to celebrating our first Christmas as husband and wife. *Kisses Marnie* I already know what I'm getting her for Christmas.

Marnie: *giggling* I've already seen it.

Autumn: Oh, God. We're fading to black. Thanks for reading and subscribe to the blog so you don't miss a post in this festive wedding series.

Yep, they're still kissing.

This is Autumn Bennett for the *Rocky Point Daily Journal.*

Small-town news delivered with big-city style.

Getting to Know: Leah Bristow

I met Leah at Marnie and James's first dinner party. When I asked why Marnie was throwing the dinner, she said she wanted an evening where everyone could get to know each other rather than her guests and wedding party being strangers up until the rehearsal. I think it turned out great, and it really set the tone for the next two weeks. Listen in!

Autumn: It's nice to meet you! Marnie's told me a lot about you!

Leah: It's nice to be here. It's a lovely town, and the resort's spectacular.

Autumn: It is. Marnie said that Jared Hollister, one of James's groomsmen, flew you in from Marengo.

Leah: Yes, he did. I've never been on a plane that small before. It was a little nerve-wracking at first, but Jared's a good pilot. He delivered me in once piece.

Autumn: Marnie would've killed him if he hadn't. Can you tell our readers a little about yourself?

Leah: Oh? Like what?

Autumn: You know. How you know Marnie, where are you from?

Leah: I was born in New York, and I've lived there all my life. I work in the city—I'm the human resources director for Outdoor Wonders. That's how I know Marnie. I hired her to be the human resources manager for the Outdoor Wonders store in Decatur. I suppose while I'm in the area I could go see the store and meet some of the employees. She does a great job, though. I don't need to check up on her.

Autumn: So you know Marnie from work?

Leah: Yes. In fact, this is the first time we've met in person. I was a bit surprised she asked me to be a bridesmaid. We've gotten to know each other through email chats and Zoom.

Autumn: That's really great. It's easier than ever before to keep in touch through social media.

Leah: Marnie was a willing ear when I needed someone to talk to, and she's turned into a good friend. I was happy to be a bridesmaid.

Autumn: What do you think of Rocky Point?

Leah: It's cute, what I've seen of it. And there's so much space. I wasn't prepared for how chilly it would be here. Jared said I'd need warmer outerwear so I'll be making a trip into town to do some shopping.

Autumn: You definitely need to be warm. Marnie has a lot of outdoor activities planned if you feel like joining in, though in a previous interview I did with her and James, she said the main focus for the next two weeks is to relax, relax, relax. I'll be working and covering as much of the wedding as I possibly can, and I look forward to hanging out and getting to know you, Leah. It was very nice to meet you.

Leah: It was nice to meet you, too, Autumn. Thanks for chatting.

Leah's a very sweet woman, and one of Marnie's closest friends. Please feel free to stop and give her a real Rocky Point welcome!

And a sweater. She looked cold.

I'm just kidding. She looked gorgeous, and I'll definitely be asking her later about her fantastic wardrobe.

This is Autumn Bennett for the *Rocky Point Daily Journal.*

Small-town news delivered with big-city style.

Getting to Know: Callie Carter

I sat down with Callie Carter, one of Marnie's bridesmaids and neighbor from Decatur, Minnesota.

I hadn't met Callie before, and we settled in to chat at Marnie's get-to-know-you dinner.

Autumn: Hi, Callie, it's nice to meet you.

Callie: Hi! It's nice to meet you too.

Autumn: How was your drive from Decatur?

Callie: It was fine. I've never had a reason to come to Rocky Point before. There's not much between here and Decatur, is there?

Autumn: No, not much, but Marengo has decent shopping, at least. How long have you lived in Decatur? How do you know Marnie?

Callie: I've lived in Decatur all my life. It was born there. I've been Marnie's neighbor for a few years now. We met when we were both doing yard work. We share a town-house wall and our backyards don't have a fence separating them. She's really friendly, and we were friends practically from the minute she said hello.

Autumn: She's always been like that. I've known Marnie forever. Tell our readers a little about yourself.

Callie: Well, I'm thirty years old. I'm a firefighter with the Decatur Fire Department—

Autumn: You're a firefighter?

Callie: Yes. I went to the academy after I graduated high school. My dad and two brothers are firefighters, too.

Autumn: What does your husband think of that?

Callie: Oh, I'm not married. Not even dating anyone at the moment. My family and occupation make it difficult, but I'm enjoying being single.

Autumn: But you're always on the lookout.

Callie: Well, I did have to have maintenance come to my room earlier. I'd let him fix more than just my sink drain if you know what I mean.

Autumn: *giggling* I'm sure he has a way with his hands. What do you like to do in your free time?

Callie: I like going to the movies. I don't have a lot of free time what with the way the fire department schedules us, but I like movies, sleeping. Going out for drinks. That kind of thing.

Autumn: I lived in Decatur for a while and there's a lot more to do there than here. Are you staying in Rocky Point for the whole two weeks?

Callie: Yeah. I needed the break. Firefighting is hard work and I've been a bit stressed out.

Autumn: Well, maybe your maintenance man can fix that, too. It was nice to meet you, Callie. I'm sure we'll be seeing a lot of each other in the next few days. Marnie has a lot planned.

Callie: I'm looking forward to it.

Autumn: So am I. Thanks for your time!

Thank you for joining me while I interviewed Callie Carter, a bridesmaid in Marnie Zimmerman's wedding party.

Next up, and interview with Jared Hollister. See you then!

This is Autumn Bennett for the *Rocky Point Daily Journal.*

Small-town news delivered with big-city style.

Getting to Know: Jared Hollister

Much to his chagrin, I caught Jared Hollister, Zamboni driver *extraordinaire,* at Marnie's meet and greet at the resort. You probably know Jared if you stopped in at the sports arena to watch a Bears game or noticed him fly over Rocky Point in his plane, but I'll let him tell you about himself. Thanks for joining us!

Autumn: Thanks for talking to me, Jared. I know how busy you are.

Jared: *sipping beer* It's no problem, Autumn. How are you doing?

Autumn: Not too terrible, thanks for asking. How are things at the arena?

Jared: Same as usual. We have a big game tomorrow night. Marnie asked me to take Leah into town to buy some warmer clothes. I'll do that before the game. Are you going to go?

Autumn: I'll be there to cover it for the blog. Can you tell our readers a little about yourself?

Jared: Everyone knows who I am.

Autumn: Humor me.

Jared: *sighs* My name's Jared Hollister. I'm thirty-six years old. Divorced. One daughter who's sixteen. I'm the manager of the sports arena in Rocky Point. I also own a plane I inherited from my grandmother, and I fly packages back and forth between here and Marengo, sometimes Decatur. What else do you want to know?

Autumn: How do you like your steak?

Jared: *blinks* What?

Autumn: *laughing* Just kidding. I was wondering if you were paying attention. You keep looking at Leah. She's pretty.

Jared: I do not, and yes, she is.

Autumn: How long have you known James?

Jared: We went to high school together. You know that.

Autumn: Our readers might not. Were you pleased when James asked you to be a groomsman?

Jared: Sure. I guess so. He's a good friend, and I'll be proud to stand up with him. Marnie's a sweetheart. They'll be happy together.

Autumn: I think so too. I'm really happy for both of them. Thanks for chatting with me, Jared.

Jared: Yep. Talk to you later.

And he's gone. Jared's been a solid member of the Rocky Point community all his life, and his daughter Briar, attends Rocky Point High and is a hockey cheerleader.

I'll pry more information out of him later. Especially about the quick glances he kept giving Leah during our interview.

Marnie and James's wedding will bring some excitement to town, that's for sure, and look to this blog for up-to-date information on it all!

This is Autumn Bennet for the *Rocky Point Daily Journal.*

Small-town news delivered with big-city style.

Rocky Point Polar Bears vs. the Marengo Jets: An inside look.

Tonight marks the biggest hockey game of the year for Rocky Point and its high school hockey team.

The Polar Bears are playing the Marengo Jets. The arena's packed and several of Marnie Zimmerman's wedding party and guests are also attending the game.

While I go to games regularly and report on some of them for the blog, I asked Marnie and James how it felt to be in their old stomping grounds again. James said it made him feel old and Marnie said she was glad she wasn't in high school anymore. I have to agree. While I had a good time in school, it was a relief to move on to bigger and brighter things.

Marnie, some of you may remember, used to be a hockey cheerleader. James never played, but the hockey games were big social events and he never missed one.

I'm sitting with Leah Bristow, one of Marnie's bridesmaids. I interviewed her earlier, and if you missed it, you can read it here. This is the first high school hockey game she's attended, and Jared was true to his word. She looks cute in a new parka and boots she bought at the Rocky Point Supply Company.

There were rumors that Blaine Hanson, 17, high school senior and valet at the Rocky Point Resort, wouldn't be well enough to play tonight, but he's in good spirits, scoring the first goal of the game.

Blaine was in a snowmobiling accident last weekend and sprained his wrist when he was thrown off the machine. He looks to be on the mend, and we're grateful that he wasn't seriously injured.

I spoke with the Marengo Jets coach, Warren Fields, and he told me there were more freshmen and sophomores on the team this year than in years past. It shows on the ice tonight and the rookie mistakes they're making much to Rocky Point's delight.

This game was over before it started, and this girl is going home and getting some sleep.

Jared, if you're reading this, the popcorn machine needs to be repaired. It really smells in here.

Congratulations, Polar Bears, on your win! Keep it up when you play the Hamden Hornets next week!

This is Autumn Bennett for the *Rocky Point Daily Journal*.

Small-town news delivered with big city-style.

Getting to Know: Mitch Sinclair

Today I sat down with Mitch Sinclair in the dining room of the Rocky Point Resort. They have a marvelous breakfast buffet if you need a recommendation and a gentle nudge to get out of the house! Mitch has been cozying up with Callie Carter who is one of Marnie's bridesmaids, and if you recall reading my interview with her, is from Decatur. If you missed that interview, you can read it here.

Autumn: Mitch, thanks for taking the time to chat with me today.

Mitch: You're welcome. I've never been interviewed before.

Autumn: It's painless, I promise. Callie survived.

Callie: Barely.

Autumn: Hey! I'm nice. Mitch, can you tell us a little about yourself?

Mitch: Well, I'm from Rocky Point. I graduated with you and Marnie, James and Jared, Logan and Ivy. I did the two years at Rocky Point Community College, and I was on the paper mill's waitlist.

Autumn: You never ended up working there?

Mitch: No. I lucked out getting hired as the resort's

maintenance man, but that worked since they shut down anyway. I'm happy here.

Autumn: Tell me about a typical day.

Mitch: I always check in with Desiree in the morning. We have a quick meeting about what needs to be fixed. I let her know about things that need more repair than I'm capable of—

Autumn: Like what?

Mitch: I'm not an electrician. So if wiring needs more attention than I can give it, Desiree has to call Rocky Point Electric. Things like that.

Autumn: I see. What else do you do with your day?

Mitch: I keep the pool clean and in working order. Shampoo carpeting if it needs it, fix anything in the guest rooms that breaks down. Keep the lobby floors buffed. Spring is horrible because everyone tracks in slush and mud. That kind of thing. Some days are quieter than others, then sometimes it feels like everything breaks down at once.

Autumn: And you live here at the resort, is that correct?

Mitch: I don't have to, but it makes Desiree happy to have me on site twenty-four hours a day. There have been a few times I've been called in the middle of the night because of an overflowing toilet. Last night I stayed up pretty late fixing a machine for Carmen, the woman who's in charge of doing the resort's laundry.

Autumn: What do you do in your free time?

Mitch: I visit my parents. They still live here in town. I like to spend time outside. I put a salt lick on the trail behind the resort and watch the deer. I use the fitness center and work out a lot. The job's easier if I stay in shape.

Autumn: What are you doing for the holidays?

Mitch: I'll spend it with my mom and dad. We don't do too much besides exchange a gift or two and eat a nice meal.

Autumn: That sounds like a lovely way to celebrate the holidays. Now that you're hanging out with Callie, will I be seeing you at some of the wedding activities?

Mitch: Yeah. Maybe.

Autumn: Great! Thanks for speaking with me. I know you didn't want to.

Mitch: That's not—

Autumn: Don't worry about it. No one does. Thanks again. I'll let you get to work.

Mitch: Thanks for wanting to talk to me.

Autumn: You're welcome.

Mitch Sinclair has been the maintenance man at the Rocky Point Resort for the past five years. Desiree Arnold made a good choice when she hired him. He's a hard worker and knows his stuff. If you stop by the resort, say hi. He keeps the resort operational, and as we know, the resort's and important piece of Rocky Point's economy.

Thanks for stopping by, and I hope you're enjoying reading this wedding blog series as much as I am writing it!

This is Autumn Bennett for the *Rocky Point Daily Journal.*

Small-town news delivered with big city style.

The Rocky Point Supply Company Gets a Little Help

I'm interviewing Helen Brunswick today. She, along with her late husband Glen, opened the Rocky Point Supply Company back in the 80s. One of the few places in Rocky Point to buy outdoor clothing and souvenirs, the Supply Company has been a cornerstone in the community for many years.

Autumn: Hi, Helen, thanks for talking to me today. How are you doing?

Helen: I'm doin' good, darlin'. We haven't had this many customers in the store at once in a long time.

Autumn: You look like you're really enjoying yourself.

Helen: Well, you know how it is. Glen passed away, and it was hard to want to keep going.

Autumn: I know. How long has Glen been gone now?

Helen: Almost two years. We knew it was coming. He'd been fighting that nasty cancer and he was ready to go.

Autumn: We were all so sorry about it.

Helen: Thanks, darlin'. It's been tough getting back on track. Leah's been a big help.

Autumn: Can you tell me a little about what Leah's been doing at the store?

Helen: That girl's so sweet. She came into the store with Jared looking like a scared little rabbit. Jared, I think, has a soft spot for her. Can't say I blame him any. She saw that I needed help and said she would. It was pretty brave of her, too. She didn't know if I'd welcome the help or bite her head off. Mostly though, I think that girl's lonely, and maybe she saw some of that in me, too. We get along real well, Leah and me.

Autumn: So she's been helping you put out stock and do a little cleaning?

Helen: The first thing she had me do was put on some

music. Perked everything right up. It took days to clean out my stockroom, but she didn't say one thing about getting paid.

Autumn: People in town seem excited.

Helen: I have to tell you, Autumn, I've sold more in the past three days Leah's helped me than I have in the last four months.

Autumn: Do you think you'll change your mind about selling?

Helen: *shaking her head* No, ma'am. It's about time I retire. Running a store's a lot of work, and I'm just too old for it now. I need a spry young thing to take over. Someone who has the energy to unpack product, get it out onto the floor. I just don't have it in me anymore.

Autumn: Maybe Leah will stick around.

Helen: I don't think you're the only one who hopes so. Jared was giving her the eye when he brought her in to buy a warmer jacket and a pair of boots. She's told me a little bit about her job in New York. That would be a mighty big move for that little mouse, but I think she needs a change. She didn't look so good when I met her.

Autumn: *sighs* I've been getting to know her, too. But we all have things, don't we, Helen?

Helen: Sure do, kiddo.

Autumn: Anything you want to add to the blog before we wrap it up?

Helen: If you can, can you add a coupon to the blog? I'd like to give 25% off a full-priced item. Maybe they can print it out?

Autumn: Or show it to you on their phones?

Helen: That works, too. Something to get more people in here. Say thanks for putting up with me.

Autumn: I'll have the design department at the paper put something together, okay?

Helen: That'd be great, sugar. Between you and Leah, you've helped me have a pretty decent holiday since Glen passed away. Thank you.

Autumn: It's no trouble, and I think Leah did most of the work.

Helen: She's a good girl, that one. She'll make Jared a fine wife.

Autumn: I don't think *that's* on their radars right now.

Helen: Mark my words. This old woman knows a thing or two.

Autumn: I just bet you do. Thanks for talking to me, Helen.

Helen: Thanks for wanting to. I appreciate the coupon.

Autumn: It's no problem at all. Thanks again.

Helen couldn't stop telling me how wonderful Leah is. She's a pretty special person, and I have it on good authority Leah will be helping Helen today as well. Enjoy the coupon, and say hello to Helen and Leah when you get a chance!

This is Autumn Bennett for the *Rocky Point Daily Journal.*

Small-town news delivered with big city style.

Getting to know: Logan Draper

I've been trying to pin down Logan Draper, one of James's groomsmen, for days. I finally caught up with him eating breakfast in the dining room of the Rocky Point Resort. Lean in while I see what he's been up to for the past eighteen years.

Autumn: Good morning, Logan. You're a hard man to track down. How are you?

Logan: Good.

Autumn: How does it feel to be back in Rocky Point?

Logan: Strange. I haven't been back since high school graduation.

Autumn: Can you tell our readers a little bit about yourself?

Logan: *sighs* I went to school in Decatur and opened a law practice with James. We're estate attorneys. I like to watch documentaries, and I take a pro bono case here and there.

Autumn: But you didn't marry?

Logan: No. I guess I haven't found that special someone yet.

Autumn: What do you do in your spare time?

Logan: Like I said, sometimes I take a pro bono case

here and there. I like to read. I work a lot and that doesn't give me a lot of free time.

Autumn: Do you date?

Logan: A little.

Autumn: This is a boring interview, Logan.

Logan: *laughing* I guess I'm a boring guy.

Autumn: I find that hard to believe. Tell me one interesting thing about yourself, then I'll let you get back to your breakfast.

Logan: *blows a breath* Umm . . .

Autumn: It can't be that hard.

Logan: I volunteer at an animal shelter two days a week.

Autumn: Awww! That's great! Are you a dog or a cat person?

Logan: Dogs for sure.

Autumn: I have two cats. They love to cuddle, and they keep me warm at night.

Logan: I'd rather have a woman do that.

Autumn: Are you offering?

Logan: *blushes*

Autumn: Just kidding! My cats would get mad at you. Thanks for talking to me, Logan. I'll see you around if you stop skipping Marnie's activities.

Logan: Sure thing.

It was fun teasing Logan a little bit. We always got a long in high school, and it's nice touching base with him again.

I love seeing so many new and old faces for the wedding!

This is Autumn Bennett for the *Rocky Point Daily Journal.*

Small-town news delivered with big city style.

Ivy and Logan, a Surprise Wedding!

Autumn: Let me congratulate the two of you! Logan, I interviewed you for the blog not that long ago, and I have to say, this took me completely by surprise. But marriage looks good on the both of you!

Logan: Thanks.

Autumn: You didn't give me any hints this would be happening.

Logan: I didn't know. I'd only seen Ivy once since coming back, and she—

Ivy: Don't say I hated you.

Logan: Okay. You might not have hated me, but—

Ivy: We've worked through a lot in a short amount of time.

Autumn: Your mom, Ivy, was in an accident not long ago. You were married in her hospital room. How's she doing now?

Ivy: She's doing okay. She's in therapy and attends AA meetings. She's going to start going to church again. Right now she's still healing from her surgery, and she's out on her own recognizance until the judge can sentence her for driving while intoxicated and without a valid driver's license.

Autumn: How did she take the news that you were going to get married?

Ivy: She was really happy for us, and like some of the others, Mitch, Leah, she's looking forward to a fresh start next year. Logan's been a big help. Rosie's lucky things weren't worse.

Autumn: Logan, your mother is also back in town. How does she feel about your marriage to Ivy?

Logan: She's very happy for us. We'll be visiting her regularly in Denver once we get settled in Decatur.

Autumn: You and Ivy will be living there?

Logan: Yep. James's and my practice is there, and Ivy wants to go to school.

Autumn: Ivy, how did you know marrying Logan was the right thing to do?

Ivy: Besides being in love with him?

Autumn: Besides that. Everyone knows that it takes more than love for things to work out.

Ivy: I grew up with Logan. He's been a part of my life for as long as we've been apart, and I knew I didn't want to live without him anymore. Sometimes it gets to a point where even if things don't work out, it's not as bad as if you didn't try. I'd reached that point.

Logan: Awww, sweetheart.

Ivy: Well, it's true.

Autumn: What do you have to say to anyone who thinks you moved too fast?

Logan: I say, you have to do what's right for you. But if you don't ever take a chance, then you'll never be rewarded. What if I never told Ivy I still loved her? What if I let our pasts decide how our future would turn out? We wouldn't be sitting here talking to you. I wouldn't be planning to ravage her later. *laughs* Next year will be a start to a life I never thought possible. Not only because I was brave enough to say something, but because Ivy was brave enough to let me in after I'd hurt her. It takes a strong woman to do that, and I'm grateful every second Ivy's that strong. It wasn't too fast. It was just right.

Autumn: Are you going have children?

Ivy: No, we're not. It's not a secret that Logan had a hard childhood, and I've had my fill taking care of my mother. It will be nice to enjoy each other without the extra responsibilities. Besides, I think if we need a baby fix, Marnie and James, and Callie and Mitch, will let us borrow theirs. From the sounds of it, we won't have to wait long.

Autumn: There's definitely something in the water.

Logan: We'll drink hot chocolate, then. I want Ivy to myself for a very long time.

Autumn: Do you have any immediate plans?

Logan: No. Enjoy the ceremony and reception. Help out my mother-in-law. Enjoy my mom's visit. Now that things with Ivy and me are solid, I'd like to appreciate the little things, live in the present. Enjoy the smile on Ivy's face first thing in the morning. Meeting her to have dinner, sneaking kisses while she's at work. *kisses Ivy's hand* The little things.

Autumn: And you, Ivy? Do you feel the same way?

Ivy: This whole thing will be an adjustment. Taking it day by day, hour by hour, sounds good to me, too.

Autumn: Well, you're glowing brighter than a lit-up Christmas tree! I'm so happy for you.

Logan: Thanks.

Ivy: Thank you.

Autumn: I'll see you two later, okay? Thanks for talking to me.

Logan: No problem.

Ivy: Bye, Autumn.

They look so good together! I'm happy for them.

It's tough for couples just starting out, and if you'd like to purchase them a wedding gift, the *Rocky Point Daily Journal* has set up a bridal registry. You can find it by clicking here.

Rosie Graves' recovery will be a long and arduous process. If you'd like to help her get on her feet, a small donation campaign has been started by an anonymous organizer, and you can donate here.

If you'd like to send Ivy and Logan a congratulations card, you can send it to them care of the paper at PO Box 1111 Rocky Point, MN 55115-1111. We'll forward the cards to the happy couple.

This is Autumn Bennett for the *Rocky Point Daily Journal*.
Small-town news delivered with big city style.

Getting to know: Autumn Bennett

We settled at Starbucks so bride-to-be, Marnie Zimmerman, could interview me. I couldn't be left out of the wedding party interviews! There was more than one person who told me to enjoy a taste of my own medicine. Luckily, I had a venti peppermint mocha to wash it down.

Marnie: Who came up with this again?

Autumn: It was Callie's idea to let you interview me.

Marnie: It's a great idea. We can't skip you since you've interviewed everyone else.

Autumn: It's strange being on the other side of the recorder.

Marnie: I'm glad you reminded me. You're a good sport. How are you doing?

Autumn: *shrugging* Okay. I'm already getting tired of the cold but blogging has kept me busy. I have quite a few posts to write up. The donation campaign Callie's dad set up for Mitch's parents met the goal and then some. Did you know that? I'm happy for Ruby and Chip. They deserve it.

Marnie: That's great! Callie's been walking on cloud nine since she met Mitch. So, Autumn, tell the readers a little bit about yourself.

Autumn: Well, I grew up here in Rocky Point. I went to the University of Decatur and majored in journalism. While I was in school, I interned at the *Decatur Herald* and eventually worked my way up to investigative reporter.

Marnie: What made you decide to move back to Rocky Point?

Autumn: Marnie! I thought we weren't going to talk about that.

Marnie: This is a small town, Autumn. Everyone knows.

Autumn: Then I don't have to say it.

Marnie: Are you being serious right now?

Autumn: Fine! I moved here for a man. That didn't exactly work in my favor.

Marnie: I'm sorry, sweetie. Are you going to move back to Decatur?

Autumn: I don't know. I like being able to see my nephew. I'd miss him if I moved, but no offense to the *Journal*—I love you, Lew!—writing for a small paper isn't the same as writing for the *Herald*.

Marnie: Do you think it will ever work out between you and Cole?

Autumn: Marnie! Did you have to bring him into this?

Marnie: Why not? He's the reason you came back. Do you still love him?

Autumn: I know this is a casual blog, but I don't think the readers care about my love life. Besides if—

Marnie: That's right. I'm sorry. You can delete this if you want.

Autumn: No, it's okay. I'd just rather keep some things private.

Marnie: Leah's living with you now. How's that going?

Autumn: It's great! I love having a roommate. You don't know how lonely you are until you're not anymore. I'm thrilled she's going to move here and run the Supply Company.

Marnie: Do you have any plans for the next year?

Autumn: I'm not sure. My parents would like me to visit, and I can't lie, a vacation sounds good. Try to do a bit more freelancing. Maybe start my own blog, though everything I have to say, I say in this one. Maybe take some online classes to earn my master's degree. The community college approached me about teaching a journalism class. I've been thinking about trying to put a curriculum together for next fall's semester. I wouldn't be ready for spring.

Marnie: You didn't tell me that! That sounds amazing! I'm happy for you.

Autumn: Thanks. I'm trying to have a full life here.

Marnie: Without Cole.

Autumn: Marnie!

Marnie: Well, I'm sorry. I'm happy, and I want my friends to be happy, too.

Autumn: You don't need a man to be happy.

Marnie: No, but it sure helps.

Autumn: Spoken like a woman who's going to be married in a few days.

Marnie: Well, sure. Ivy and Logan tied the knot, and Mitch and Callie aren't far behind, and Leah and Jared can't stop making goo-goo eyes at each other.

Autumn: I'm the only one left.

Marnie: It's not as if Cole doesn't—

Autumn: Marnie! Is there anything else you want to ask me before we wrap this up?

Marnie: No, I guess that's it. *wrinkles her nose* You're a good friend, Autumn.

Autumn: You're one of my best friends, too. Thanks for taking the time to interview me.

Marnie: No problem. Come on, let's go to the Viking. I'll buy you a drink for making you mad.

Autumn: I'm not mad.

Marnie: Then you need sex.

Autumn: *sighing* What happened to the drink?

Marnie: Wine first, then sex.

Autumn: For you, maybe. I'm taking control of this interview. Say goodbye, Marnie.

Marnie: Goodbye, Marnie.

Thanks for reading my interview by Marnie Zimmerman, bride-to-be. The rose-colored glasses she's wearing are covering up the hearts in her eyes, but we wouldn't have her any other way!

This is Autumn Bennett for the *Rocky Point Daily Journal*.

Small-town news delivered with big city style.

Lives Saved, A Child Found

I'm sitting in my empty kitchen, a cold cup of coffee at my elbow. Many of you know now that my nephew, Ty, was kidnapped by Buck Drayton, a man I was engaged to while I lived in Decatur.

The Rocky Point Police Department did all they could to find him, and I owe a special thank you to Layla and Trevor for their extraordinary assistance and unwavering faith that Ty would be found and brought home safely.

At 4 AM on Thursday morning, Buck called my cell phone and said he took Ty from his bedroom. He offered an exchange: Ty for me. Under the direction of the police department, we agreed, and the exchange was made in the newspaper's parking lot.

Buck drove me out of town to an abandoned hunting shack.

Lots of things go through your mind when something like that happens. You try to think of ways to escape. You hope if he kills you, he does it fast. You think of all the people you didn't get to say goodbye to. You hope if he doesn't kill you, he won't hit you or rape you. Most people in Rocky Point won't ever face something like that unless they watch a program on TV. I wouldn't wish what Buck did to me on my worst enemy.

I was scared. Not only for myself, but for Ty because I didn't know if he was safe.

There's a certain amount of guilt I'll always carry

because I was engaged to that psychopath, and in my own way, led him here when I moved home.

Layla followed us and ended up taking his life to protect mine and hers. Buck was armed and he shot at both of us.

I'm lucky to be alive.

Ty's okay, and the child psychologist seems to think the damage the kidnapping caused will be minimal, if any. Buck didn't hurt him, and I thank God for that.

You may also have heard of the bomb my sister and Ty's mother, dropped on us. I'm sharing it with permission. Cole McClure is not Ty's biological father. My sister admitted this during the investigation while Ty was missing.

This doesn't mean Ty's not Cole's son, and Cole will continue to love and take care of him in that capacity.

I'm not normally so revealing in these posts, but I know a lot of you helped search for Ty, and I feel I owe you the courtesy of the truth. Besides, it's better to reveal all the details rather than let rumors run wild.

In that vein, you all know my sister was not the mother she could have been or should have been, and she's stepped back from that role.

Cole asked me to marry him, and I said yes. We're going to raise Ty together.

There are some of you who won't agree with that we're doing. There will be some that will accuse us of shutting my sister out to create a family with her child.

All I can tell you is that she stepped aside voluntarily to pursue dreams that did not include being a mother. Not all women want to be mothers, and they shouldn't be punished. The citizens of Rocky Point have not had favorable opinions of Summer for a long time and I don't expect that to change, but when you're cowering under an evergreen branch in the middle of the night hiding from a madman who wants to kill you and the temperature's minus five, it puts things into perspective real fast.

I spoke with Leah about it. She had the same revelations when she fell through the ice while ice fishing during her second day in town. In a situation like that, it's easy to think you're going to die. If Jared hadn't been looking for her, she might have.

We only have one life. We only have a handful of years to make our mark, create something meaningful to leave behind. We only have a few short years to be happy.

I wasted a lot of those years holding on to resentment, and in doing so, Cole lost those years too. I was blaming him when I had no right.

I'm not going to waste any more time because of resentment or guilt. We both made mistakes and it's time to put those away.

Ty will be okay. Cole and I are going to give him the stability and love he needs to thrive. We're going to be his parents, and the residents of Rocky Point can be happy for us or not.

To be honest, dear reader, I don't care either way.

I'm happy.

Finally.

That's all that matters to me. I love Cole with all my heart. Ty's my angel, and we'll move forward. Together.

If you're unhappy, fix it. Life is short.

Ask Leah.

Ask me.

Ask Logan and Ivy who married just days after being separated for eighteen years.

Ask Mitch who didn't think he'd find anyone who would understand what he'd gone through, much less love him despite it.

Find that happy and hold on tight.

This is Autumn Bennett for the *Rocky Point Daily Journal.*

Small-town news delivered with big city style.

It's here! The Wedding Day!

It seems like forever since James and Marnie announced their engagement. These two weeks have seemed even longer because of all the craziness that's happened. If you would have told me beforehand everything that was going to take place during these two weeks of festivities, I would have said you were delusional.

But, I guess, looking back, our lives needed shaking up.

Rocky Point needed shaking up.

Mitch and his parents didn't deserve to live the way they had since his accident, and Callie coming to town definitely had an impact on their situation. Perhaps it didn't turn out quite like they expected, but in the end, the Sinclairs are doing what's best for them. Unfortunately, that means leaving Rocky Point like so many others did when the paper mill closed. Whether the citizens of Rocky Point believe it or not, we're losing some good people when they move. Ask Desiree Arnold, the manager of the Rocky Point Resort. She's having a tough time filling Mitch's maintenance man shoes. If you know of someone who can fix almost anything, give her a call. She'd appreciate the referral.

Leah, as well, has made a positive impact on the community. Not a day goes by that someone doesn't approach me and tell me all the wonderful things she's doing for the Supply Company. After her husband died, Helen Brunswick had a difficult time keeping the store going, and many admitted that the store closing would cause a gaping hole in Rocky Point's economy. It means a lot to the people of this community to be able to run into the store to buy a pair of boots, or a warmer jacket, or a pair of mittens one of their kids lost for the millionth time. The little department store that carries more of our day to day items wasn't meeting the demand, and it was a relief for the whole town when Leah took over. Helen will still be a part of the Rocky Point Supply Company, and I encourage you to drop in to see them.

When she came to town, Leah changed more lives than just those of the shoppers in this area. Everyone who knows Jared Hollister and his daughter, Briar, also knows that they've struggled since Rita, Jared's ex-wife, moved to New York. Leah gave Jared something he and his daughter can build their lives on. Not to mention, Leah has turned into a very good friend of mine and I love that she's staying in town. While Decatur isn't that far, sometimes it's nice to know that a close friend is only a few blocks away.

If you've been reading this blog series, you've read that Ivy Graves and Logan Draper said their own vows not long ago. Logan came back to Rocky Point to be one of James's groomsman, and Leah and Callie aren't the only ones who found love. Ivy has had some tough times since her brother, Joey, passed away twelve years ago, and her mother, Roseanne Graves, has had a difficult time dealing with the past. We always like to think that we can handle things on our own, but sometimes we have to let go of our pride and accept help when it's offered. Logan did that for Ivy, but make no mistake, she's helping him, too. If you'd still like to offer them congratulations by sending a card or a gift, you can click here for that information in a prior blog post.

My life has changed as well since everyone came to town for the wedding. Cole and I finally admitted that we were both at fault for the way things have gone, though Ty's disappearance may have speeded that along. Ty's doing great, by the way. It seems he'll have no lasting effects after what happened. As for me, sometimes I still have nightmares about running through the woods and Buck shooting at me, but I don't wake up alone. Cole will always be there for me. While we won't be getting married as quickly as Ivy and Logan, (or Callie and Mitch and Jared and Leah, *ahem*) Rocky Point will have its share of weddings to look forward to in the coming years.

I'm writing this as the reception carries on around me. There is so much joy in this room tonight, I think we could power the whole town for the next year if there was a way to harness the energy.

Marnie looks lovely in her dress, and the ceremony went off without a hitch. Cole's taken plenty of pictures, and I'll be posting some in the coming days as I get Marnie's approval.

The new year will bring some changes. A lot of them good, maybe some not so good. Life's like that, I guess. No one can guarantee just how things are going to go. We all suffered some bad times and came out the other side. I'm sure we'll be put to the test time and again, but if I found out anything in these two weeks, it's that you don't need to suffer alone. You don't have to be alone. There's help out there.

If you feel like you don't have anyone to ask, talk to me.

Stop at the Supply Company and talk to Leah. Ask to have a word with Cole at the paper, or Jared at the arena. We're a tight-knit community and we hold each other up.

I need to go. The love of my life is asking me to dance, and I think I just might accept.

I hope you enjoyed the wedding series. If you have any ideas for future blog posts, drop them in the comments! I would appreciate the leads.

This is Autumn Bennett for the *Rocky Point Daily Journal.*

Small-town news delivered with big-city style.

A NOTE FROM THE AUTHOR

Thank you so much for going on this adventure with me! I loved the city of Rocky Point, and I based the little town loosely on my hometown of International Falls, MN. It's a town less than 10,000 in population, and like Rocky Point, it sits on the Canadian border.

While I grew up, I did several of the activities that my characters also enjoyed: ice fishing, snowmobiling, and ice skating. International Falls is home to several resorts that offer fishing all year round, and the resort where Jared takes Leah to feed the chipmunks really does exist—I've fed the chipmunks several times (but always in the summer!).

While there are some trials living in a small town, there's also a charm "living away from it all" and being part of the small-knit community made my childhood a memorable experience.

Thanks for reading!

Vania Rheault

Do you like billionaire romance? Sign up for my newsletter and receive a free standalone novel, an ugly-duckling billionaire romance, *My Biggest Mistake*. There you'll be the first to know of sales, new releases, and what I'm working on. Don't miss out! Go to www.vmrheault.com/subscribe.

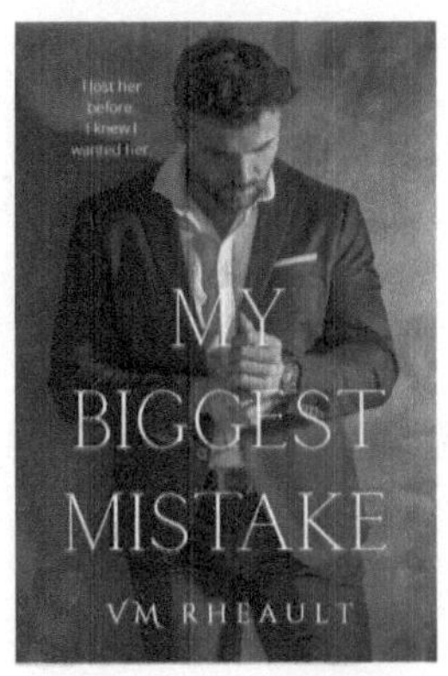

ALSO BY VANIA RHEAULT

Don't Run Away

(Tower City Romance Trilogy Book One)

Chasing You

(Tower City Romance Trilogy Book Two)

Running Scared

(Tower City Romance Trilogy Book Three)

The Finish Line

(Tower City Romance Trilogy Book Four,

Bonus Novella)

Wherever He Goes

(A Steamy Forced Proximity Standalone)

The Years Between Us

(A Steamy Age-Gap Standalone)

All of Nothing

(A Steamy Enemies to Lovers Standalone)

His Frozen Heart

(A Rocky Point Wedding Book One)

His Frozen Dreams

(A Rocky Point Wedding Book Two)

Her Frozen Memories

(A Rocky Point Wedding Book Three)

Her Frozen Promises

(A Rocky Point Wedding Book Four)

As VM Rheault

Captivated by Her (Cedar Hill Duet Book One)

Addicted to Her (Cedar Hill Duet Book Two)

Rescue Me

Give & Take (The Lost & Found Trilogy Book One)

Lost & Found (The Lost & Found Trilogy Book Two)

Safe & Sound (The Lost & Found Trilogy Book Three)

Faking Forever

Twisted Alibis (Ghost Town Trilogy Book One)

Twisted Lullabies (Ghost Town Trilogy Book Two)

Twisted Lies (Ghost Town Trilogy Book Three)

A Heartache for Christmas

Cruel Fate (King's Crossing Book One)

Cruel Hearts (King's Crossing Book Two)

Cruel Dreams (King's Crossing Book Three)

Shattered Fate (King's Crossing Book Four)

Shattered Hearts (King's Crossing Book Five)

Shattered Dreams (King's Crossing Book Six)

ABOUT THE AUTHOR

Vania Rheault has lived in Minnesota all her life. In 2003,
she graduated with a BA in English with a concentration in
creative writing from Minnesota State University,
Moorhead. When she's not writing, she's sleeping, working
her day job, or going to movie night with her sister.
Find her at vmrheault.com

www.ingramcontent.com/pod-product-compliance
Lightning Source LLC
Chambersburg PA
CBHW050904130726
47900CB00015B/2044